SWEET SURRENDER

SAV R. MILLER

SWEET SURRENDER
KING'S TRACE ANTIHEROES BOOK ONE
Copyright © 2020, 2023 by Sav R. Miller

Cover Design: Bitter Sage Designs (Bee)
Editors: Jenny Sims (Editing 4 Indies), Justine (Cultivate Expressions Editorial Services)

This is a work of fiction. Names, characters, businesses, places, events, locales, and incidents are either the products of the author's imagination or used in a fictitious manner. Any resemblance to actual persons, living or dead, or actual events is purely coincidental.

For Emily
I honestly don't think this book would exist without you. Thank you for reading all ten-thousand versions of it.

"There are darknesses in life, and there are lights, and you are one of the lights, the light of all lights."

— BRAM STOKER, DRACULA

NOTE FROM THE AUTHOR

Sweet Surrender is a dark mafia romance and contains graphic violence, sexual assault, profanity, sexually explicit scenes, and heavy discussions of certain topics that some may find triggering. Content may not be suitable for all audiences.
Reader discretion is advised.

For a more detailed content warning list, visit savrmiller.com

This is the republished edition with minor changes from the original version. ©2020, 2023

PROLOGUE

ELIA

"W<small>IPE THAT FUCKING FROWN</small> off your face, *figlio*. Your despondency is making me look bad."

Sloshing the ice around in my tumbler, I glance over at my father. Even in his prime, the man didn't scare me, despite having one of the largest body counts on the East Coast. To me, he's only ever been Dad.

A shit dad, but Dad nonetheless.

"No one's paying you any attention, Pop." I gesture around the fenced yard at the faces turned away from us. We've set up shop on one side of the Pasinis' backyard, beneath the wide, bamboo parasol meant to shade us from the sun and haven't moved in an hour. "Besides, it's your fault for making me come here. Seriously, what grown man throws himself a birthday party?"

My father sighs, leaning back in his lounge chair. "It's his stepfather, I think. We stopped throwing you parties when you were, what, sixteen?"

Try seven. But no one wants to talk about that, least of all me. Instead, I nod, scanning the crowd for the fiftieth time since settling in with my whiskey.

Luca went all-out on the alcohol; I'll give him that. Almost as if he anticipated animosity among the family and King's Trace commoners.

If I didn't know any better, I'd think this was a party for Senator Harrison, Luca's uncle by marriage. The gray-haired, beady-eyed thief keeps his eldest daughter strapped to his side, touting her around like a pussy parade.

Caroline's beautiful, and it's not exactly difficult to comprehend why he brings her everywhere. She's the prim and proper foil to her younger sister, who's starred in more sex tapes than the average porn star.

The Harrisons are legendary around town, although they give off a vibe of secrecy. Something in the way Dominic's always leering, looking for someone to introduce his daughter to.

I rake my gaze over the girl—woman—again, absorbing her appearance for the hundredth time; her golden hair shimmers down her back, grazing against the creamy skin exposed in the short, rose-pink sundress she has on. Her blue eyes remain cast down at the ground as though she's afraid of what she'll discover if she looks up.

Well, she should be scared. I've been unable to move my gaze from her curves since I first noticed her. Can't stop thinking about what it'd be like to get her alone; how soft her plump lips might be—if she tastes as sweet and innocent as she looks.

Shifting in my seat, I adjust myself discreetly. A hard-on with kids around would make my father *really* look bad.

My eyes find the pair again; I don't like the way the senator's arm curls around her, keeping her breasts flush against his side. His nails dig into the exposed skin of her bicep, making her squirm.

"What's the deal with him?" I ask, jerking my chin in the senator's direction. Dominic's rounded belly jiggles as he laughs, and Caroline grimaces, a flicker of annoyance flashing in her baby blues.

"He's auctioning his daughter off or something. I don't know if he's paying off his debts or collecting on campaign promises. This is why we don't get involved in fucking politics; they'll sell you anything if it keeps them in power." My father shakes his head, tipping his beer bottle to his lips and taking a long gulp. He pulls it away, pointing at them with the mouth. "Imagine selling your fucking *daughter* to a criminal. *Cristo*, your mother would castrate me from the afterlife if I tried something like that."

Pain throbs deep in my chest, cracking the cavity open like someone's reached inside and gripped my heart in their cold hands. I clear my throat and bring the glass tumbler up, taking a quick drink. *If he doesn't stop talking about our life in New York, I'll cut his dick off myself.*

I set the glass down and fold my hands over my stomach. "Who do you think will get her?"

"Kieran Ivers."

My eyebrow quirks up. "Pardon?"

He shrugs. Flesh sales aren't that uncommon in our world, but that it's happening here, out in the open, and in favor of a rival outfit, is nearly unfathomable. "Look, son, put your petty rivalry with that boy to rest, at least while we're here. Harrison owes all of us money, and we aren't going to take a body as payment. That's absurd. It's not even on the same level."

"*Petty* rivalry?" I glare at him, my hands gripping the

armrests on the chaise. "I inherited the fucking thing. Even if Kieran wasn't a total freak, don't act like I had a choice in who my enemy is."

"You have a choice to continue it."

Heat scorches beneath my skin, pressure building in my temple as I try to rein in the rage. Any other man would be properly splattered on the floor right now for insubordination, but I can't act that way with my father. Not Orlando Montalto. Our parent outfit, the Riccis in Boston, would have my head on a fucking platter within the hour.

Heaving a heavy sigh, I pinch my eyes closed, trying to erase the memory of this girl from my brain. Who she's getting sold to should be of no consequence to me, except that I can't shake my dead mother's nagging.

Everyone in this life has a choice, my sweet boy. Please don't ever forget that.

Mommy issues aside, anything that beautiful should be kept from Kieran, who loves to destroy precious things. He'd eat her heart as soon as they exchanged rings and let his men use her lifeless body after.

Unwarranted possessiveness blooms like a cactus inside me, pushing me to my feet as the girl finally wrenches herself from her father's arms and heads for the door to the house.

Glancing around the crowd, she locks her eyes on mine for a moment, widening when I refuse to look away. The dull fire burning there tells me all I need to know about her. She may look pure, but there's dirt on her soul—a skeleton handcuffed to her wrist that she's been forced to drag around for as long as she can remember.

Her hips sway as she walks away, my pants tenting

uncomfortably when she pauses and gives me one last glance, a small smile lighting up her perfect face.

And holy fucking hell, I want her. Want to break her body in half as I dive inside, filling her veins with my blood.

At the very least, I want her before Kieran has her. Not because I'm better for her but because he deserves to lose.

"Elia..." My father's voice comes from behind me. A warning. "Don't do something you'll regret."

Smirking to myself, eyes glued to where she disappeared through the French doors, I brush some dirt off my Armani suit jacket and yank on the lapels. "Sometimes, regret's the only emotion worth a damn."

Caroline

If I could drag my father's body to this corner of the house and stab him with the pocketknife I keep tucked into my underwear, I would. Without a single thought as to whether I'd regret it after—because I wouldn't.

I'd never regret hurting that man. Not after today and not after the last ten years.

First, he asked me to dress conservatively to avoid drawing attention away from him. Then he told me not to drink or stray too far because he had *investors* lined up, different men vying for my hand.

Stupid and defiant, I'd pulled on a light-pink dress that barely skims the tops of my thighs, relishing in the way my father's eyes bugged out of his head. It takes a lot to shock Dominic Harrison: senator and bad dad extraordinaire.

But I'm beyond done playing his filthy games. Games I never should've been involved in to begin with. The man could take my childhood and push it neatly under his dirty little thumb, but he won't have my adult life, too.

Shortly after we arrived at my cousin Luca's birthday party, did our obligatory family greetings, and spread out to socialize, my father's intent became abundantly clear.

Luckily for me, Kieran Ivers hasn't come out of his not-so-ivory tower in the weeks since the murder of his brother, a former organized crime associate in Stonemore, the corrupt town bordering ours.

Unfortunately, my father likes theatrics. Kieran's absence didn't exonerate me, and he still plans to hand me over to the highest bidder. The leers from his colleagues and men with blood on their hands don't help matters, either.

With shaking fingers, I work a cigarette from the pack in my clutch, not caring that I'm inside, and my aunt Carly will be furious if she discovers me here.

Whatever. She should try being forced into marriage and see how many cigarettes she feels like smoking.

I press the end of the smoke between my lips and rifle through the clutch for my lighter, cursing when it's nowhere in sight. My father probably confiscated it when I went to the bathroom before leaving our house.

"Let me help you with that."

The deep, velvet voice startles me, and I jump back, the cigarette falling from my mouth.

Turning around, I feel heat flare between my thighs. Elia Montalto stands a few inches away, Zippo lighter in hand, offering it to me. I exhale slowly, bending to scoop up my cigarette, unable to stop my gaze from sweeping over his fit body.

Even though this party is casual, he stands there in a three-piece suit—all black, the way I imagine his soul. The

6

top buttons of his undershirt are undone, revealing a light swatch of dark hair. My mouth dries up at the sight.

He's tall, maybe half a foot taller than me, smiling down like the cat that caught the canary. A predator circling his prey.

Sorry, sweetheart, but I'm no one's victim.

After catching his attention outside, I hoped he'd follow me.

My heart beats rapidly against my chest, threatening to bust right out and launch itself at him. Nerves and something else—a quiver in my stomach I can't quite identify.

A few beats of silence pass between us, and he clears his throat, reaching for my wrist. The breath stalls in my lungs at his soft touch, at odds with the calloused fingertips he presses against my skin. Sharp, torn ridges hiding what lies beneath.

He uncurls my hand and takes the cigarette, fitting it between his lips. They're dark pink and pillowy, the bottom curving over a slight cleft in his stubbly chin that I want to push my tongue into.

Jesus, Caroline, get a fucking grip.

Cupping his hand around the Zippo and flicking it open, he lights the tip of the cigarette and takes a long drag; his cheeks hollow and his throat bobs, and I can't tear my eyes from the movement. Everything he does seems to happen in slow motion, and it's captivating as if he calculates each move and consequence ahead of time.

The logic of a killer.

My core throbs, moisture pooling between my thighs, as he removes the cigarette from his mouth and exhales clean smoke through his nose. *Has there ever been anything sexier?*

He offers it to me, and I know it should annoy me that he

took it upon himself to take the first drag, but I find that I don't care. In fact, I quite like the indirect contact of our lips as I go to inhale. Menthol flavors explode in my mouth as my lungs fill with smoke. I breathe out slowly, trying to look casual.

Elia cocks his head, studying me. His gray eyes are dark and impossibly deep, enticing but guarded. Clouds gorged with rainwater just before they burst. "Those things kill people, you know."

I repeat the inhale and exhale, leaning against the rosy wallpaper. Aunt Carly really did a number on this suburban hellhole. "I hear you kill people, too. What do you think will get me first?"

He takes a step toward me even though I'm already plastered against the wall. A small, devilish grin splits his chiseled face, and he runs a hand through his dark locks. They fall forward, disturbed by the movement, just long enough to sweep over his forehead.

I slip my hand behind my back to keep from pushing them out of his face.

"So you know who I am, then."

"I don't live under a rock, and I'm not a tourist. Of course, I know who the self-imposed king of King's Trace is."

And it's true. Everyone in town knows the Montaltos run this place and funnel in more revenue with their drug racket than the rest of the town pulls in combined—that the thirty-year-old *capo* is one of the most dangerous men in the state of Maine.

"Hmm." Taking another step until his body is just a breath away from mine, he reaches for my cigarette, plucking it from between my teeth. He places it in his mouth again, stealing another puff, and irritation simmers in my gut. It's the last one I have, and he's ruining my relief.

His mouth falls open, smoke billowing out in wisps, brushing against my face. I close my eyes as he props his hand on the wall above my shoulder, leaning in. "I heard the king is looking for a queen."

My eyes pop open, taking him in carefully. "How exciting for him."

Shrugging, he drops his hand and grazes my bottom lip with his thumb, propping it open to push the cigarette inside. He holds it there while I inhale, sucking deeper than before like I have something to prove. His eyes watch my mouth work, blazing with a heat I'm not used to. It makes my thighs clench in anticipation.

"I suppose there are worse fates."

I snort, releasing the cigarette. "You equate marriage to fate? Women must be lining up at your door for your hand."

"Women have been lining up on my doorstep since word got around about my massive cock." He says this so casually as if it's supposed to impress me. It does, embarrassingly, but I don't let him know that. "Besides, what's wrong with my analogy? Not all fates are bad. Most aren't even consequential."

"Fate, by design, is catastrophic. Nothing good can come from having your choices taken away."

"Interesting. So you're a fan of choice."

My eyebrows pull together. "What person isn't?"

"You may be surprised, *amore mio*. Many of us decide against choice because of duty. Loyalty."

I ignore the fact that he just called me his love in Italian. Tilting my chin up, I meet his gaze head-on. "Who are you loyal to?" My voice is throaty, desperate from having this sinfully good-looking man so close.

"My family." Dipping his head, he presses his forehead into mine. From the corner of my eye, I see him dig the lit end of my cigarette into the wall. A dark burn appears, tearing at the paper, but I can't bring myself to care. He drops the butt and brings his hand to my lips, tracing them with the tip of his index finger. "Myself, when it comes up."

I swallow over the hard knot that's formed in my throat, trying to remember to breathe. "That's a good person to be loyal to."

He chuckles, bending to glide his nose down the slope of my neck, brushing hair off my shoulder as he descends. His lips trail over me and back up across my collarbone. Pausing, he traces the tip of his tongue over the dip in the middle. One hand comes up to grip my waist, and he moves, fitting his pelvis against my stomach.

I can feel *all* of him.

Fuck me. This is probably the hottest thing that's ever happened to me, and it's happening with one of the most dangerous men on the freaking planet.

Why does that make it immensely hotter?

"You do have a choice, you know." His free hand pinches my chin, forcing me to look down at him while he slips his tongue beneath the neckline of my dress, between my breasts. My nipples stiffen immediately, brushing against the soft material, the friction driving my blood south. "About who you marry."

I sigh softly, tentatively bringing my hand up to run my fingers through his hair. *Of course, he knows about that.*

Unlike his hands, his hair is unnaturally soft, begging to be tugged. My fingers flex in his roots, and he grunts once, biting my nipple through my dress like he's struggling to maintain control.

My pussy aches, apparently in favor of him letting go. "You don't know my father."

Elia scoffs, righting the top of my dress and dropping to his knees. His hands come to my thighs, disappearing under the hem of my skirt. I suck in a breath as they inch higher, my clit pulsing as it waits. "You're an adult. No one can force you to do anything."

"Dominic Harrison can."

He freezes, hands just below the bottom curve of my ass, and frowns. "What does he have on you?"

I shake my head, bringing my hands to his cheeks. The dark stubble lining his jaw is rough against my palms, and I smooth over it, trying to commit him to memory. "It's not your problem."

"Maybe not, but I want to help."

"Why?"

"Do I need a reason to help a girl in distress?"

"First off, I'm not a *girl*, and I'm not in distress. I'm perfectly capable of helping myself." My fingers walk up to his hair, unable to stay away. "Second, you don't know me."

"Do I need to know you to help you?"

"You ask a lot of questions for someone who doesn't answer any himself."

"You haven't asked me anything."

"Nor do I want to. I'm not interested in getting to know you. If you want to help distract me from this god-awful party, be my guest. It's the least you can do after hijacking my cigarette. If not, kindly leave me to sulk alone."

Don't leave. Please, don't leave.

"*Gesù Cristo.* You've got quite the fucking mouth, *amore*

mio." His fingers skirt up and dig into my ass, hard enough to leave bruises. The slight bite of pain feels exquisite, like teetering on the precipice of danger and ultimate pleasure. He bunches my dress around my hips, exposing me in the dark alcove, and glances at the knife tucked into the waistband of my panties.

One dark eyebrow arches.

I shrug, and a grin stretches across his face. He brushes against the handle, almost reverently, hooking his thumb in the crotch of my panties and yanking it aside. "Fucking perfect."

Cool breath skitters across my bare pussy, sending a shiver through my veins, and his lips meet the inside of my inner thigh in an open-mouthed kiss. My back bows, fingers tightening their grip in his hair, holding him in place. "Fucking hell, you're gorgeous. I cannot wait to destroy you."

Coming down from the almost-high, I shake my head, trying to push him away. "No, we can't do anything. Anyone could walk in—"

He sucks on the skin he just kissed, pulling it between his lips until my knees buckle. "That's the point, baby. Let them come in and find me with my head between your legs. I bet dear old Daddy won't want to marry you off after you embarrass him."

A squeak falls from my lips when his tongue makes contact with my clit, delving between my folds with little finesse. He dives in—a man on a mission—and takes what he wants. And while his determination turns me on, I can't help but wonder if I'm making the right decision.

Still, no one's ever done *this* to me, and it feels really fucking good. Elia uses his fingers to spread me, lapping at the bundle of nerves like water, and he's lived his entire life without a single drop. He grunts and huffs against me, the sounds of my arousal obvious in the small room we're in, heating my cheeks and making my legs shake.

"It won't work—"

One long finger swirls around my entrance, pushing in gently. *Oh my God. I'm being fingered by a mob boss in my cousin's house. Can it get any more depraved than this?*

Sitting back on his heels, Elia curls his finger inside me, stroking against my front walls. A fire low in my belly grows, orange and red flames dotting my vision as the pressure mounts.

"Marry *me*, then."

1

CAROLINE

"WHAT DO you *mean* you're getting married?" my younger sister, Juliet, asks from her spot on my bed. She tosses the *Cosmo* magazine in her hand to the wastebasket and sits up, crossing her legs. "I didn't even know you were dating someone."

Shrugging, I pull on a pair of pink flannel pajamas with snowboarding dogs on them. I can at least find comfort in these old rags while the rest of my life spirals out of control.

"Because you're never home—too busy making sex tapes and getting tossed in jail for public urination."

"Uh, *intoxication*, thank you very much." She sticks her tongue out at me, pushing a strand of hair behind her ear, fingering the gold, heart-shaped locket draped around her neck—a present I gave her when she turned eighteen that she hasn't taken off since. "And anyway, we have cell phones. We talk at least once a week, but somehow this guy's never come up until now?"

"I don't know, Jules. I guess maybe I just didn't want to make a big deal out of the whole thing."

"But it *is* a big deal! Daddy's been trying to marry you off since you grew boobs!"

Inwardly, I cringe because she's not wrong. There hasn't been much kindness from my father in the past ten years.

When not doing his damnedest to keep me dependent on him by only paying for college if I agreed to live at home, refusing to buy me a car, and holding my relationship with my sister hostage, he was dragging me along to fundraisers, galas, and other political events—desperate to pawn me off on someone.

Luca's party was only one in a long string of attempts.

I know my father likes to believe I'm inept and useless, but that's only because it's the narrative I've been feeding him. Revenge is a lot easier to exact on someone when they don't think you're capable.

He's in DC campaigning for a friend, but I can almost feel the anger resonating over state lines. News travels fast around King's Trace, and when it's about the Harrisons, the local papers hike into overdrive. When he hears about my engagement, he'll freak. And I can't *wait*.

I flop onto the bed beside Juliet and stretch out. "I guess I'm just not the kind of person you can set up."

She eyes me, looking for a wall to break down. I hate to tell her they're impenetrable, although my future husband put in a good dent. At Luca's party, Elia just waltzed in and obliterated every visible defense, like a Viking pillaging a village. When he asked—no, *demanded*—my hand in marriage, it seemed like my only choice was to agree.

His scent, his body—all of it bewitched me, a sorcerer casting his spell, capturing his victim. It wasn't until much, much later, as I came down from the high of having his mouth on me, that I worried he might be bad for me.

A man disguising venom beneath his custom-tailored suit.

But there wasn't time to think with logic. My father's decree to hand me off to the first pervert to clear his debt was already in motion. I could practically hear the ink drying on our marriage license.

If my fate is tied to marriage, the least I can do for myself is find someone attractive. Then when our union inevitably goes up in flames, at least I can say I had a good-ass time.

And Elia's mouth on my skin is the purest pleasure I've ever known.

"So..." Juliet says, dropping to her back beside me, bumping her shoulder against mine. "Who is it?"

"Who's who?"

"Oh Jesus. Don't start."

I can't stop the grin from spreading, despite the turn of events my life has taken. "I don't know if I should say."

"Okay, well, you can't just keep it a secret. How will that work at the wedding?"

Chewing on the inside of my cheek, I glance at her sheepishly. "There isn't going to be a wedding."

She blinks once. Twice. Three times. On the fourth, she shakes her head as if dispelling some kind of fog. "I'm sorry, what? No *wedding*?"

"Nope."

"*You* don't want a wedding? Since when?"

It comes out accusatory, highlighting her contempt with me. I get it because, to her, I'm the golden child our father smiles down upon, but I don't let her see the truth. She doesn't know what he's done to me—what he'd do to her if given the chance. Ignorance keeps her safe.

"Since now, I guess, Jules."

"You're eloping?"

"Yep."

"Okay, this is officially insane. You've *always* wanted a big wedding. I mean, Jesus, you even wanted to bake the cake yourself, like no one else in town would have the skills to please you." Her blue eyes, clear and bright just like mine, widen, and she jerks backward, clutching the comforter. "Oh my God! Are you pregnant?"

"What? No!" I whisper-shout, eyes flickering to the door.

Our mother's just down the hall in her room soaking in her Jacuzzi, pretending as if the outside world doesn't exist, as usual.

"You totally are! Oh God, this is hilarious. Miss Perfect and Responsible, having a shotgun wedding." She starts laughing, the sound bouncing off the walls of my bedroom.

It brings a small smile to my face, but I push it down, clamping a hand over her mouth. "Would you stop? I said I'm not pregnant. That would require having sex." *Which I haven't in a year.*

She pries my hand from her mouth, one finger at a time, and shrugs. "Luca said you disappeared with someone for a while at his birthday party."

"I had a cigarette," I half lie, clenching my jaw. I'm going to end up killing Luca, too, one of these days. "Would I do that if I were pregnant?"

"Maybe the baby-making came after?"

"*No!*" Huffing, I launch myself backward on the bed. The frame shifts, creaking under the sudden weight. "God, if I tell you who it is, will you *shut up*?"

"I make no promises."

Sucking in a deep breath, I close my eyes and envision his perfect face, the sharp contour of his cheekbones, and the harshness in his gray eyes that makes my stomach somersault. "Elia Montalto."

Silence beats down around us, thick in the air. Suffocating. I roll to my side and prop my head on my hand while Juliet stares at the ceiling, unmoving. Pressing my finger beneath her nose to check her breathing, she snorts and shoves me away, finally coming to life.

"Sorry, I thought for a second I'd died and gone to heaven. It sounded like you said you're getting married to a Mafia boss."

I don't say anything.

"What the hell? Daddy tried to pawn you off on dozens of men, but you pick the biggest criminal in the entire state of Maine? Are you insane, or do you have a death wish?"

A little of both.

"I don't know, Jules. It just kind of... happened. It was an impulsive decision, but there were no other determining factors, I swear." My heart presses painfully against my chest at the lie, hating that I can't sit and explain how my decision protects her. How I wish I didn't have to marry *anyone* and that our father would just keel over, but I can't.

Not yet.

"Well, all right." She shakes her head, twirling a lock of hair around her index finger, lost in thought. "Can I at least be a witness in the ceremony?"

"It's not going to be anything super special, you know. Just us at the courthouse."

"I know. I'm okay with that. You *do* need witnesses for that, right? You won't cut me out of that part of your life, too?"

Tears well in her eyes, and I grind my teeth together, wishing she knew why I hide myself. Wishing I could

SAV R. MILLER

confide in *someone*. But telling her risks her safety, and I won't let our father get her, too. Elia promised he'd make her off-limits. I'm sure that involves the exchange of money in some capacity, but if it means my dad doesn't get to touch her, I don't give a shit.

Up until I hit puberty, Juliet and I were connected at the hips, our souls intertwined and inseparable. Only three years younger than me, she was the closest person I was allowed in my life, and she mirrored everything I did. It felt good to be able to go through things first, like I was conquering demons and showing her how to handle them.

In the years since my father started dragging me around with him for appearance purposes, we've grown apart. My allegations of abuse, pleas I made with my mother to open her eyes and see reality, went unheard, and Juliet always sided with them. She never knew any better.

Distancing yourself from the people who are supposed to show you unconditional love is hard when the evidence is covered up.

Eventually, an invisible wedge formed between us; with me instead just trying to shelter her from the pain I endured at our father's hand, and her acting out any way possible.

My best friend Liv says I have a hero complex, that I want to save those around me, even if that means sacrificing myself in the process.

Juliet calls me a martyr.

Neither of them knows the truth.

I lean down and wrap my arm around Juliet's waist, pulling her slight body into mine. Laying my head on her shoulder, I tap my fingers on her side. "Of course, you can be there. I can't imagine doing it without you."

20

WE MEET my father at the airport when he arrives back in King's Trace. He's *livid* when he sees me; news in DC must really travel fast. His face turns beet red, jaw tightening, and he grips my bicep harshly, fingernails ripping into my skin through the long-sleeved T-shirt I have on. It's early, and my mother and Juliet have gone to grab coffee, so no one is around.

But it's not the abuse I focus on—not this time.

Over a week has passed since the last time I saw Elia, and my nerves are starting to get the best of me. I gave him my number, so why hasn't he called or texted? On my end, it's been complete and utter silence, as though he forgot who I am or rescinded his proposal.

The thought of being sold to someone else makes me nauseous. The prenuptial agreement I got in the mail yesterday with a note reminding me of our court date did little to appease my fears.

Even as my father shoves me up against the wall in an isolated corner of the airport, his hand curling around my throat in a grip meant to rob me of all my air, my brain is on Elia—wondering what he's doing and who he's doing it with. Jealousy prickles low in my belly, fierce and unwarranted.

Jesus, he's not even my husband yet. Why should I give a shit what he's doing?

"Are you even listening to me, you stupid fucking tramp?" My father spits in my face, and I close my eyes, trying not to laugh at the ridicule. Like he hasn't been trying to pimp me out to the people funding his campaign since I was a teenager. "Do you have any idea how much shit you've fucked up for me?"

His free hand comes up and wraps around my neck as well, squeezing hard. This isn't a new dance, but the force with which he's applying pressure is amplified—probably exacerbated by my defiance.

A smile works its way onto my mouth; I can't stop it. I love seeing him like this. So powerless after the last decade of being in complete control. And he can't do a thing about it.

Except kill me. Although he'd be doing me a service by freeing me, I'd only be failing my sister.

"Guess you'll have to find someone else to do your bidding," I grit out, barely able to inhale enough oxygen to speak. My vision explodes with light at the corners, heat slamming into my head as his grip tightens.

"Yeah? And what's to stop me from using that bratty little sister of yours?"

I bare my teeth at him. "Touch Juliet, and I swear it'll be the last thing you do."

"You're going to get us all killed." With a nasty grunt, he releases me, and I gasp, my lungs trying to refill as quickly as possible. My hand flies to my throat, rubbing at the prints I already feel forming, and he turns away from me in disgust. "I always knew you were a bitch, but I didn't think you were stupid, too."

As he walks away, not stopping even to see if I'm able to come after him, my heart shatters. *What did I do to make you hate me?*

The kid in me aches, unsure of what changed between the point when I hit puberty and everything that came before. He wasn't always like this—angry, violent. I *know* there was a time when he read me bedtime stories about princesses slaying dragons and let me fantasize about my dream wedding, saying no man would ever be good enough for me. Normal dad things, and all of a sudden, they were gone, replaced with an evil determined to destroy me.

With no way to distinguish what I did, what exactly caused him to act this way, I've been forced to absorb it, internalize it. But I never stopped wondering *why me*. Worst of all, I can't stop wishing he'd come back. Be my dad again.

Parents have that ability; they create you, and in return, you spend your whole life craving their approval, even if they don't deserve it.

Especially then.

I scramble to my feet, glancing at myself in the window's reflection. Red fingerprints bloom on my skin, evidence of my father's rage. Digging into my purse, I pull out a sheer scarf and quickly tie it around my neck, enough to at least cover half the bruising. Running to catch up to where my father now stands with my mother and Juliet, I can see the question in my mother's eyes, but she doesn't say a word.

She never does. That'd mean facing the monster she married.

My pain feels invisible, like a tiny shard of glass embedded into my skin. Something stepped on and absorbed but otherwise imperceptible to the naked eye. It's not, though. It's real, and it splinters inside me each time no one notices. But there's nothing I can do about it.

Yet.

2

ELIA

THE LITTLE REDHEAD sits back on her heels between my thighs, freshly manicured hands gripping my knees through the black slacks I wear, her mouth dangerously close to my dick. If we didn't have an audience, I'd kick her ass out for being so annoyingly forward.

"Is something wrong, Elia?" Siena's piercing green eyes peer up at me from fluttering lashes, fingers squeezing me. She's completely naked, her pale, freckled body on display in my office even though my father, Orlando Montalto, sits across from us, his gaze trained on the oak surface of my desk. Not my fault he came in while she was attempting seduction.

She does it this time every week, trying to rekindle whatever mediocre flame we once had that amounted to nothing outside of sex. My numerous rejections do nothing to deter her.

I ignore Siena, staring daggers into my father's hollow face. His fingers tap on the wood between us. My office is nestled in the upstairs corner of Crimson, the club we've owned and operated since our arrival in King's Trace, so while music from downstairs bleeds through the walls, it's still relatively quiet. We could do this for hours and not be bothered.

He leans back in his leather wingback chair, crosses an ankle over his knee, and cups his jaw.

Waiting. Watching. A made man through and through, several times over.

The speculation is killing me.

Crimson is a front for Mafia business; King's Trace is a massive tourist town because it's so small and nearly off-the-grid, so rich folk from Quebec and Portland like to vacation here and party hard during their visits. We set up deals in the back alley during the day when we're less likely to be raided, and at night, they come back and pump money into cover charges, overpriced drinks, and sex in our VIP lounge, occasionally with dancers.

I'm not a huge fan of the whole prostitution thing, but I let the girls make the final decision. Most of them don't double because they're paid enough with my gig, but a few do it for the control.

Siena doesn't like control. She wants to be treated like dirt, which is why she continually throws herself at me despite the multiple rejections.

Uncrossing his legs, my father shifts, the rustling fabric of his Brioni suit the only sound in the room. Even the ice cubes in our glasses are still, as if the discomfort swarming around us froze them in the liquid.

The temptation to take Siena up on her offer, just to spite him, is heavy. Unfortunately, spite has played a major rule in my life and our relationship as is, and right now the flames between us burn bright enough that I don't need to add fuel to the fire.

I'm the first to break our silence, desperate to know whether he approves of my decision. "Okay, would you just fucking say something?"

"Not until you excuse your little harlot."

Rolling my eyes, I brush Siena away, tossing her dress in her direction. She pulls it over her head, taking the hint, stiletto heels clacking against the hardwood floor as she exits the room.

My father clears his throat. "What would you like me to say, son? That you're royally fucking up here? Forcing this girl to marry you just to stick it to Ivers?"

"I'm not *forcing* her to do shit. It was a suggestion, and she accepted. Almost immediately. Makes me wonder what the fuck is going on at home."

"Whatever's going on at home is none of your concern. We have much bigger problems, now that someone's stealing from our direct supply in the warehouse. Or did you forget we're missing product?"

I roll my eyes. "Of course not."

"Then why aren't you focusing on that? I know for a fact that Giacomo and Marco have rounded up several men as leads, and I'm told you haven't interrogated a single one."

I'm a little offended, though not at all surprised, that my two right-hand men are telling my father about the things going on around here. I'd be more surprised if they left him in the dark.

Shifting in my seat, I shrug. "*I* don't do that. That's what Kal is for."

Kal Anderson, the doctor we keep on payroll because of his affinity for torture and clean hits. He's infinitely better at it than I am. Swallowing, I swirl my fingertip along the rim of my glass.

"Then bring him in."

"He's not in town."

A deep sigh, from low in his chest. "All right, we'll put Marco on it."

My father leans forward, leveling me with a steely gaze. It doesn't scare me, per se, but my spine does stiffen a bit. His nostrils flare, a clear indication he's pissed.

Well, join the club. I propose to a woman, and she gives me a fake fucking number. If I hadn't been so distracted by the sight of her coming on my tongue, I would've thought to check the number before we departed, but my mind had turned to mush the second I tasted her.

I don't appreciate her ploy, though. As if I'd give her up now or wouldn't be able to find her.

That's my exact plan when I leave the club tonight, but my father's interference is ticking me off. I don't need micro-managing.

"You know, son, how a boss leads his men says a lot about what kind of husband he'll make. Are you sure you're up for that particular task? Because your disinterest in being involved with the business and your immaturity tell me you're not ready for any of it. Maybe I should call Rafe down here and have him dissolve the outfit, take the rest back to Boston with him."

It's a thin threat, considering Rafael Ricci spread his operation thin to avoid federal detection in the first place, and he's not particularly looking to bring drugs back to his city. No, our official capo prefers to spend his time networking with law enforcement and the media, leaving the dirty work to the smaller branches of Ricci Inc.

I clench my jaw, my fingers balling into a fist at my side. It takes more effort than I'm willing to admit not to snap, take my father's throat in my hands, and demand to know what he thinks of the kind of husband he was—one that allowed his wife to be murdered while his son lay there, helpless.

But I can't. I don't want to dredge up the memories or hash out sins past. My mother haunts me regularly; I can only hope she does him as well.

"Maybe you should." I shrug instead, forcing nonchalance.

I can tell he isn't expecting my response, and it makes my chest cave with the weight of how little he knows me. His brown eyes narrow, looking for a piece of my soul to penetrate. But my soul is tarred, black and thick, and in desperate need of redemption.

Too bad men like us don't get that chance.

"What the hell's gotten into you? That girl's pussy can*not* be *that* tight."

Aside from the fact that I've merely tasted Caroline, the way he so blatantly disregards the woman I've chosen to be my wife grates on my nerves. "I get you're used to doing things a certain way, but this is *my* job now. *My* business, *my* wife. And you *will* respect all of it."

"Am I supposed to respect the several million dollars you wire transferred into Harrison's account, as well?"

"It was a business transaction, just like anything else. I had to sweeten the pot so he'd hand Caroline over." And because she asked me to protect her sister, and money is the only thing that speaks to people like Dominic.

A knock on the door jars us from our conversation, and

Benito, my personal guard, pokes his bald head inside. "Giacomo for you, Boss."

I wave him along, irritation spiking my blood. My father's mouth presses into a thin, hard line, and he stands, exiting the room as Gia enters.

"Boss." Giacomo Marelli's large frame and buzzcut fill the doorway, blocking the view into the hallway behind him. He's dressed in casual clothes, light-wash jeans, and a black sweater like he isn't my second-in-command. The only tell is the .22 strapped to his waist, mirroring the weapon on my hip. He averts his eyes from my father's retreating form, scratching at his forearm. "Am I interrupting?"

"Actually, you're late." I push back in my chair, settling behind the desk. Gia looks at me with narrowed eyes, shifting back onto his heels, appearing uncomfortable. I bristle. "What's going on?"

He sighs, looking apologetic. "I guess that depends on what you want to hear first."

"How many fucking problems *are* there?"

"Well, I received word that Kieran is looking for an outfit to poach clientele from and debts to collect."

"How the hell can he do that from that creepy house he lives in?"

"Ivers International has hands in every pie; organized crime is only the tip of the iceberg where their computers are concerned, and Kieran's a hacking phenomenon."

I stroke a hand over my chin, considering this. "And he thinks I owe him something?"

Gia frowns. "He *knows* you do."

Goddamn Dominic Harrison.

If I weren't such a fucking sap, there'd be no wedding. No war with a man lacking a soul.

And that's saying something, since all made men sell a part of themselves for this life. My soul reeks of destruction, but Kieran's is missing altogether. I've only met him once, and only in passing, but it was enough.

What kind of bastard *smiles* during his own brother's funeral?

I sure as fuck didn't smile at Ma's. How could I, knowing what I'd done? The guilt follows me around like a lost ghost, which drove me to help Caroline in the first place. A form of atonement I'm not sure she's capable of offering.

Reaching for the scotch at the corner of my desk, I tip my head back and down the remainder of my drink, admiring the burn as it glides down my throat. Slamming it back on the wooden surface with a grunt, I level Gia with a look. "Does he know I'm not giving her up?"

He nods, shifting and crossing his legs. Gripping his knee in one hand, he flicks a piece of lint off his jeans. The picture of ease, though *my* insides are boiling. "Do you really want to keep her?"

Blinking, I narrow my eyes. "Why the fuck wouldn't I?"

"I don't know. It isn't like this is a marriage that's really benefiting *you*. I mean, wasn't Siena just here?"

The slight bite of jealousy in his words makes my chest squeeze. Gia keeps quiet about his sexuality, but I know a small crush simmers beneath the surface of my best friend. "Yeah, so?"

"*So* why not give Caroline an out, let her marry Kieran, and move on with your life?"

"I don't want to do that. Besides, I've paid my dues. If I'm going to be out a few million dollars, don't you think I deserve to get something out of it?"

To keep my promise to Caroline and provide protection for both her and that bratty sister of hers, I had to outbid Kieran, which meant paying Dom's hefty debt to him. And even though it barely made a dent on my bank, my pride still suffered.

"You're starting a war by bringing her here, and you don't seem to really care."

"I *don't* care." I shrug, suddenly feeling trapped in my expensive suit. I don't know what it is exactly about this subject that makes my skin crawl, but I'm quickly becoming irritated with the conversation. "Caroline belongs to me, regardless of how this arrangement benefits either of us. She will be my *wife*, and I promised to protect her. As my oldest friend, I thought you of all people would get my desire to honor my word."

Bowing his head, he uncrosses his legs and braces his forearms on them. Giacomo and I grew up in this life together; his family followed my father and me shortly after Ma was murdered in New York, starting the Montalto operation under the thumb of the Riccis. When my father retired and Gia's father was shot and paralyzed, we naturally assumed their previous roles and have been running the unit ever since.

His older brother, Angelo, serves as one of my soldiers and constantly causes trouble. Most times, Gia's only job is to keep an eye on the unruly fucker.

As boss, my father only ever admired one trait in a man —loyalty. Dominic Harrison never had any; always looking for a way to steal a quick buck. The senator began as a book-keeper for Ivers International but quickly expanded his business. Using money he skimmed from the Ivers's company, he secured a seat in the legislature and began borrowing from organized crime units throughout the state, promising the moon and more.

Most of the campaign money at this point is stuff he's straight-up laundered from our businesses, using connections as a front and funneling the money into his own account. He's playing a dangerous game; one I suspect he's close to losing. Few steal from the Mafia and live long enough to tell about it.

But regardless of whatever the fuck is going on with him, the little *topolina* is *mine*. I have a feeling she might be worth it.

"LOTTA PUSSIES DRYIN' up today, my friend." Marco Alessi, head of shipments and imports, claps his hand on my shoulder, shaking me. Considering how many trips he's made to the bar and the stench of vodka on his breath, I'm guessing he's wasted.

Phoebe, the petite brunette bartender he insisted we staff, glances at him warily as she adjusts my cuff link. I don't know how I managed to rope her into helping me dress for my elopement, but she seemed happy enough to leave her post at first. Now, she just seems annoyed.

I can relate. "Goddamnit, Marco, you're not supposed to get drunk until after the wedding. That's what the reception is for."

"Sue me." He shrugs, swinging his arms at his side and scanning the room. Crimson's club floor is split level, half for the dance floor and bar, the elevated half a VIP area with dancers and sticky, red leather booths. My eye catches Siena's red hair as she works a pole from above, shaking her ass like her life depends on it, and I quickly look away. Marco, though, zeros in on her, a wicked grin slicing across his face. "Excuse me."

He takes the stairs quickly, immediately sidling up to the side of the stage Siena's on, leaning against the edge as she shimmies around. I roll my eyes, but not because I give a shit who he fucks. My men deserve release, so long as they're smart about it.

For some reason, my nerves are getting the best of me; it's been over a week since I got the correct number and made plans to meet Caroline at the courthouse, and a part of me worries she won't show. If she doesn't, I'll have to chase her father down and shake him for a return, which I know he won't give easily.

I'm not sure she'd forgive me for putting a bullet in his head.

And it wouldn't even solve her problems—as if Kieran wouldn't come after her anyway, demanding payment in whatever form she'd give it. Even if she didn't *give* it, he'd rip it from her the way a dairy farmer rips a newborn calf from its mother. She wouldn't even see it coming.

I don't know why, but there's this strong urge inside me to keep that from happening, which is what has me signing my life over today, abandoning bachelorhood, and choosing duty over freedom.

Nothing good can come from having your choices taken away.

My heart races at the memory of her words, her determination not to let others rule her life—at least, anyone who isn't her father. I need to find out what the fuck he has on her to make the girl so subservient to his every whim.

Phoebe pokes my wrist with the Montalto family cuff

link, drawing my attention back to her. She forces an apologetic smile. "Sorry. I'm not feeling all that well."

"Relax, Pheebs, it's a dull cuff link, not a knife." I take my hand from hers, step off the overturned milk crate we've been using as a platform, and look at myself in the mirror she dragged down from the dressing room upstairs. "Well, what do you think? Do I look like a groom?"

Her big doe eyes stay focused on the stage above us. "You look great, Elia."

"Phoebe."

"Like James Bond, even. Or Michael in *The Godfather*."

I glance again at my all-black Armani suit, because anything more is just false advertisement and obviously more expensive than the one he wore in that movie. "Phoebe," I repeat. "You're not even looking at me."

Blushing, she tears her eyes from Marco and Siena dry humping in a booth. *What the fuck is that about?*

"Sorry, sir." She gulps, then takes me in for real, a slow, shy smile spreading across her face. If not for her demure nature—and the fact that Marco is hopelessly in love with her but clearly a dumbass—I'd probably have had a taste of her delicate flesh, but we work better as colleagues. Friends, even.

And my mind is stuck on a feisty blonde, who, after tonight, will legally be *mine*.

Phoebe's jaw drops as her gaze reconnects with the scene upstairs, watching as Siena crawls on her knees to Marco's lap, head disappearing as her red locks drape over him. I reach down and close her mouth with the tip of my index finger, offering her a sympathetic smile. "Why don't you head home?"

Her eyes snap to mine, and she straightens her back. "I don't need—"

I shake my head, cutting her off. "Look, this place will probably be packed tonight for the reception. You don't want to be here for a Montalto celebration. They're notoriously raucous and always getting shut down by police."

"I thought the police were on your payroll."

"They are, but they've still got to keep up appearances from time to time." She tries to steal another glance upstairs, but I grip her chin firmly, keeping her head straight. "*Go*, kid. Trust me when I say you don't need to see that shit."

Her chin jerks in my hand, resisting, but after a minute of me not relenting, she finally sags beneath my touch and nods. I release her, adjusting the collar of my shirt as she walks back over to the bar, scoops up her coat and purse, and walks out the front entrance without another glance.

I should probably tell Marco to get it on somewhere less public, but I don't have time. One look at the thick gold watch on my wrist tells me I'm somehow running behind, and there isn't a chance in hell I want to miss this.

3

CAROLINE

NAUSEA BUBBLES inside my stomach as I tilt my head, peering up at the King's Trace courthouse. It's an ancient building nestled in the heart of downtown with tall, beige stone walls and stained-glass windows, and sits across from the public library and a couple of local businesses.

And because this isn't a normal wedding or town, Main Street is lined with dozens of cars and folks dressed in their Sunday best as though they'll actually get to be a part of the ceremony.

Juliet's hand clasps mine as we make our way up the front steps, sans our parents, who thought it best to come separately. Something about taking advantage of the large crowd and spinning my marriage to my father's benefit.

I gather the skirt of my dress—a simple white, floor-length sheath with a plunging neckline covered by a thin lace shawl draped strategically around my neck. It hugs my curves and draws attention as we move into the building, causing heat to stain my cheeks.

My sister squeezes my palm, giggling as the tall, metal

doors fall closed behind us. "This is the wildest thing you've *ever* done."

The unease in my stomach spreads, knotting my intestines. "Please stop reminding me."

"Why? You're not thinking of backing out, are you? Wouldn't that crush your fiancé?"

Crushed is not how I imagine Elia would feel if I called off this sham. I've considered showing up at his club several different times this week to falter on my end of the deal, but my father's rage holds me back.

I'm just not sure how I'm supposed to trust this man I'm giving my life away to. Exchanging one prison for a relationship that will undoubtedly erect another just because I like the way his head fits between my thighs? Because he said he could protect me?

Maybe my father is right, and I really am stupid.

As we make our way to the courtroom where my parents and Liv stand by the door, tension threads through the muscles in my chest, restricting airflow. I stumble slightly in the Versace heels I borrowed from Liv, and catch myself on the golden handle, pressing all of my weight into the fixture.

I feel my best friend's hands on my back as Juliet's slips from mine, leaving me cold and alone again as my heart bleeds.

For Juliet. For us.

For me.

Cool fingers wrap around my arm, and suddenly, I'm being half dragged to the ladies' room, where Liv positions me in front of a sink and splashes cold water on my face.

"Hey, be careful! You'll ruin her makeup." Juliet's at my side, dabbing beneath my lower eyelid with a napkin.

Liv rolls her brown eyes, a tight black curl falling from

the updo she has her hair twisted in. She holds a paper towel beneath my chin as the water rolls down my face. "Okay, well, I'm more concerned with the fact that your sister looks like she's about to pass out. Jesus. Did you eat anything today?"

I shake my head slightly. "Didn't want to get sick on my honeymoon." Not that I'm actually getting one, but they don't know that.

"You have to make it through the ceremony to get the honeymoon. Jesus, Care." Liv sighs and unzips her purse, a cream-colored clutch that almost glows against her brown skin. Pulling out a nutrition bar, she splits the package open and hands it to me. "Just don't get any filling on your dress."

Juliet tilts her head, pulling the neckline of my dress up. "Are you sure you want to do this? It's not too late to back out."

Liv nods. "Yeah, say the word, and we'll skedaddle right now. You can move in with me and put that culinary art degree to use since I have no idea how to cook. Hell, I'd even let you come work for me at this point."

"As tempting as the offer to be an unpaid intern at your startup sounds," I say, forcing a smile I hope looks more genuine than it feels, "I'm okay. I want to do this."

Bringing the bar to my mouth, I take a small bite and chew slowly, just noticing my mother in the mirror behind me. She looks so similar to Juliet and me, with her dyed-blond locks—prompted by early graying—and big blue eyes. That's where the comparisons stop, though, because everything else about Lynn Harrison screams *frigid*.

She somehow manages not to notice the bruises lining my neck, just like all the times my father dragged me into his office and screamed until my ears felt like they were bleeding, and she went on about her business—too absorbed in her own understanding of the world to care that someone else is experiencing differently.

Her eyes bore into mine, searching for an explanation. Every time she tries to speak to me, I feign being tired or not feeling well to avoid the conversation. None of it matters anymore, anyway. This train is too far along the track to pull back now, even if my stomach still flips as we leave the restroom.

My mother holds her arm out, barring passage, and then speaks to Juliet and Liv. "Go ahead, girls. We'll be there in a second." They nod and trot off, matching gold dresses sashaying with their retreat. She turns, folding her arms across her chest. "Look, I know you're going to do your best to evade my questions because you're a private person. And while that's something I've put up with thus far, I need to know why you're putting your family through this."

Tears prick my eyes, burning like a grease fire. Everything is always about *us*. I can't exist as a separate being.

I look up at the ceiling until the tears subside, and then I swipe the back of my hand across my nose, meeting her gaze. "Putting us through what, Mom?"

She cocks her head to the side, frowning. The question is ignored when she notes, "Caroline, you barely know this man."

"I know all I need to."

"Oh? So you're aware he's a murderer? A drug dealer?" She scoffs as if it's crazy I could accept someone living that kind of life. Like my father is any better.

Elia's words from Luca's birthday flash in my mind, indicating the inability to choose between loyalty and duty. And maybe if I had more time and more resources, I could afford

to turn my nose up at his career. But I can't. He's too important, and my loyalties lie with *me* now.

"Suspicion does not equal guilt," I say, taking a step back
from her. "*Dad* knows that better than anyone."

The lines around my mother's Botoxed lips deepen.
"Caroline... whatever it is he's doing to you, *tell me*. I want to
help you."

Biting down hard on the inside of my cheek, I consider
the offer but decide against it. If she wants to pretend to be
ignorant of what's been going on under her nose, I can't
trust her.

"You can't help me. I'm not in any danger."

"Caroline, sweetie. You don't do stuff like this. Why won't
you let someone in for once?"

*Because it hurts that I have to give someone an opening. That
no one has ever cared enough to barge in and force the truth
from me.*

Because you turn your head and let it all happen.

"It's done, Mom. I'm marrying Elia, and that's that."

"What are you going to do if things go south? Do you
know what it's like being married to a criminal? They're paranoid, fickle, always looking over their shoulder." She sniffles,
glancing down at her feet. "I never wanted that life for you."

I shrug. It's not like I'm keeping the life; if I make it to the
end of our six-month prenup agreement, I'm out of there
anyway. "There's always divorce, you know."

She laughs, but it's humorless. Fake. A hollow spot rips
open in my heart, accepting all the pain it can fit. "Not with
men like this. He won't let you go."

An excited jitter runs the length of my body, but I shove
it away, compartmentalizing the thought. I can't let the desire

I feel for this vile man cloud my judgment more than it already has.

Even if I can't stop thinking about what it'd feel like to have Elia on top of me. Inside me.

What it'd be like to let him keep me.

Heaving a frustrated sigh, my mother leans in with watery eyes. *Fuck, I could really use a cigarette.* "Are you pregnant?"

Jerking back, I roll my eyes so hard I'm afraid they might fall into my brain. "Jesus, have you been talking to Juliet?" She waits, eyebrows raised. "Fuck, *no*, Mother. I'm not fucking pregnant."

"Not *yet*, anyway."

My eyes widen at the smooth voice, so close I'm afraid to turn around and greet its owner.

But temptation wins out, and I spin on my heels, meeting Elia's steely gaze. It wracks over my form, darkening exponentially, and a slow, simmering grin spreads across his glorious face, brightening his features like lightning striking through a storm cloud.

Sliding his arm around my waist, he nods down at my mother. His all-black suit makes him look even more terrifying than usual, like a fallen angel, and I briefly wonder if he owns anything in color.

"You must be Mrs. Harrison. What a pleasure to meet you, although I do wish the circumstances were a bit different."

"Different?" my mother asks, eyes narrowing at his arm.

I try to squirm away, but he tightens his grip. "I think, typically, families meet prior to the wedding day. You'll understand, of course, that this courtship was sort of a whirlwind, and there was simply not any time. I trust you won't hold it against us."

Her lips purse as if she's trying to determine whether he's speaking down to her, but he just keeps grinning with me pinned to his side.

"Yes, well, I suppose I can understand that," she says finally, easing some of the tension from my shoulders. "Although I still wish the ceremony were bigger. Caroline has always dreamed of a big wedding."

"Is that so?" Elia turns his eyes to me, and I feel lost staring into them like he's letting me see past his normal defenses as he tries to peer into my soul. *Not happening, dude.* "Well," he quips, recovering from the onslaught of information, "perhaps she'll let me throw her a big celebration down the road once business settles."

"And you're sure she's not pregnant? Caroline likes secrets, so forgive me if I'm not exactly convinced."

His hand glides farther around me, palm pressing lightly into my abdomen. My muscles clench beneath his touch, anticipating something more, but it never comes. "Mrs. Harrison, you'll be the first to know when that happens. Now, if you don't mind, we have an appointment, and I hate being late."

As he guides me toward the doors, we leave my mother behind, dumbfounded by his mere presence. I look up to thank him—why, exactly, I don't know. It's not like I didn't have that under control—but he just shakes his head, tossing me a quick smile. "Let's fucking do this, *amore mio.*"

"Wait." I freeze in place, pulling against his hold. "How come I haven't heard from you since the party?"

"Missing me already, *carina*?"

Mouth twisting down, I slip out of his grip and fold my

arms over my chest. "No. I just think it's rude to propose to someone and then ghost them."

"Ghost?" He frowns. "I'm unfamiliar with the term."

"Jesus. How old even are you? Do you know how to use context clues?"

"I'm thirty, and yes, I understand context. Like how the blush staining your pretty cheeks tells me you aren't really angry, just trying to hide how being in my presence turns you on."

Heat spreads from my face to my neck, and my fingers dig into my palms. "I'm actually angry."

"If anyone has the right to be angry, it's me. You gave me a fake number."

I blink. "No, I didn't. Why would I do that and still sign your prenuptial agreement?"

He shrugs. "Okay, well, then it was all a misunderstanding." He moves forward, trapping me against the doors, his pelvis brushing against my stomach. *Christ*, I forgot how tall he is. I swallow as he stares down at me, gray eyes flicking over my face. "Have I mentioned how ravishing you look?"

"No." I'm breathless, making a liar out of myself. How is it I barely know this man, and he's already making me lose control?

"You do." Bending down, he traces his tongue along the curve of my ear, lips landing just beneath my lobe. "Now, let's get inside and do this, so I can get you home and underneath me."

My head swims as he sweeps me inside the courtroom, desperately trying to keep up with this impossible man.

He's electric, fast and splintering, and I can feel myself being drawn in despite my reservations, a conductor begging to be shocked.

My idiot heart should know to run for cover.

MY NEW HUSBAND'S hands feel like snow in mine, as if the blood pumping through his body is made of ice. We've been married all of thirty seconds, and it's the only thing I can focus on—not his father off to one side and not my sister on mine, flanking us in case we change our minds.

Like we can back out now.

I can't even focus on the fact that, for the first time, we're about to kiss as a married couple.

Our first kiss, at all—we didn't exactly get around to mouth kissing at Luca's party.

Nerves race up my arms as he steps close, sending a shiver through my body.

He frames my face in his large palms and tilts my head slightly, forcing me to look into his eyes. They're half lidded, totally devoid of the love and joy he promised me for the rest of our lives just moments ago.

Lifeless.

This is the man who proposed to me, hard and domineering, as he guides me to the position he wants me in. Like I'm a piece of meat and no longer a human.

And I just married this monster.

My heart stutters, conflicted, as those gray irises darken and drift down to my lips; they part in an unwelcome invitation from parts of my body that I'm not proud to admit he awakens.

"*Amore mio,*" this dangerous man whispers, pupils dilating. I curse the way his words make my insides quake. I don't know why he keeps calling me that, considering this is a marriage of convenience—a strategic arrangement and little else.

Barely even that.

When I don't respond—what can I even say?—he steps in closer, a fist tangling at the base of my curls. He angles my head even farther back, forehead perpendicular to the cathedral-style ceiling of the courtroom and leans in so his lips move over mine.

Holy Mother Mary.

Elia presses closer, deepening the kiss despite our audience.

The gesture enraptures me, an uncontained fire consuming my flesh. The heat of his mouth licks down my spine and sets my skin ablaze. I start to protest, but he ignores it and pushes his tongue in, sweeping against the roof like a scavenger on the hunt for scraps of food.

I've been kissed before, but never like this. Not by Elia Montalto.

No man has ever ravaged me this way, and I find it strangely tantalizing, the promise his body makes juxtaposed with the reality of our situation.

One of his hands leaves my hair and glides down my back, curling over the curve of my ass to shift me against him. I feel *all* of him, and I can't deny the way my core throbs with excitement.

We're full-on dry humping in front of a district judge and our closest family, but my husband seems completely unfazed.

I suppose, as a mafioso, he's used to doing unpleasant things in front of others.

Something hard and oddly shaped digs into my hip. Without breaking away, I can tell by the outline that it's a pistol. Having the weapon pressed against me is arousing, the danger this man exudes making me unsteady.

He finally pulls away, allowing me a chance to drag breath back into my lungs as the depravity of this settles in. A soft smile graces the sharp contours of his face, and his hands drift down, pulling the shawl from my neck. I don't have time to object, my head still trying to catch up with the blaze that kiss left.

There's a sharp intake of breath that snaps me back; Elia's fierce gaze locks onto my neck, one hand coming up to shield me from our audience. He leans in, pressing his forehead against mine, and when I think he's about to kiss me a second time, he exhales, closing his eyes, still as a statue.

"What the hell is that?" He speaks through clenched teeth like he's having a hard time maintaining composure.

I swallow, trying to retreat, but his hand keeps me in place. "Nothing."

"Don't fucking lie to me."

My eyes narrow, and I pull back harder, bristling at his tone. He releases me, and I snatch the fabric from his hand, wrapping it around me quickly. Luckily, Juliet, Liv, and Orlando are speaking to the judge and no longer paying us any mind.

"Who did that to you?" Elia growls, reaching for me.

I twist away, shooting him a nasty look. "Just drop it, okay?"

"*Drop it*? Where the fuck would you like me to put it, Caroline?"

Shaking my head, I cross my arms over my chest, closing myself off from him and the confusing things he makes me feel.

This marriage isn't supposed to be like that.

He huffs harshly, rapidly tapping his hand against the wooden railing in front of the defendant's stand, and then grips my wrist and pulls me from the room before I've even had a chance to tell my sister goodbye.

Like I'm actually about to give up any information.

He has his secrets, and I have mine.

4

ELIA

I'VE BEEN MARRIED to this nymph for all of five minutes, and I can already tell she's going to cause me problems. That fucking bruise on her neck is all I can think about, clogging my brain with thoughts of murder.

Why the fuck won't she tell me who did it?

Granted, we barely know each other, and I suppose I can't fault her for not wanting to divulge every secret to a stranger. But still. How can I protect her if she won't tell me what danger lurks ahead?

Tugging her behind me, I burst through the courthouse's front doors, ignoring how she struggles to keep up with me. My Town Car sits at the curb, Benny behind the wheel, and I elbow my way through the small crowd collecting on the sidewalk, throwing open the back passenger door and shoving her inside.

At least, I try to. My palm flattens on top of her head, but she braces her palms against the roof, resisting. "Get your hands off me," she snaps, her voice low to avoid eaves-droppers.

My eyes flicker to the cameras behind us, taking the scene in for all of King's Trace to see. "You really want to do this out here? Our first lovers' quarrel, where everyone can listen and use our words against us?"

Her top lip curls over her teeth in disgust. "We are *not* lovers."

"No? What would you call what we did at Luca's party?"

"Nothing that involves the word love, that's for fucking sure."

I inhale, closing my eyes, trying to tamper the heat rising in my bones. *This girl makes me insane.* My dick stiffens, and I move forward into her, fitting it into her backside. "Careful, *amore mio.* Someone might hear and think you have ulterior motives for defying dear old Daddy."

"Yeah? And what were *your* motives? Because if you think I'm one of your little whores who'll do whatever you say, you have another thing coming." She glares at me over her shoulder, fingers flexing against the rubber material on the inside curve of the car doorframe.

Her tight, plump ass feels soft against my groin, and I throb with desire. It flares in my feet and zings up my spine, flooding my vision. My hand comes down on one cheek, twisting the material of her white dress. "I'd watch that pretty little mouth if I were you."

Even though we're surrounded by a throng of people, strangers with fabricated investment in our lives, she has a glint in her eyes as she meets my gaze over her shoulder. A flame ignites, though I can't pinpoint its origin. "I thought you liked my mouth."

A guttural moan vibrates in my neck, my forehead dropping to her shoulder. "It's the best thing about you, *cara mia,* but it's about to get you in a lot of fucking trouble. Get in the car. *Now*."

She tosses her hair over her shoulder, the scent of tropical, flowery fruit assaulting me as she finally ducks into the vehicle. I slide in beside her as she moves to the opposite door, smoothing her dress down over her legs. We buckle in silence, and Benny pulls away from the sidewalk, inching through the crowd.

"Now," I say, crossing one leg over the other, "let's talk about the bruises on your neck."

"You can't just tell me what to do, you know. You're not my father."

"Thank fuck for that, considering he's a massive piece of shit who *sold* his daughter."

She tosses me a heated glare, nostrils flaring, cheeks pinkening. *Fuck, that blush makes my throat burn.* "How lucky for me that you got there first."

"Kieran Ivers would've bent you over the bench in that courtroom, fucked your likely virgin ass, and then slit your throat before thinking twice about his audience. I think you should count your goddamn lucky stars I even offered to marry you."

"I didn't ask you to do that."

"You didn't object, either. Seemed pretty eager when I had my head between your thighs, worshiping your pussy until you came all over my fucking chin."

We've veered so far off topic, but it's hard to stay focused when the hatred for me emanates from her body like the warm glow from a campfire on a cold winter night. It draws me in, the light irresistible, but I'm afraid someone's left a few dead leaves too close to the pit, and it's beginning to spiral out of control.

Clearing my throat, I try to redirect the conversation. "Just tell me who touched you."

"I don't want to talk about it."

"Too damn bad." My voice is sharp, the jagged edge of a broken glass shard, and she flinches. Swallowing, I try to force some of the tension from my body, aware that I'm being an ass.

What is she doing to me?

With anyone else, I wouldn't care. I'd lean into the fact that she finds me intimidating and use it to get what I want.

Montaltos don't bend to anyone, yet I feel my gut deflating, trying to allow room for her to breathe.

"Caroline." My voice softens, but I don't want her to get comfortable with it. I lean over the seat and grip her chin in my hand, forcing her to look at me. Better she learns I'm a prick now rather than later. "I don't tolerate secrets."

"Well, that's a shame, *husband*, because I have many."

My eyes narrow, searching her flawless face for signs of distress. She's cold and aloof, using her attitude to throw me off, but I'm not so easily deterred. "Tell me what happened to you. The last time I saw you, your body was unharmed."

"Wrong, *Capo*. My body hasn't been unharmed since I was a kid."

"What do you mean?"

She sighs softly, shaking her head, and I release her. Turning to look out the window, she presses her forehead against the glass, watching the world flash by. We pass by the streets leading out of downtown, flush with pine trees while lush landscapes flank the cracked sidewalks. To an outsider, King's Trace is your average, cutesy tourist town, but I know the danger that lurks beneath.

I *am* the danger.

It feels wrong to be the most powerful man in the state yet unable to get your brand-new wife to open up about her demons.

A million miles stretch between Caroline and me, shifting something between us I wasn't even aware existed. An invisible force, blocking her from me.

Settling back in my seat, I close my eyes and try to focus on strategizing for work. Certainly, when Kieran hears that we went through with our nuptials, he'll want a meeting, and I'm sure as fuck not giving him that. Not when I'm sure he's involved in our missing product.

"Why'd you ask me to marry you?"

Opening my eyes, I look over at my wife; Caroline still stares out the window, but her fingers curl into the tops of her thighs, knuckles blooming white. "Does it really matter after the fact?"

"I guess not."

"Look. I just wanted to help. It seemed like you could use it." A smirk tugs at the corner of my mouth, and I try to shift the tone of our afternoon. "It helps that you're beautiful."

"What, did you think that by marrying me, I'd pull my skirt up and let you dick me down whenever you need it?"

I choke on a surprised laugh. "*Dick you down*? Jesus, your mouth. What does that even mean?"

"What's it *sound* like? Come on, Elia, that big head of yours can't be completely empty. Stupid men don't run criminal organizations."

I'm not comfortable with how much she knows about my work, but I suppose that's the curse of living in a small-ass town and being the daughter of a man deeply invested in the world. "Keep talking like that, and I'm going to throw you over my fucking knees, *carina*. I told you to watch your mouth."

"And I told you, I'm not going to just do whatever you say."

My jaw ticks; I can feel my blood pressure rising, shifting quickly from arousal to indignation. No one fucking talks to me like this, yet... I don't mean it when I tell her to stop.

Some idiotic part of me finds it amusing. Interesting, almost, how defiant she is given her apparent submissiveness where her father is involved.

"Why'd you agree to it?" I shouldn't ask. Shouldn't care. But none of this adds up. Her own mother said she's not the impulsive type, and she's made it clear she isn't interested in being like the other Mafia wives. So what the fuck is in this for her besides a little protection?

It's not like she couldn't just disappear. Kieran would go after her father for sure at that point, and the others Dominic owes money to would just follow suit.

So what's keeping her here, tied to me?

Her eyes stay trained out the window, but I don't miss the way they glaze over, the way her throat bobs with a thick swallow. Something isn't right with her, but I don't have time to figure out what exactly because, in the next second, Benny pulls into my driveway, announcing our arrival and pulling her from the conversation entirely.

The gray stone walls on the exterior of the restored Victorian mansion look like every other house on the Lake Koselomal strip. They're homes for a few of the uber elite, surrounded by iron fencing and white cedar trees, overlooking a lake no one ever swims in.

Benny opens the car door for Caroline and helps her out. The urge to make a cutting remark about how easily she accepts help from him briefly scalds my tongue, but I tamp it down at the sheer look of wonder taking over her face. She peers up at the house like it's a castle, and she's a princess finally moving in.

A foreign sensation blossoms within me at the realization that I want her face to stay that way forever—pure, angelic, unfettered. Like all her past ghosts and sins are behind her, forgotten.

"*This* is your house?" A wide grin breaks out, showcasing her perfect white teeth.

I shrug, making my way up the stone front walk. "Yours, as well, now."

"Holy shit." She stands in the circular driveway for a few more seconds, then scrambles to catch up as I step onto the porch. "It's gorgeous. Like something out of a fairy tale."

My eyebrows scrunch together as I look to the mansion, trying to see what she does. But all I see are armed guards and a heavy-duty security system at the front door, making the home seem more like a prison than anything else.

What kind of fairy tales are you reading?

Choosing not to burst her bubble, I key in the door code and wait for it to unlock.

Stepping inside, I share a nod with Benny that lets him know to stay outside and watch as my wife—my *wife*—gazes around at the tall ceilings, the abstract paintings on some of the walls, and the clean and barely used furniture. The white of my home against the white of her dress makes her look like the spring goddess she is, innocence just waiting for the stain of destruction.

I've never liked the lack of color; it's always felt like a personal dig from the interior decorator—like she knew my secrets and filled my home with items I was bound to dirty up.

The white marble flooring, the quartz countertops, and the Viscaya furniture with its gold borders, dark woods, and white velvets make the house feel like a coffin, a lonely shell reflective of the life within.

Yet she gazes around as if she's never seen anything more beautiful.

A small smile plays on my mouth as I watch her, but it disappears as my gaze drops to her neck. She unwinds the sheer wrap, unaware of my inspection, and drapes it over one of the sofas. Trailing her fingers along the soft material, she turns, finally facing me.

If she notices the hard set of my jaw, she doesn't say anything. "This is beautiful."

Again, I shrug because I'm not really sure what else to do here. I don't know what happens after this. All I can think of is finding out who put their hands on her and stuffing my fist down their throat.

"I can't imagine it's that different from your parents' house." The Harrisons live in Locust Grove, a gated community on the other side of town, situated just behind the mayor's mansion.

She scoffs, pushing a curl behind her ear. "It's hardly a home, first of all. And second, houses in Locust Grove are just cookie-cutter shacks hiding tragedy. They're not places for people to live or raise families. Not like this. There are so many possibilities here."

Taking a step closer, I gaze down at her, inhaling her rich scent, wishing I could commit it to memory. Maybe even bottle it, keep it for the nights she inevitably refuses to warm my bed. "What tragedy happened at your house, Caroline?"

Her blue eyes meet mine, and I swear I want nothing more at this moment than to lose myself in their depths. The sadness within is endless, a sea of untethered, repressed memories nearly mirroring my own.

She offers me a tight smile but nothing else.

An invisible force draws me even closer, until our body heat mixes, and I can't tell where I end and she begins. Warmth rises to my neck as her perfume envelops me, and I bring my hand to her throat, sweeping over her broken skin with my fingertips. She leans into my touch, her eyes drifting closed like she feels safe here.

With me.

When she absolutely shouldn't.

When all I can think about is fucking devouring her, crawling inside her skin and stitching myself into the walls of her being, grinding myself into dust and sprinkling it on her bones. All the ways I could destroy and leave my mark on her.

"Fuck," I breathe, my heart swelling and shattering like the tide pulling back and crashing against the shore. Her eyes open, and she stares up at me from hooded lashes, daring me to take her.

Taste her.

Eat her alive.

So I do.

5

CAROLINE

FOR THE SECOND time in the short span we've been married, Elia knocks my freaking socks off with the sheer intensity of his kiss. Well, at least, that'd be the reaction if I was wearing socks.

One second, we're standing there, wallowing in our contempt, and in the next, he's fusing our mouths together until I can't distinguish my breath or heartbeat from his.

It's like he's trying to consume me the way someone might their last supper.

My soul temporarily leaves my body as his lips continue their assault, hands tangling in my hair; it orbits around us as we maneuver through the living room, stopping only once we've hit resistance at the wall by the grandiose staircase. He pushes his hips into my stomach, and I can feel him grow hard in time with his ragged breathing.

Jesus. His erection scorches me through my dress; I raise one leg as he reaches and grips my thigh, hooking it around his waist. My dress bunches at my waist, the new angle granting him better access to my core. The friction of him against my clit causes stars to dance across my vision.

I gasp, my mouth opening at the sensations awakening in my abdomen, and he takes the opportunity to shove his tongue inside, swirling and tasting like I'm the most delicious delicacy he's ever had.

Our tongues war for dominance, twisting and pushing, fighting like two serpents. His free hand cradles my jaw as he tilts my head, deepening the kiss.

From this position, it feels like I can swallow him whole.

And a strange part of me, one I've never tapped into before, kind of wants to.

Finally, he breaks the kiss. I'm not expecting it, though, and find myself jerking forward, trying to chase his mouth. He grins at me, using the tip of his thumb to swipe some saliva collected at the corner of his lip. His chest heaves with each breath, and his hand doesn't move from my thigh—like he's not quite finished.

My pussy pulses at the idea.

"I want you." His eyes darken, thunderstorms trapped in his gaze, and my entire body temperature rises. Goose bumps prickle along my skin as his hand on my thigh travels higher, cupping just below my ass, and squeezes hard. "So goddamn bad."

Sweeping my hands up his chest, I revel in the taut planes beneath his suit, gripping the edges of his lapels. I pull him close and lick the shell of his ear, whispering, "You shouldn't."

Close to the curve of my neck now, he eats up the distance, pressing his lips into my skin. A soft moan escapes my mouth even though I bite the inside of my cheek to keep it in. "What's that supposed to mean?"

He sucks just below my ear as if he's trying to rip the flesh from my body, making me shiver. "Just that you shouldn't want people you don't know everything about." My response is shaky and delayed as he continues his assault.

Releasing me with a succulent pop, he bites down on the raised spot, definitively marking me. God, when my father sees that, he'll probably lose it—even if this man is my husband.

I'm not stupid enough to think my problems have ended.

If anything, I've just exacerbated them.

Elia's head straightens and his eyes bore into mine. He drops my thigh, my shoe smacking against the marble floor and making my body vibrate. "Is there something you're trying to tell me, *carina*?"

"No."

His lips purse, eyes roaming over my face as he searches for answers I'm not willing to give.

I drag in a stuttered breath, trying to calm my racing heart. How many times does it need to break before it learns its lesson and stops yearning for things that can't be?

If I go into this and immediately forget why I've signed my freedom over under the guise of protection, it's all for nothing. I can't let this handsome face—no matter that he's sex on legs—distract me.

Disentangling my limbs from his, I duck beneath his arms and cross the room, leaning against the kitchen counter. Space, that's what we need right now. He gets in my personal bubble, and every bad thought I've ever had about his world and men dissipates into thin air.

He clears his throat, adjusting the collar of his shirt and unbuttoning his suit jacket. "Very well. I have a few things I need to attend to at work, so I regret that I'll be unable to join you for the majority of our honeymoon."

I shrug. "I knew what I was getting into."

We stand there for a few beats, silent, staring at each other. A fire dwindles in his gaze, and my body begs me to rekindle it, but I refrain. *Do not let him distract you.*

"Caroline, I—"

"I'll be fine, Elia. I'm entirely capable of being left here by myself."

"I wouldn't think you're incapable." He frowns, eyebrows pulling inward. "I was just going to say Benito will remain on duty even after I'm gone. I never know how long I'll be, so if you need to leave the house for some reason, just make sure you tell him so he can take you."

"Oh, that isn't necessary." *Like I want his crony tailing me on every trip I make.* "I'm fine walking."

"Walking?"

"That's what I said."

He reaches up and cups the back of his neck, rubbing at the spot. "Caroline, I'm sorry, but I'm afraid you can't just go walking around town any longer. Not without a security detail."

"Why not?"

"Why *not*? I thought you said you knew who I was."

"I do, but what does that have to do with me?"

Exhaling, he drops his hand and shakes his head. "Just...tell Benito when you need to go somewhere. He'll take you wherever."

"And if I don't? If I leave by myself?"

Crossing his arms over his chest, he takes a few steps toward where I'm standing until he's so close he has to turn his head all the way down to look at me. It makes me feel two feet tall. Vulnerable.

"You don't want the answer to that." His voice is harsh, strained, and my ears crave more. More loss of control, more desperation—I want him to unleash the beast I feel percolating beneath the surface of his skin, hiding out in his veins.

I want to push him the way I've been pushed, to see how long it takes him to break.

My soul salivates for his—wants it as a trophy. Proof that I'm not the broken girl my father always said I was or just a prize to tout around.

"But I *do*." My eyes lock onto his, and I see the monster lurking there. It calls out to mine, but I ignore it because that isn't the game we're playing here. "What do I have to do to make you hurt me?"

"Why the fuck would I want to do that?"

I sigh softly, reaching out and smoothing my hands down the front of his suit, flicking my fingers over the belt buckle. My hand grazes the unmistakable bulge in his slacks that hasn't lessened since we pried our faces apart, and he inhales a sharp breath at the contact.

Men are so fucking easy.

Pinching his eyes closed, he shifts his hips forward into my palm, and I squeeze, ignoring the moisture slickening my thighs. Elia Montalto might be the king of King's Trace, but he's no match for me.

Like every other man before him, a quick stroke of his dick sends him into a frenzy, making my task here so much simpler.

He'll never even see it coming.

Just as that thought flashes in my mind, Elia jerks back, breaking the connection. He moves, trapping my body between his and the counter. His hand curls around my throat, the pressure of his fingertips a startling contrast to how it felt having my father's on me last week.

It's light, just enough to prove his authority. Not like he wants to hurt me, but a warning that he absolutely could.

"I don't think my pain is the kind you'll recover from." Dropping his hand and yanking away as if I've burned him, he turns on his heel and marches to the front door. "And I don't know what game you're trying to play, but I should warn you: I don't lose. Ever. Now, stay here while I'm gone, and we can talk logistics when I return. Don't leave this place unless Benito is in attendance. I don't think I need to inform you that people rarely cross Montalto men and live."

The door closes behind him, the sound echoing against the tall ceilings in this loveless castle, and pleasure floods my heart at his parting remarks.

That's exactly what I'm counting on.

I'M NOT a stranger to having someone tail me when I travel; as a senator's daughter, it comes with the territory. But it's an entirely different feeling when it's not your father following you, and instead, a beefy bald man who looks like he could crush me with one thumb. At least he let Liv tag along.

Benito drives me to Locust Grove, stopping at the curb of the last house in the neighborhood. And even though it's only been forty-eight hours since I last stepped foot inside, it feels like an entire lifetime.

It doesn't help that Elia hasn't been home since the afternoon we got married; Benito won't tell me where exactly he went, just that he'd be home whenever he finished the job.

Of course, if I'd known his version of "protection" meant hiring a babysitter, I wouldn't have bothered with the union at all.

He did, at least, send Luca over with groceries and a few evening gowns, for the occasions in which we might need to make an appearance. I tossed them to the back of the walk-in closet I'd made my own in the guest bedroom and clung to Luca's arm, vying for information on what Elia's been up to.

Unsurprisingly, he gave very little information, too busy trying to resume our long-dead and much-regretted relationship. His parting piece was to inform me that my father was still trying to negotiate his freedom or find a way to rip mine away. And that he had flown to Las Vegas for business meetings—which meant, temporarily, my house would be free of the scumbag.

When we've packed all the items in my bedroom into as few boxes as possible, Benito helps us load them into the car. Liv leans against the sedan, folding her arms across her chest and fiddling with the zipper on her raincoat. She won't meet my eyes, and it's starting to grate on my nerves.

"What's up?" I ask, coming around with my last box. Setting it gently on the ground, I stand beside her, mimicking her pose.

She runs a hand through her curls. "Nothing, really. I just hate all of this for you."

"You hate that I'm married and moving out of my parents' house? Come on, Liv, you moved out at seventeen and married your career right out of college."

After graduation, she secured a small loan from her father, a lawyer for Stonemore's Minority Business Development Agency, and opened up her own marketing firm.

Now, Liv offers services to residents in King's Trace and our surrounding areas trying to make their mark on the world.

It was an immediate success, propelled partly by her parents' influence and connections around town. The hours are grueling even a year later, but she seems entirely satisfied with the results. Jupiter Media flourishes, priding itself on its creativity and leadership.

"It's not that I'm upset about it." She swipes a finger beneath her eye, flicking away dried mascara. "When do *you* get to live your life, though? I thought you were gonna open up your bakery finally. Cater to the tweaked-out tourists of King's Trace."

That was before my father stole my startup money and used it in bad investments. Before the Mafia got involved, and my name was thrown in as collateral—as payment.

I laugh, bumping her shoulder with mine, ignoring the pain radiating in my chest. "That's still the dream. There have just been a few... hiccups along the way. But trust me when I say Elia Montalto will not be a problem."

"I don't think he'll be anything *but* a problem, but I'll reserve judgment for now. Let's go get you unpacked and then drink until we're belligerent. Three-day weekend and all."

"Wait. Why? It's the middle of May; there isn't a holiday for another week."

"I know." She winks, pushing off the car. "I took tomorrow off because I'd planned on being hungover, anyway. You don't want me to look like a liar to my employees, do you?"

"Liv, you're the boss. Who cares what they think?"

"A *good* boss trying to set a good example. Most of my

underlings are interns. They need to see a boss who keeps their word, or they're gonna start asking me to pay them."

My stomach sinks as she climbs in the back seat of the car, ready to leave. There's still something inside I've yet to get, and if I don't do it now, I miss my chance.

Benito rounds the trunk and gestures to the box at my feet. "Done with this?"

I nod as my gaze drifts to the large red front door of my childhood home, my body moving of its own accord before I have a chance to stop it.

Inside, I pad across the hardwood floors to the double doors leading into my father's office. Glancing around to make sure my mother and sister haven't returned yet, I push the doors open and close them gently behind me, inhaling the deep, musky scent in the air. Dusty bookshelves line the walls, and ostentatious cherry furniture takes up the floor space, making it look like the den of a man with something to prove.

I walk to the desk and unlock the combination to the bottom drawer. When we came here, I hadn't planned on taking this, but now that we're about to leave, I don't want to go without it. Upstairs, I pocketed my knife and the ankle sheath I sometimes wear when it doesn't fit in the band of my underwear—useful in a pinch, but *this* is the ultimate betrayal. His only defense.

The pistol is heavy in my palm, the metal cold and scintillating in the dim sunlight pouring in from the window. My fingers mold around the barrel like the weapon was made for my hands.

I stand and tuck it into the back of my jeans; it digs into my skin as I exit the house, an uncomfortable reminder of the life I'm trying to avenge.

6

ELIA

GIA SHAKES a cigarette from the pack tucked in his suit jacket, offering it to me. I wave him off, ignoring the way my blood warms at the slight tobacco scent. "I quit."

"Really? Luca Pasini seems to think you left quite the opposite impression on his mother's foyer."

Pushing off the metal wall, I stuff my hands in my pants pockets and turn to the garage door, waiting for Marco to let us inside. "Luca Pasini should learn to keep his stupid fucking mouth shut."

"Must run in the family."

I scrub a hand over my jaw, ignoring the jab. Not because Gia deserves my ignorance, but because my mind is completely stuck on whatever Caroline might be doing at the house. It's been a couple of days since I've even been able to get back, and I hate that there wasn't time for me to show her around and help get her settled.

And even though Benny's at home watching over her, I can't stop my heart from beating erratically at the thought of something happening to her. Which is completely irrational, considering I've known her officially for all of a week and a half—but still.

My legs itch to carry me back to the car and the club, where I can sit behind my computer screen and keep watch over her. Something about her screams trouble—both causation and attraction; a delicate bird with a damaged soul, looking for something to prey on, with no idea of how small and ineffectual she is.

"You seem on edge." Gia takes a drag of his cigarette, propping his foot against the wall as he examines me. "Married life not all it's cracked up to be?"

"What are you, a fucking shrink?" The heels of my hands dig into my eye sockets, rubbing until a kaleidoscope of colors obscure my vision. "And anyway, I've not even been home long enough to experience domestic bliss."

"Ah." He flicks ash onto the ground, smoothing it into the pavement with his boot. Black counter-tracking boots without tread, keeping our involvement at the warehouse anonymous. "So *that's* your problem."

If Marco isn't here in the next sixty seconds, I'm liable to rip out Gia's jugular. "What is?"

"How long's it been since you got laid?"

"Why, you offering?"

He cocks a brow but doesn't say anything. Doesn't have to.

I feel a slight flare of remorse at the taunt, but not enough to draw out an apology.

Crossing my arms over my chest, I grit my teeth, trying to reel in the irritation lacing my blood. His self-righteousness really puts a damper on our friendship. "Anyway, it's none of your damn business."

"*Testy.*" Snapping his fingers, he cracks a smile, the

tension leaving his face. A rarity. Montalto men don't smile, except when we're throwing our power around or trying to get pussy. My fist balls, desperate to erase it from his face. "Oops, sorry. Wrong word."

"Are you twelve, G? Because only a fucking prepubescent child would find that funny."

"I'm just saying. I thought part of the *benefit* of this relationship would be you getting to bend that prim and proper ass of hers over any time you please."

You and me both.

At my sides, both my hands curl into themselves, nails digging into my palms. I feel the skin break, feel the blood under the nails, and feel my heart rate kick up until I can hear it in my ears. It pounds mercilessly, drowning out every other thought. "I didn't ask for your goddamn opinion. Shut the fuck up, or I'll put a bullet through that thick skull of yours."

He clamps his jaw closed just as the garage door finally slides up, Marco's lanky form appearing from behind. He's in black jeans and a black muscle tee, revealing his heavily inked body. Must have just left Siena; she's a sucker for tattoos, and he rarely walks around with them on display. Too identifiable.

My mother had two full sleeves, tattoos she got before she ever met my father. They were bright floral patterns and birds, tracing from her wrists to her shoulders.

They're visible in every picture I have of her, making her a clear target. Not many tattooed Danish women in New York City ever shacked up with an Italian underboss, so she was easy to find when they needed to.

I've only got one: a *sort sol* like she used to talk about. A phenomenon of birds gathering to nest for the night that sometimes blocks the sun. She took the flock as a sign of fate.

She should've known its translation, *black sun*, could've never meant anything good—for the world or for me.

As the thoughts worm their way through the pounding in my ears, Marco hurries us inside, slams the door shut as soon as our feet clear the threshold, and crosses over to where a few decrepit, polyester couches sit. Swiping a black button-down shirt off the arm of one couch, he pulls it on and leaves it hanging, gesturing around at the stacks of packaged coke lining the tables.

"You're fucking late." I make my way around the pallets, inspecting the packages for tampering. If we hadn't already been balls deep in the drug trade when I took over as *capo*, I would've let the antiquated process die with Gia's father's career. Unfortunately, King's Trace tourists are coke fiends willing to pay a pretty penny for a quarter ounce.

Now, I have to make weekly trips to the warehouse and make sure shipments are coming in clean. Until we figure out exactly who's skimming off the top, I have to be vigilant. Colombian exports are expensive, and losing money makes me look like a shitty *capo*.

Marco side-eyes Gia, who shrugs. "Don't mind him. He's grumpy because his wife is giving him permanent blue balls."

"Jesus Christ." Tilting my head back to look up at the rafters in the ceiling, I press past the anger dancing inside. Killing my second-in-command wouldn't be a good look and could jeopardize Caroline's semi-freedom since he's investigating her father's finances.

Coming over to stand beside me, Marco sweeps his hand out over the bricks filling the room. "As you can see, everything comes prepackaged, and I'm sure as shit not messing with anything. No desire to do blow here, Boss."

"Would probably get in the way of your addiction to alcohol." I move through the aisles, glossing over each minute detail. Some bricks are packaged individually—for tourists who make it to town about once a year and like to shell out a cool twenty-five grand for a kilo of aggressive fun. Others are packed in a baker's dozen, running a good quarter of a million dollars, sold in bulk only to reputable, returning customers and other organizations.

Each pallet appears to be intact, sealed with industrial-strength plastic wrap and reinforced with packing tape. At the end of the far aisle next to Marco's cluttered desk sits a locked crate that I know is stuffed full of guns of varying sizes in the event anyone ever discovers this little hellhole.

"If everything comes in off the truck intact, and we've not had any issues with our suppliers in the past, our best bet is that someone in our own ranks is skimming the product before delivery, and then telling the Stonemore gang where we sell in exchange for a cut of the cash."

Marco nods, solemn. "Any ideas who it might be?"

"Not a fucking clue." I look at Gia, who stands off to the side, surveying the area. Always on the lookout.

He meets my eyes, and I don't even have to mention his older brother's name before he lets out a heavy sigh, shoulders slumping. "Fuck. Angelo?"

"Unfortunately, he's the only one of my men ever to have a coke problem, and the one constantly testing his boundaries with me."

"For the record, I've never told that fucker about this place." Marco strokes his chin in thought. "If he's stealing, it means he knows where this is, potentially making it a target."

"Anywhere we go is a goddamn target. That's why we carry."

Gia frowns. "I'll talk to Angelo, see what he knows."

"Good. In the meantime, we'll double security here and at the drop-off locations. No one delivers by themselves anymore. I don't put it past Kieran Ivers to leave that Gothic castle of his just to come down and ambush us during a deal."

"What are you gonna do if it's Angelo stealing?" Marco cocks an eyebrow, shoving his hands into his jeans.

"I'm gonna fucking kill him."

We double-check each pallet for missed details, lock up the warehouse after stationing two guards at both entrances, and head back to Crimson as the sun sets along the King's Trace skyline.

The pink splashing against the clouds reminds me of the heat dotting Caroline's cheeks when I say something particularly crass or rub my erection up against her. The flush that coats her creamy skin when we kiss—like the mere connection of our mouths sends her blood singing. My body aches for hers, like a sore muscle in desperate need of a massage, and the desire coursing through me makes me nervous.

Something strange is going on with her, and I know I shouldn't trust her or let my guard down in her presence. She could kill me. Maybe not physically, but this attraction is dangerous and part of the reason I've been staying away. I only married her to appease the ghost of my mother, and to piss off Kieran and Dominic.

Yet I can't deny the way the base of my neck knots up at the mere thought of her, and that's a huge problem.

Instead of indulging my perverted fantasies when I return to Crimson by calling her, I spot Siena in the VIP lounge, dressed in skimpy leather lingerie, and drag her to my office. She stumbles inside as I slam the door, not bothering to lock it. "On your knees."

A little grin lights up her face as she kneels before me, reaching to adjust the cup of the studded bra barely large enough to contain her tits. "I thought for sure you were done with me now that you're married."

Undoing my belt buckle, I slide the leather band out from the loops around my waist and unzip my slacks. "I don't remember asking you to fucking speak."

Licking her lips, she bounces on her heels and moves forward, cupping me through my black boxer briefs. For a moment, as I stare down at her, the red of her hair morphs to a golden blond, and it's almost possible to imagine this is Caroline and not some common whore.

That I'm in a regular marriage where my wife isn't plotting something, keeping secrets, and not sleeping with me; that I don't need to turn to one of my own dancers to relieve myself of the dark thoughts swarming my mind when I think about Caroline Harrison.

Fuck. *Harrison.* Siena slips her fingers beneath the waist of my boxers, tugging down until my cock springs free, and the face of the senator flashes through my mind, causing my hands to ball into fists at my sides.

My gut tells me he's the one who put those bruises on her neck, but I can't figure out why. Why he'd do it, and why she'd let him. I need to figure out what's going on there before it ruins everything.

Siena's lips close around the tip of my cock, which is only half hard at this point and becoming softer the longer I get stuck in my head. I grip a handful of her hair, trying to force myself into the moment, but it just isn't working.

I want only one set of lips on me, and they're nowhere around the club tonight.

My brain is stuck on going home and fighting with Caroline until her face pinkens, imagining how easy it would be to make her blush. I'd grasp the back of her neck and pull her body into mine, enjoying the resistance she'd inevitably put up. Pressing my hips into hers, feeling the heat emanating from her pussy, I'd bring my face to hers and revel in the sharp intake of breath and uptake of her heartbeat.

I'd bring my mouth to hers, fusing our lips in a kiss rivaling the greatest of fireworks, and strip her bare before she even realizes what's happening—before she has a chance to fight back.

The thought of her putting up walls against my touch, of pretending she doesn't want me as badly as I do her, has me yanking Siena back, disgust softening my cock.

I shove away from the redhead, ignoring how she laps at the saliva dribbling down her chin from my sudden withdrawal—like she's trying to tempt me to return. For some reason, the gesture only serves to disgust me further. Siena is too fucking easy. A puppy vying for my attention.

I want the lioness—the woman I have to work for. *Beg for.* It'll make her surrender all the more sweet.

Walking around my desk, I grab a tissue from the box in the top drawer, then wipe my dick off and tuck it inside my pants. Siena stands and comes over to me, taking a tissue for herself and dabbing at her chin. She perches on the corner of the desk as I sink into the chair, leaning so her massive tits are level with my eyes. I ignore her.

"Honestly, Elia, if you were gonna take me as your mistress, you could've just told me before you went and got married." She laughs, tossing her hair over her shoulder as if the notion is hilarious.

"Who the hell said anything about you being my mistress?"

Her green eyes widen slightly. "Well, you did just bring me up here to fuck my mouth."

"And stopped before it progressed even that far." I lean back in my chair and point toward the door. "You can go now."

She blinks. "Are you kidding?"

"Do I look like someone who makes jokes?"

Her jaw drops. "Elia, you can't be serious. I-I'm your girl. Before that fucking prude wife of yours came into the picture—"

Her tone grates on my already electrified nerve endings. I react with a cruelty rarely seen on this level of the club. Violence is usually reserved for the basement and our fixer.

"I'm going to go ahead and stop you there." Pushing back from the desk and getting to my feet in one smooth movement, Siena doesn't have time to digest what's happening. My palm curls around her throat, my grip harsh and not at all reminiscent of the way I've held Caroline. I don't give myself time to process that before I squeeze, cutting off her air supply.

Her fingers come up to scrape against mine, searching for traction. But I'm too large, too strong.

"Need I remind you who signs your paychecks, who ensures you're able to safely dance at this club, and who runs this fucking town? *Me*, princess. You will not speak to me like I'm the scum beneath your shoe, nor will you refer to my wife in *any* way that isn't entirely and outrightly flattering. You've serviced my cock for years, but that time is over, effective immediately. You may rest assured when I say I won't hesitate to slice your chest open and crush your bitter little heart if you ever call me *Elia* again. I'm *Mr. Montalto*, or *Sir*, to you, and nothing fucking else."

"But—"

My grip tightens, my free hand joining to lift her off the ground. Her claws wrap around mine, desperate in their attempts to get me to relinquish control, but I hold still. Dark-red splotches crop up along her cheekbones, coloring her otherwise pale and dull skin.

"The time for talking is over between us. You will not mention this to a single soul. If I think you've even breathed a sigh regarding this afternoon, I'll have your head mounted on my wall by the end of the day. I'm not fucking around, Siena. And I'm not taking a mistress. *Capisce*?"

She tries to nod, but my hold impedes her ability to agree with me.

With a harsh shove, I release her neck; my heart thumps erratically in my chest as she slumps to the floor, a sob wracking her body. Turning on my heel, I cross the room to the large window overlooking downtown and people-watch for a few moments in silence.

The door closes softly at her departure, and the tension coagulating in my shoulders softens, balmed by the loneliness permeating my office. And as I continue watching those below, picking out the locals from the normal tourists, I lean my forehead against the cool glass, trying to calm the beat of my heart. *Why the fuck does it suddenly feel so empty?*

7

CAROLINE

I'VE BEEN STARING out my bedroom window for half an hour ever since Elia got home. He didn't acknowledge me despite it being the first time we've been under the same roof in a couple of days.

Instead, he stopped just inside the front door, watched me mix cake batter for a few silent moments, and then stomped up the stairs to his bedroom. The door slamming shut told me I probably shouldn't go after him.

Not that I wanted to, anyway; it's not my responsibility to cure his bad mood.

I was taking my strawberry cake out of the oven when he returned with a crossword puzzle book tucked under his armpit, dressed in a black long-sleeved tee and swim trunks.

Still, he ignored me, so I went upstairs to avoid seeing him again. Passing by a hall window, I caught a sliver of tanned, chiseled flesh diving into the pool on the back patio and found myself glued in place.

I haven't moved since. Can't stop ogling my husband as

his body cuts through the water, an unstoppable bullet of energy. Like he's being chased.

What ghost is he trying to outswim?

The sun sets with me still standing, watching. Drooling. He pulls himself out of the pool after one final lap, falling back on the ledge and throwing an arm over his face.

God, he's attractive. The kind of man who clearly made a deal with Satan, because his good looks are just other-worldly.

My clit throbs just looking at him, imploring me to go down and invite him upstairs. But my pride and past keep me from extending the offer. Though I'm sure he'd oblige, considering the other times he's been more than happy to grind against me, I can't make myself do it.

He pulls his crossword puzzle booklet off the black chaise lounge, positioning a pen between his lips and dunking his feet into the water as he scrutinizes the page. Silently, I watch his brow furrow as he marks spots on the booklet, concentration making him a thousand times hotter.

Jesus, he could probably kill someone in front of me right here, right now, and I'd lay back and spread my legs like nothing happened.

And *that* is why I stay in place, why it feels like my feet have grown roots. We're only a few days into this union, and I already feel like I could give Elia my soul.

I have no idea what he'd do with it, given the chance, but I don't want to test the theory, either.

Later, I'm spreading homemade buttercream icing along the outside of my cake, finally having ripped myself away from my husband's glorious body, when he pushes the back door open, strolling inside.

Water drips from his dark hair, the strands sticking to his

forehead; unfortunately, he's put that black shirt on again, as if afraid of what me seeing him in any state of undress might do.

He's right to be afraid. I want to devour him.

Focusing on my spatula, I smooth the icing along the edges of my cake, ignoring his presence. He comes and stands beside the island, leaning one hip against the side. "I didn't know you bake."

"I'm sure there are many things we don't know about each other." I glance up, meet his intense gaze, and immediately drop back to my cake. "I didn't know you like crosswords."

"They're relaxing."

"Is there a lot of stress in your line of work?"

"You know there is." He cocks his head, eyeing me. "But not just with work, anymore."

I swallow, nodding like I totally understand that. And maybe I do since he's pretty obviously talking about me, but whatever. I didn't ask him to marry me.

"Do you need help?" he asks.

Straightening my back, I push icing down toward the mouth of the pipette, considering him. "Have you ever decorated a cake before?"

"Not since..." Trailing off, he clears his throat, scratching at his chest. "Not since I was a kid."

"Well, if you're sure you want to help, you can go behind me and space out flowers with this pipette." I pick up the smaller baggie filled with a light blue icing, topped with a star-shaped nozzle. "Just make sure you don't put them too close together, or I might have to kill you."

Taking the tool from my hands, he follows me in a circle around the bottom edge of the cake, dotting every few inches with tiny, perfect accents. He's careful and considerate with where he places each one, and it makes my chest tighten.

Any time I tried to bake with Juliet or, at one time, my parents, they took over and ignored all my suggestions. Eventually, it became a hobby I had to do by myself.

"*This* is relaxing, too," he says after a few moments, putting the finishing flourish on the last flower. "How long have you been baking?"

"My dad had me in the kitchen at three. Eventually, I graduated to harder stuff like scones and artisan breads, but cake is the easiest, so I make them more than anything else."

"So things with your dad weren't always so bad, then?"

I look down at the counter, my gaze circling a glob of batter that didn't make it to the pan. "Nothing's *always* bad, right? If you look hard enough, you can find the good in anyone."

Our eyes meet when I lift my face, an electric current pulsing between us.

"I can relate. Things with my pops have been weird for a long time."

"Since your mom's death, right?" He raises an eyebrow, and I smile sheepishly. "Everyone in King's Trace knows she died before you guys moved here. I swear, I didn't google you."

Nodding without answering, he swipes a finger into the icing, bringing it to his mouth. His tongue swirls around the end, tasting, and it makes my stomach tense. "Well, this is delicious, in any case. I can definitely tell you love the craft."

Sighing, I smooth my spatula over the hole he made, covering it with more icing. "That I do."

"What else do you love?"

My gaze slides back to him slowly, one of my brows arching. "Why do you ask?"

"I don't know. Is it wrong for me to want to get to know you?"

"Kinda. I mean, six months from now, none of this is gonna matter, right? So I figure, what's the point?"

He frowns, head whipping back like I've just slapped him. "You're really sticking to that prenup."

"It's a contract, Elia. The only thing protecting me from you and my father."

That's the wrong thing to say; his eyes harden, deep-seated anger branching out over the contours of his perfect face. *How can someone look so delectable and so frightening at the same time?*

"Why the fuck do you need protection from me? I'm not the one leaving bruises on you."

He's right, but I don't say it. We don't acknowledge the insinuation that my father is the one leaving them on me instead. Maybe I wasn't as discreet about that as I thought.

"I just mean my reputation. My namesake. I want to make sure that when all this is over, I'm not left completely bro—defenseless."

Crossing his arms over his chest, he glares at me, studying my face. "Right. *When* all this is over. Got it."

"Elia, come on. We're days into this, and we barely know each other. There's a prenup, and an expiration date. We aren't—"

He shakes his head, turning away from me. "I came here tonight because I felt like an asshole for leaving you here for a few days while I took care of things at work. I thought you'd be scared, confused, maybe even a little needy. Silly me, I married a girl who doesn't fucking *need* anyone."

"Why are you acting like you suddenly want more than what we agreed on?" My heart stutters, fear clogging its chambers. "Oh God..."

I'm not egocentric enough to believe he's in love with me, but the look in Elia's eyes has me questioning his intentions. I scan his face, a pit forming in my stomach at the thought of things developing beyond the terms we established.

Beyond what I'm comfortable with.

Scoffing, he turns, showing off his profile, backlit by the pool lights outside. "Don't be stupid, Caroline. I was just hoping you'd warm my bed tonight."

The comment warms my insides, a mix of shame and delight erasing my previous hesitation.

Heat scorches my cheeks, and I set my pipette down, rubbing my thighs together to relieve the ache between them. *God, I so want to.* His bed would be preferable over sitting up in my misery until sleeps steals me away. But again, I decline. "I don't think that'd be a good idea."

"You're probably right."

As he stalks away from me, feet pounding against the stairs on his ascent, my head throbs, wishing I could answer him from before. Tell him what really needs protection when it comes to him.

My heart.

8

ELIA

GET A GRIP, Elia.

Inside my bedroom, I lean against my wooden dresser and let out a long, contemplative breath, thanking the stars above for giving me the strength to walk away from that infuriating woman.

If I'd stayed downstairs even a second longer, I would've ended up bending Caroline over the dining room table and showing her exactly what she should be afraid of.

How badly my body wants her, how it *knows* we'd fit together like missing pieces of a puzzle.

But the fear and confusion in her eyes, coupled with the bewildering feelings soaring in my chest, gave me pause. Pissed me off because all I wanted in the first place was to spend a little time with her, get a glimpse of the girl beneath that hard shell. I thought maybe we could make this situation a bit more bearable if we became better acquainted, so I hung around, waiting for an in.

Still, she shut me out. Though I suppose she doesn't have

much reason to give me an edge inside, considering I've been MIA since our wedding.

Later, I pull on a pair of flannel sleep pants and a white T-shirt, I travel across the hall and knock on her bedroom door. Only a few moments had passed after I locked myself in my room before I heard the light patter of her feet on the stairs, then the soft click of her door shutting, as if she too were afraid of what would happen if she stayed in place.

I didn't go to her immediately. Waited for activity to cease in her room and the rage boiling in my heart to calm before heading over.

I'm not sure why. Maybe because waking her would undoubtedly cause irritation to scramble her pretty face, and I like seeing her frustration. Something about her makes me want to push her buttons and see which ones keep her on.

Perhaps because she drives me mad and has since the day I first saw her. It stands to reason I would want to return a bit of that insanity.

She pulls her door open, rubbing sleep from her pretty blue eyes, and I inhale, trying to seal her scent into my lungs.

Jesus, you've got it bad, man.

"Elia?" She blinks up at me, then looks over her shoulder. "It's midnight. Is something wrong?"

I shake my head, reaching out and cupping her chin. Because fuck me, I just can't refrain from touching her. "I think I owe you an apology."

She leans into me, her skin cool against mine. "You don't. This is a weird situation we're in, and it makes sense. We don't know each other, don't know if we even like each other. I get it, trust me."

A confession eats away at my skin like a necrotizing

bacteria, threatening to reveal my darkest secret—that I've been inescapably enamored by Caroline since I followed her into her aunt's house and forced my way into her life.

Blood rushes between my ears in time to the pulse jumping in my neck. "I like you," I whisper, the sound so soft I'm not sure she even catches it at first. When she pulls back, I know she heard it.

It's disturbingly honest. More honest than I've ever been, and my stomach cramps with the words. I can practically taste her rejection before it's even passing her lips.

"Elia..."

"I don't know why or how. And I know things are new and weird between us, but God help me, I do."

She looks down, scuffing her bare toe against the floor. "We should get some sleep."

Disappointment heats my veins, and my hand drops to my side, deflated. I open my mouth to say more, but the turmoil on her face stops me. "Right... good night, Caroline."

She begins easing the door shut as I turn and go back to my room. As I push mine closed, I watch her watching me through the crack before she caves and closes hers entirely, barring me from her life.

I'm not sure what I expected her to do, all things considered. As tough of a front as she puts up, the woman's clearly a terrified bird who thinks I've trapped her in some gilded cage. If she recoils from my touch half the time, I don't know why I thought an emotional admission might sway her.

Still, something about her calls out to me. Something sinister and unkind that seems to feed off her discomfort, keeping the regret from my confession from settling in my being.

I focus on the blackness outlining those feelings, emphasizing it in my mind. I want to break her—own her. Erase the darkness inked on her soul. Use her innocence for myself; harvest it so she lives on in my bones.

And I won't stop until she's given me everything.

9

CAROLINE

ONE DAY, after the incident with Elia on both levels of the house, my cousin shows up on my doorstep. I take a peach cobbler from the oven as he enters, hands on his narrow hips, blue eyes and nose pinched as if he smells something rotten.

"Didn't your mother ever tell you it's rude to enter someone's kitchen looking like you've just smelled sour milk?" I shuck the red oven mitts off my hands, tossing them to the counter, and turn to face him.

Across the room, Benito gives me a quick nod and heads back to his post outside the front door. I swear, I've never met a more stoic, work-oriented man. It makes me want to crack him open and see what's shriveled up inside.

Luca perches on a barstool at the end of the kitchen island and leans his elbows against the marble counter, schooling his features. His honey-brown hair is slicked back with some gel product, making him look older than his twenty-four years. "What the hell are you doing, Care?"

I glance at the dessert on my stovetop, then back at him, brow furrowed. "Baking. Is that not obvious?"

"I mean, what are you doing *here*?"

Confusion clouds my vision. My eyes cut to one end of the room and back. "I live here."

"Yeah, I fucking know. *Why?* You married my boss, a fucking *capo*. All for what? A nice new kitchen to bake pies in?"

Frowning, I rest my weight on the cabinet behind me. "This is a cobbler, not a pie. Please respect the difference."

He rolls his eyes. "Fuck off with that, Caroline. You're deflecting, and you know it. Why haven't you followed through with your plan yet? What the hell are you waiting for?"

My insides somersault. I *knew* getting Luca involved would come back to bite me, but I figured I'd have an excuse for him when he finally showed. As one of my oldest friends and technically family, I thought maybe his insight would be beneficial to my plan. And it was, but he keeps harping on the situation as though he has some personal stake in it.

Only one person besides me has a personal stake in this, and he doesn't even *know* it.

Elia's confession from the other night flashes in my mind, making me dizzy. "*I like you,*" he'd whispered. A foreign sensation shot through me, trying to reconcile how he can feel that way when he barely knows me.

And why I want him to mean it, even if I can't let him know that.

"I'm waiting for an *opportunity*," I tell Luca. "Not that it's any of your business."

"Oh, so suddenly, your safety isn't my business?" Standing, he walks over to me and mimics my stance, crossing his arms over his chest. He's wearing all black, a Montalto staple, though the contrast of the dark fabric against his skin is entirely different from Elia's.

Luca looks unnaturally pale, flushed like he ran all the way here.

The heat from his side collides with my own, burrowing deep. Mystifying. I reach behind me and grip the underside of the countertop, trying to steady myself. "I'm *married*, Luca. It's not your place anymore."

"You're only married because you wouldn't accept my offer."

"Because you didn't have the money or power to throw around with my father. And you're my cousin."

"By marriage only." His hand drops, sweeping over and prying mine from the counter. He links our fingers together in a gentle reminder. "Besides, that didn't seem to bother you a year ago."

"Things change." But I don't move my hand away, if only because it feels like ages since I've had a semblance of human contact. Benito is not exactly a cuddler, and I can't risk it with Elia.

"Does he know what you're planning?"

I shake my head. "He can't find out, either. I don't need any extra complications."

Elia Montalto *wants* to be someone's white knight. He doesn't know how I'm already making him mine.

"I could still help you." Luca side-eyes me, inching closer. His body against mine is warm and comfortable, but that's it.

Instead of sending goose bumps along my spine, like he did all those months ago when I asked him to help erase the memories of the hands before him, all I feel is regret.

Regret for changing our relationship, for giving that part

of me to him just because I couldn't stand the thought of a grown man touching me before I even knew what I was doing—before I knew just how wrong it was.

Doing Luca didn't extinguish the nightmares, though. Only one man has been able to touch me since then and not have it feel like spiders crawling over my skin.

I turn and inspect the cobbler while he keeps his hold on me. The golden-brown crust sits just below the glass rim of the casserole dish, cracked and ready to dig into. I rarely eat the food I make because sampling while baking fills me up, but this cobbler is an exception.

My stomach growls, and my body feels desperate to indulge in *something*.

"I don't need help." Facing Luca again, I disconnect our hands and bodies, not missing the way his eyes seem to dim slightly. But I don't comment on it.

His disappointment isn't my problem.

"So what, you're going to just dismantle the patriarchy of King's Trace on your own? Exact revenge on a bunch of perverted higher-ups all by yourself? Do you even know what you're doing? Have you ever killed someone before, Caroline?"

The condescension dripping off his words makes my fingers curl, itching to sink into his skin. My nails dig into my palms instead.

I glare up at him, gritting my teeth. "Why, want to give me pointers?"

One eyebrow quirks, and a slow smile tugs up one corner of his mouth. "I mean, I definitely think I'm a good teacher. Or have you forgotten the lessons I've already imparted on you?"

Heat floods my face, flushing my chest beneath the

slinky pink tank top I have on. "That's not really an appropriate conversation, Luc."

"You're too concerned with appearances." He steps
toward me, one hand coming up to push a wayward strand
of hair behind my ear. His palm cups the skin beneath my
ear, holding me in place as his deep ocean eyes gaze at me.
"Why can't you just live a little?"

As he leans in, bringing his chilly lips to mine, I think
about how different Elia's lips feel. Where Luca freezes me in
place, rigidity lining my bones, Elia's touch melts me, a soft
flame incinerating my entire body the second we connect.

Still, there's a comfort present in Luca's arms. He's the
only one who really knows what's going on, and it relieves
some of the burden from my shoulders.

His hands flatten against my back as he pushes his
mouth forward, deepening the kiss and pressing my ass
against the counter. I'm trapped, my brain warring with the
familiarity of being here with him versus the kitchen we're
doing this in—a kitchen belonging to my new husband.

Someone I haven't even seen in days. Just a couple of
texts checking in, making sure I'm still breathing, nothing
about his confession from the other night, or an ETA on his
return.

Luca's tongue pulls me back to the matter at hand,
delving into my mouth at the same time he palms my left
breast over my shirt. His hips drive into mine, seeking me
out, and I open my thighs in reflex, letting him in.

"Jesus, Care." He pulls back briefly to pepper kisses
along my jaw, under my ear. "I forgot how fucking explosive
we are together."

I bite my lip to stifle the laughter bubbling at the base of
my throat. We're certainly not anything *close* to explosive, but

this is still kind of nice. "Luca, I don't... We probably shouldn't—"

His lips land on mine once again, silencing me, and after a few seconds, I force my brain off, letting myself fall into the moment. I close my eyes as he explores the full expanse of my neck. When he wedges his hand into my jean shorts and teases the seam of my sex, it's almost easy to imagine this isn't him at all.

"Well, well. Isn't this fucking cozy?"

I murmur an *mm-hmm* against Luca's lips, loving that I hear Elia's deep, velvet voice in place of his. Safe and protected in one's arms, I still get to enjoy the danger attached to my attraction to a man I want to despise.

Wait. What is he even talking about?

My heart skips a beat as realization dawns on me. The muscles in Luca's back tense under my touch the moment he also notices we aren't alone.

Luca freezes, our mouths still pressed together; I pry my eyes open, staring into his equally wide ones.

He jumps back in a flash, wrenching his hand from my shorts and putting several feet between us. Backing into the refrigerator, he finally stops, out of places to go.

Elia leans against the bottom railing of the winding staircase, the division between the living area and kitchen, with an unreadable expression on his face. One elbow sits propped on the banister, the other stuffed inside his suit pocket, the picture of calm and collected. But the twitch in his left eyebrow tells me on the inside, he's anything but.

And for some really fucked-up reason, the rage I see hiding there turns me on.

10

ELIA

THE BEAUTIFUL NYMPH licks her lips, erasing the evidence of another man's saliva on her flesh. She rights her tank top, smoothing her palms down over her toned thighs, eyes locked on mine like she's afraid to look away.

Good. I want her afraid. Want to cultivate her fear and work it from her body the way you extract honey from a honeycomb.

My plan coming home had been to convince her to come to my bed, at least for a few hours. I haven't been able to stop thinking about her and thought maybe we could temporarily quell the animosity between us, or at least let it burn bright for a while by fucking.

But that's all gone to shit now. I can't stop envisioning Luca's hand in her shorts, his mouth on her delicate, delicious flesh.

My fucking employee, kissing my fucking wife.

I don't move from my spot at the bottom of the stairs, in part because I'm afraid of what I'll do if I get too close to them, but also because my legs feel like they're stuck.

Rooted in a tar pit, burdened by the scene I just stumbled upon.

Not that I have much room to talk, considering my actions with Siena.

But still. Caroline fooling around with one of my men is a liability. If anyone found out, not only would my credibility be shot, but she'd be in danger.

More so than she already is. Just by marrying me, there's a target on her back, and it doesn't help that Kieran and her father are still sniffing around, looking for ways to take her from me. If they knew we were unfaithful to each other, even just a little, they'd use it against us.

My immobility has nothing to do with the way my heart spasms when I imagine someone else touching her—nothing to do with how my lungs constrict, how breathing feels like inhaling fire.

Luca, for his part, has the decency to look ashamed.

But it's not enough. Not for this.

One of my fingers taps along the wrought-iron banister, the dull thud somehow deafening in this house. Neither of them moves or blinks. They keep their eyes trained on me, waiting for the strike.

"When I said to make yourself at home, *amore mio*, this is hardly what I had in mind." I aim for humor, trying to rid myself of the vibrant green coloring my vision. "Certainly not with your cousin."

"Step-cousin," Luca mutters.

Caroline sucks in a breath, pressing one hand into her stomach as if to steady herself. "Elia, that wasn't what it looked like."

"No?" I cut my gaze to Luca, whose shoulders seem to slump forward slightly at her insistence. Sliding my eyes back to my wife, I raise an eyebrow. "What was it, then? Were you, or were you not, making out with a man you're not in any way married to?"

She swallows, the curve of her neck rippling. "I was, but it's not—we aren't—it wasn't like that. Nothing is going on here."

"Interesting." Pushing off the staircase, I meander farther into the kitchen and prop myself against the island. A quick sniff fills my senses with fresh baked goods, nearly sending me back in time to a period of my life I refuse to acknowledge, and I shake my head to collect my thoughts. "Pasini, do you concur with Mrs. Montalto?"

"*Harrison.*" He drops his chin, tearing his eyes from mine. His voice is so soft, I almost don't catch the response.

"Excuse me?"

I see Caroline shift forward from the corner of my eye, inching her way in my direction. I'm not sure if she wants to choose sides or get close enough to attempt to incapacitate me, but I have some serious news for her if she brings her tight little body any fucking closer.

My heart swells in my chest as her sweet scent assaults me. *Fucking hell, she's distracting.* Behind the seam of my pants, my cock stiffens, coming to life at her proximity.

But I'm on a mission, and Montalto men are nothing without their willpower.

His eyes linger on her—a desperation I recognize all too well stuffed down as far as he can get it. There's a longing as he watches her, silently pleading. "Caroline, please. Don't do this."

Fuck. That.

As I cross the distance between myself and the young soldier, eating up the space like a man starved for violence, flames burn low in my abdomen, clenching around my organs. My heartbeat kicks up, a rapid-fire against my rib cage, making me light-headed.

Rage clouds my vision and judgment, and before I have a chance to consider the consequences, my fist connects with Luca's jaw, sending him sprawling onto the ground. Spittle squirts from his lips as he bounces against the floor, hands immediately flying to his face.

I expect a scream, or a gasp, from behind me, but there's only silence. Adrenaline pumps through my veins, igniting my every nerve ending until all I can see and think and feel is *murder*.

Bending down, I grip the roots of his hair and strike his face against the marble floor before he has a chance to get back up. Blood spurts from his eyebrow as it breaks open, and I can hear the faint crack of his nose as it collides with the floor.

Getting to my feet, I dust off my suit jacket and exhale through my nose, steeling myself against how fucking good this all feels.

My black soul vies for the violence. The corruption. *The power.*

It's been so long since I really allowed myself to give in, but now that I have, I'm afraid I might not be able to stop.

My mother is probably rolling in her grave.

Pulling my calf back, I position my boot so it's aligned with his groin and kick forward with every ounce of anger coating my blood. It feels thick and evil, like hot molasses in mid-July blurring my eyesight.

I kick until the only thought piercing my conscience is about my wife and that this man had his hands on her. Something I vowed to protect her from, regardless of intent.

Shame floods the recesses of my brain, a lighthouse calling me to shore as I realize my absence this week maybe drove her to him.

What kind of a fucking husband just disappears on his wife?

My foot seems to continue of its own accord, propelled by the darkness within me, repeating the motion until his gurgling is the only sound present in the entire room. The distant noise of curdling liquid pulls me from my thoughts and grounds me in place.

I blink, feeling as though I've just woken from a blackout.

Luca's body curls into the fetal position, the response probably a reflex and defense mechanism as he chokes on his spit and blood. I slam my fist once into the wall to shake myself out of this—to keep myself from killing him right here in front of Caroline.

Caroline.

Wheeling around, I notice she hasn't moved from her spot by the island. Her clear blue eyes hold mine, a sea of emotion swirling in their depths.

But I don't give her a chance to act on them—to run. Instead, I close the gap between us, cup her jaw in my bruised, bloodied hands, and crush my lips to hers.

There's only a hint of hesitation, the slightest gasp as she opens her mouth, and I tilt my head, adjusting so we fit better together. So I can climb deeper inside.

And then, while her cousin—the man she nearly reached third base with—lies in agony, she raises on her tiptoes and kisses me back.

11

ELIA

"OH GOD." Caroline drags her lips from mine, pushing against my chest. "What the hell are we doing?"

"What *married* couples have done for centuries."

"You just beat the shit out of my cousin."

"*Amore mio*, I told you no one would ever touch you again. I fucking meant it." My hips piston forward, pinning her into the island, my erection hard and heady against her hot, sweet core. I need to get these layers out of the way.

Need to be inside her already.

I drop my mouth to her jaw, feathering kisses along the smooth ridge, feeling her fingers curl into my biceps.

Off to the side, Luca's groans grow more insistent, like he's fighting the black fog threatening to take him under. I can almost feel Caroline's eyes on his slumped form, can feel the moment she distances herself from this between us in favor of caring for him.

Her shoulders tense, her head tilting back farther in an attempt to escape me. She presses hard against my arms, trying to push me off, but there will be no reprieve from this tonight.

She's been my wife an entire week, and I've not tasted her once since the party where we met.

An entire week of her clouding my thoughts, my every fucking fantasy, of wondering what she was doing at home and when I'd be able to get back to her.

The surveillance I have posted around the house keeps me somewhat updated, but there's nothing like being here. No substitute for experience. I can only bust a nut watching her undress through a screen so many times before I need the real thing.

And right now, that's all I want.

Her body, her soul, all of it. I want to bend her over this counter in front of the fucker who thinks he has a claim on her.

"I'm going to fuck you until you're raw—right here, right now—if you don't tell me to stop." My fingers grip her jaw tight enough to leave bruises, but I can't stop the punishment. The monster inside me grabs hold, unyielding as it salivates for her.

It seeks out her inner demons, the dark stains marring her innocence, looking to add insult to injury. It's still mad about my confession, about the mounting feelings I have toward her that remain unreciprocated.

But what does she have to reciprocate? I know more about her than she does me, so how can I expect her to find something decent within me to latch onto?

Ignoring that thought, my free hand pops open the button on her shorts, pushing the fabric aside with a heated fervor. Her chest heaves with each breathless pant, her wrist circling mine before I can delve to her hidden paradise.

"*Wait.* We can't do this here."

Chuckling, I press harder on her throat, loving the way it flexes beneath my grip as she tries to swallow. I dip down and lave my tongue along her collarbone, enjoying her warm flushed skin as a dizzying arousal surges to my dick. It throbs behind my slacks, my balls aching for release.

"I can do whatever the fuck I want, baby. This is my castle, and I'm your goddamn king."

"Elia," she whimpers, hips jutting forward and connecting with mine. Her hands slide up my arms and around my shoulders, nails biting the skin at the back of my neck. But she doesn't try to push me away or duck out. Instead, she leverages against me, hoists herself onto the island, and wraps her legs around my waist, pulling me in close. "I want you to fuck me, but I don't want to do it here. Not in front of Luca."

My nostrils flare against her skin, and I pull back, straightening my spine to look in her eyes. "Well, *carina*, the choice is yours. Either we do this *now*, and I let your little boy-toy walk, or I head back over there and put a bullet in his mouth, then fuck you beside his corpse. It doesn't make a difference to me."

"Isn't it enough that you *nearly* killed him?"

"No." I give her an incredulous look. "*Cristo*, Caroline, you honestly don't know how men like me operate."

She licks her lips, dropping her gaze to my mouth. "How are you any better than Kieran Ivers if you do that? If jealousy clouds your judgment? How can you keep from hurting me if you kill the people I care about?"

"I would appreciate it if you didn't utter that name when I've got my hands on you." Just the mention of that Irish prick has my dick softening.

SAV R. MILLER

She leans forward, pressing her tits into my chest. Through the thin fabric of her tank top and bra, I can feel her puckered nipples brush against me, hot enough to sear a hole through my dress shirt. "You married me and then left me alone for a week. We married out of convenience. I'm not mad about the fact that you smell like perfume right now, why are you so livid about this?"

Part of me wants to note that I work in a strip club, so odd perfume cloying to my clothes is often part of the job. I haven't interacted with Siena since the night in my office, and she avoids even looking in my direction now.

Still, I don't point that out because I don't have a real answer to her question. I don't *know* why I'm so angry. In the past, it has taken far more than this to rile me up, and yet Caroline seems capable of unraveling me all on her own.

There's a persistent sensation pooling in the back of my mind, in the dark part of my heart, that wishes she were more. More than some girl I married out of spite or some savior complex, and more than someone I have an expiration with. Something that wants her to be my saving grace, my redemption—a spring goddess, wrought from the earth to heal me even though I am entirely undeserving.

But I know she doesn't want that. She has some hidden agenda, some secret reasoning for marrying me, and it pisses me off that Luca seems to know about it—that he has an in with her, and she won't give me *anything*.

Thinking of him with his hand in her shorts, sharing her secrets and mouth, sends electricity up my spine, hot enough to sever the cord from my brain. I slide my hand from my wife's neck around her back, palm flattening and fitting her flush against me.

"I don't fucking care *what* this is," I growl into her hair-

100

line. "You're *mine*, and I will destroy anyone who thinks they can take you from me. And I won't stop until these streets run rampant with their blood. Now, turn around and put your hands on the counter."

"Elia..."

"*Caroline.* I'm losing my patience. Either turn around or get on your fucking knees."

"I think we should talk about boundaries and expectations. We hardly know each other, and I'm just not sure getting hot and heavy every time we're together is doing us any favors."

"Honestly, I don't give a shit what you think. Turn around and spread your fucking legs before I do it for you."

Heat flashes in her eyes; she hesitates for a moment, defiance flickering like an electrical fire, wild and out of control.

In truth, if she rejected me, I'd let her. I have no desire to take such a thing from her. It's much less appealing when they don't want it.

But I can't let her know that. The irritation that colors her face turns me on too much, and I still don't wish for her to be too comfortable in my presence.

Not when I feel like I'm on fire in hers.

After a moment, she pushes my arms aside and turns around. Jutting her perky ass into my groin, she flattens her hands against the marble, arching her back and glancing over her shoulder.

Holy. Fucking. Hell.

Has there ever been anything sexier than this? The prim and proper, fiery daughter of a US Senator submitting to her Mafia boss husband. *Fucking perfection.*

My dick's never been harder, and it pulses painfully against her. "Jesus, *amore mio.*" I swallow over the knot forming in my throat, suddenly nervous. The gentle curve of her ass, clad in these shorts, beckons me, a siren leading sailors to their death. I run my hands over her, cupping the backs of her thighs.

She starts to turn her head toward Luca, whose moans have silenced in the minutes since I beat him senseless, but I reach forward and fist her hair, using it to press the side of her face into the counter. "I didn't tell you to move. Remain absolutely still, and maybe we'll both make it out of this alive."

Her fingers stretch, body tense. "What's that supposed to mean?"

"Oh, I think you know." My free hand explores her body, squeezing her tit through her shirt and sliding around to hook in her waistband. "Are you wet for me, *cara mia*?"

She doesn't answer, and a slight chuckle works its way from me as I push her shorts down over her hips. This is the first time I'm actually seeing her bare, under bright lights; as her luscious ass and the half-moon of her pretty pink pussy come into view, I find myself following the movement of her shorts, unable to keep away.

Releasing my grip on her head, I fall to my knees, the sight of her dripping and swollen and *vulnerable* knocking the wind out of me. I shuck off my suit jacket, tossing it somewhere over my shoulder, and shove the sleeves of my shirt to my elbows, pushing my clunky *Cartier* watch farther up my arm.

"I've never seen anything more beautiful." Reaching up with both hands, I spread her pussy lips wide open, thumbing through the juices collecting at her entrance and spreading them up to her clit.

Her hips buck, banging into the cabinetry, as I pinch the bundle of nerves, probing her seam.

"You're such a liar, Caroline. You're *drenched*."

"I never said I wasn't," she breathes, leaning to press her forehead into the countertop. The angle gives me more access, spreading her wider, and I nudge her thighs apart even more, fitting my head between them.

She cries out at the first lash of my tongue against her slit, legs shaking by my ears. I grip a thigh with one hand and shove a digit inside with the other, continuing the ministrations of my tongue in needy, circular motions.

The sweet scent of her skin makes my dick leak in my pants. I adjust my angle, plunging deeper, scissoring her open with two fingers now and using my tongue like a whip against her sensitive flesh.

"Would you have let Luca fuck you?" I say into her, refusing to pull back for even a moment. Like I want to miss a second of this.

"I—what?"

"Answer the question, Caroline." I speed up the lashings of my tongue, spearing between where my fingers pry her open, and drag it up between the crack of her ass, rimming the puckered little hole. "*Fuck,* you taste amazing. The sweetest, purest sin I've ever indulged in."

A strangled sound rips from her throat, and she beats her palm against the counter.

I push a third finger into her as my tongue pierces her ass, massaging the ring of muscle. My knuckles breach her lips, my fingertips meeting resistance, but I don't stop pushing, even though I'm sure it must be uncomfortable. She jerks into the pressure like she loves the bite of pain.

"*Answer* me."

"Jesus! I already did."

"Already did what?"

"Fuck him. I fucked Luca."

I freeze, my tongue snapping back into my mouth. "Wrong answer, *amore mio*."

Her pussy flutters around my fingers, and I can tell she's holding off, trying to deny herself the orgasm for as long as possible. Maybe until I'm buried inside her.

White-hot rage burns through me, zinging up through my thighs and rushing to my brain. I yank my hand from her body; she cries out at the loss but quiets when she hears the clink of my belt buckle. Her fingers flex against the counter as I undo the buttons on my pants, letting them drop to my knees, and shove my boxers down.

My cock, angry and red, bobs free, immediately curving against the swell of her ass. I pump it a few times in my fist, running the tip between her cheeks, and then line up with her entrance.

She braces herself, planting her toes into the floor until they bloom purple, hands white-knuckling the edge of the counter.

I shift my hips forward, my tip splitting her lips as it disappears into her, inch by glorious fucking inch. It takes a few thrusts before I'm fully seated, but once my pelvis sits flush against her perfect little ass, both of us let out low groans of pleasure.

I've never in my life felt anything as heavenly as this. Her pussy is warm and so goddamn wet, clinging to me like rain-soaked clothing. Gliding in and out, I push even deeper on each thrust in, hitting what must be her cervix.

Small body and tight little pussy, meet my massive cock. Happy to be of service.

"*Cristo*," I grit through my teeth, the muscles in my ass clenching as I rut into her. "Your pussy is *tight*. Fits my cock like a goddamn glove. Didn't think it'd be this perfect, did you?"

She makes some unintelligible sound, twisting her head on the counter. My hand rears up, palm covering her face, keeping her from getting distracted. "Ah, ah, ah. Don't look at him. Don't even fucking think about him."

Pulling out, I watch as I disconnect from her body, landing a harsh slap on her ass. Then I fist my shaft and line it back up, a low groan emitting from deep inside my chest as I shove back inside. Her pussy swallows me whole, the sounds of her arousal as I fuck her filling my ears.

It's a flood down there, sloppy and succulent, a symphony I want to fall asleep to for the rest of my life.

That's how I know I'm already in trouble.

12

CAROLINE

Up until this point, I've only *really* been with two other men in my life, although I don't like to count the first. Maintaining the prudish daughter image so that I'd look good while my father groomed me didn't exactly leave a lot of room for fooling around. If I even looked at a man he didn't have plans or debts with, there was hell to pay.

The first was someone I chose thinking he'd be kind. Of all the men my father ran around with, he'd always been the nicest. Until he wasn't.

The other was Luca. A different kind of choice, but one I regretted all the same.

My sister Juliet, on the other hand, has left her mark on nearly every man in town. Free to do whatever she chooses since our parents never seemed to give much of a shit about her in the first place.

I could never decide which fate was worse.

In any case, while my minimal experience and her stories had me thinking I understood what the average dick looked and felt like, *this*—being fucked over my new kitchen counter by my husband, while my cousin lies in a bloody heap of flesh to the side—is unlike anything I ever could've imagined.

Because, holy *hell*, Elia is huge. Definitely bigger than average in girth and length, and he ruts into me like a mad bull on steroids.

His grunts, hot and moist in my ear, make my inner muscles clench, and his calloused fingertips pressing into my skin make me feel pure and innocent.

Loved, even though that's the furthest thing from the truth of our situation.

A harsh knock on the front door pulls me from the impending orgasm dreamland I'm floating in; Elia's thrusts stutter, and he presses as deep inside me as he can go, freezing, his tip nearly puncturing my womb. His front is flush with my back, curled over me in a somewhat protective manner, and I force my body to relax and not read too much into the situation.

If someone's at the door, I can only assume he doesn't want them seeing me naked. Simply because he's possessive and domineering, and not because he cares about the shame it might cause me.

Despite the promises made when we first wed, I don't fool myself into thinking this is anything more.

I can't afford that theory. Don't want to acknowledge what it might mean.

He rolls his hips again, a rough move that sends my pelvis into the counter, eliciting a squeak from my throat. The doorknob rattles, the banging continues, and he pushes my hair over my shoulder and licks a trail up the back of my neck, nibbling lightly.

My vision blurs at the sensation, like being pricked by tiny needles coated in liquid ecstasy.

"Elia," I whisper, frantic, as the lock unlatches to the front door. The movement seems to happen in slow motion.

Without answering or removing his body from mine, he turns and tugs me to the opposite end of the island. We drop to the floor, and then he's rolling, slipping out of me and propping his back against the cabinets.

"Ride me," he commands, his voice low and gravelly. His eyes are half-lidded, blazing with a fiery lust I feel all the way to my toes. Stretching his legs out, he yanks me down on top of him so I'm straddling his thighs, finally seeing his cock in the light for the first time.

And what I see gives me pause.

"You're not wearing a condom." I bite my lip at the creamy arousal coating his dick, which twitches slightly under my perusal. Yep, he's definitely bigger than I imagined, with thick purple veins and a slight curve to the right. It's a wonder he even fits inside me at all.

"So what? I'm clean, and I know you are, too."

I press up on my knees, putting distance between our bodies. My breaths come in sporadic bursts, matching the tempo of his. "What do you mean, you *know* I am?"

He tsks. "*Amore mio.* Did you think I wouldn't do my homework on you prior to establishing a legal, committed relationship?"

"That's extremely creepy."

Hands come up and grip my hips, squeezing lightly, trying to coax me down. "It's creepy to want to protect me and my assets?"

"I signed your stupid prenup. It's not like I get anything if this goes awry."

He frowns, clearly not understanding my sudden vora-cious anger. *Yeah, well, join the club, bud.*

Men don't *get* me, though it's never stopped them from trying to.

I barely even *get* myself.

Elia peers at me, and suddenly there's a softness in his stony eyes. "If this were a normal relationship, you must know I'd give you everything I have." He brings his hands up, cupping my jaw, and my body melts into his.

At least, as much as it can without reconnecting, because I'm weak for this man, and we barely know each other.

"Besides," he continues, dropping my face and reaching around to cradle my ass, "what do you need my money for, when you're the daughter of a senator?"

I glance over the countertop at the front door, which has ceased opening for the time being. Maybe it was Benito, and he thought better of coming in. "I'm not getting an inheritance."

"You're not?"

"No." I half-laugh, tipping my chin down to look at his face. I want to run my tongue along his dark stubble, want to fold myself up and let him consume me, and that worries me because I'm on a mission here.

I'm supposed to be using him, not the other way around. He's not supposed to confuse me, make me feel things.

But the way he stares has me reconsidering everything, and that does me no good. Not getting revenge means not reclaiming my power. My body. *My innocence.*

It means the stains on my soul won't ever be washed out and replaced by the blood of those who've wronged me.

"If my father even has any money left at this point, he's

certainly not giving it to me. Not after I disobeyed him and married you."

My husband blinks, fingers flexing into my skin. It's almost like we're not still naked, dripping with our need for each other—like all of this is ordinary. "Your father's not a good man, is he?"

The hard glint in his eyes tells me he suspects more than his question might initially let on, and I don't have the energy to fight him on his hunches. Instead, I shrug. "None of the men I know are good men. Some are just better at hiding it."

His gaze narrows, his grip on my flesh tightening. "What has he done to you?"

"It doesn't matter, Elia. I'm not there anymore, right?"

"It *does* matter, and I want to know."

"Well, I'm not going to tell you. Maybe you should've dug deeper before you married me."

"Caroline, I—"

But he doesn't get to finish, because the front door flies open, banging into the wall with such force, my teeth almost rattle. Although, it could be less because of the force and more because of the figure standing there, meeting my gaze over the countertop. I'm still sitting atop Elia, partially naked, his half-mast erection plastered against my thigh. My father's eyes darken, a sinister smile stretching across his face.

Speak of the fucking devil.

Elia

"Christ, who the hell is that?" I snap, twisting around to

get a look across the kitchen, but Caroline's thin arms wrap around my neck, pulling my face into her chest. Though she still has her tank top on, I can't deny that I could get used to this position.

"It's my father," she hisses in a low voice. I can tell by the strain in it that she's clenching her teeth. Her spine tenses, and I raise one hand to smooth along the ridges, trying to calm her.

"What the fuck is he doing in my house?"

She shakes her head, but nothing comes out. As she shivers in my arms, I glance around for the suit jacket I discarded earlier. It's a few feet away, tossed haphazardly on the floor, and I use my leg to drag it closer, draping it around her shoulders.

"Is that any way to greet your father-in-law?" The bastard's voice is close, far too close for my liking. When I manage to wrangle my head free of Caroline's breasts, I glance up and see him standing above us, a perverted grin plastered on his rotund face.

"It is when he shows up unannounced and then lets himself in."

"I didn't let myself in. Your guard finally put me through after I spent nearly fifteen minutes convincing him that I am, *in fact*, Dominic Harrison." He stuffs his hands in his khaki pants, pressing them in a way that showcases his semi-hard dick straining against his zipper.

What the ever-loving fuck?

Stroking my hands over Caroline's body to ensure no part of her shows under my jacket, I tuck my chin over her shoulder and glare up at him. "I prefer people don't make house calls. Especially those who owe me and the rest of the state of Maine money."

SAV R. MILLER

He scoffs, pulling out a hand to run it over his hair, greased back with so much product he looks like he just climbed out of my pool. "I just came to see my daughter."

"You came to see my *wife*, who lives in my home, for which *you* need an appointment." I push Caroline gently from my lap, keeping her turned away from this man, and tuck my dick back in my pants, getting to my feet. If the gesture embarrasses him at all, he doesn't show it.

In fact, he simply keeps his gaze trained on his daughter, waiting for her to acknowledge him.

And for some reason, one I can't explain, I don't want her to.

I step in front of him as I zip up my slacks, shielding her from his gaze. It surprises me that she seems to cower in his presence, at odds with the spitfire nature I've become accustomed to in our short time together, but maybe it has more to do with the fact that she's naked than anything else.

At least, that's what I tell myself.

"What can I do for you, Harrison? Need another bailout? A soul? I hate to break it to you, but I damaged mine a long fucking time ago."

Shaking his head, he finally peels his eyes from where they landed on my thighs, his face pinching like he's just sucked on a lemon. "I suppose I should ask about my nephew's body in the corner, but I'm sure it has something to do with my whore daughter. She never was very good at keeping those legs of hers closed; I can't say I'm surprised marriage hasn't changed her."

A dam breaks inside my chest, setting free the vilest, cruelest parts of me. I clench my fists at my sides, resisting the urge to throw one into his cheek or to sucker punch his round gut. He wants a reaction from me, to test the waters and see how much I care for the damsel I bought.

If I take the bait, he'll use it against me, use her against me.

But I'm no fool. Instead of rushing to her defense like my heart demands, I stay silent. Watching him. Fuming.

Something inside me dies with my silence. I don't dare look at Caroline.

"In any case," he says, studying me with black eyes, "I came to formally congratulate you two on the wedding. Not exactly who I saw my *princess* auctioned off to, but I suppose it worked out for the best, regardless."

He throws me a wink, and I suppress the violence clawing its way through my veins. The way he calls her princess in such quick succession, after calling her a whore, laces my stomach with hot nausea. I don't know what's going on here between them, but I don't like it.

It'd be so easy to wrestle his disgusting body to the floor and pin him there until his face pinkened, eyes went bloodshot, and the last measly breath escaped his lungs. So easy to torture him until he apologizes or tells me what the deal is with them.

But I don't. Because it'd be messy, and I promised to protect Caroline, even if I don't trust the feelings she evokes in me. I don't think she'd appreciate me manhandling her father and meddling in her affairs.

"Great. Thanks." My voice is tight, deadpan, but he doesn't seem to notice or take the hint.

"I'd also like to invite you two to a fundraising gala I'm hosting in July. Black-tie, at the Montalto Arts Center. Your appearance would do wonders for my reelection campaign, and I'd love to get to be the one to introduce you as a married couple to the world for the first time."

The thought of being stuck at any event with him makes my ulcer flare, but I nod anyway, hoping to usher him out. "Sounds good. I'll have to check my schedule, but I'm always looking for events to attend. It's good to keep up appearances, wouldn't you say, Senator?"

His eyes narrow, his gaze attempting to dart back to his daughter, but I wedge myself further between them. With an exasperated huff, he smooths down the blue sweater vest he has on, clears his throat, and exits the same way he came in.

Benito pokes his bald head inside, an apologetic look on his face, but I shake my head. I'll deal with his stupid ass later.

Caroline climbs to her feet, clutching my jacket around her, and the sight of my clothing swallowing her has my mouth drying. But the look on her face, gaze downcast and sullen, her features somehow sunken, has me retreating.

She glances at Luca's passed out body, then up at me through watery blue eyes. I don't understand what's happening, why the fight's suddenly drained from her life force, and it throws me off-balance.

I want to reach out and draw her to me, promise her that whatever the hell's going on, it'll all be okay. That I can help her, keep her safe. But something tells me she won't believe me.

Won't let me in.

As she turns on her heel, leaving her shorts across the room and me with her injured cousin, I'm sure of it.

13

CAROLINE

AN INVISIBLE CHASM opens up between Elia and me in the weeks following my father's unwanted drop-in, not that we necessarily needed the help. It's hard to get close to someone who spends all his time at the elusive Crimson—a place I've been instructed not to step foot into—or in our pool out back, swimming laps like he's trying to escape his demons.

I guess he doesn't know how they embed themselves in your skin, locking in with a ferocity that can't be outrun—only slain.

That day, I found myself wishing I could end mine for good. Hot embarrassment coated my skin like a sheer film of sweat, and instead I found myself unwilling to even face him, letting Elia take the lead instead.

Normally, I wouldn't have cowered from my father's leering gaze, but being fully naked around the man brings back memories I'm just not willing to let resurface. It's taken a lot of willpower to get over some of the things he did and said to me, things he made me do, and I won't suddenly let myself regress.

Elia wanted answers, I could tell, but I'm not looking to give them. This particular battle is my own to fight, and although I married him so he'd take care of some things for me, I'm not actually looking for a savior. Just some revenge.

The distance between us shouldn't matter, especially considering my growing attraction to him. But still, when I'm assigned a new bodyguard—Leonardo Fanucci, a brute of a man who doesn't speak or blink or seem to even breathe—I can't help feeling like I'm being punished.

And, well, maybe I am. I did almost fuck one of his soldiers, and without established boundaries and expectations, it's hard to know where exactly we draw the line. Apparently, he draws it at that.

Good to know.

Liv comes to visit not long after that debacle, during one of Elia's frequent stretches where he sleeps at his office and only checks in a few times a day to make sure I'm not dead. I'm working on cranberry-orange muffins, a recipe handed down through generations on my mother's side, when she saunters in, black hair tightly braided and pulled back off her neck.

Leo stands just inside the front door, hands crossed over his lap, watching me. *Always* watching. Like the cameras hidden around the house aren't enough for my husband.

"Oh, good, I'm starving." She's wearing a beige pantsuit with a deep purple undershirt, indicating her departure from work, and I can't help the soft stab of envy that pricks my stomach.

I'd always expected to own a little bakery by this point in life, and to be spending my time baking professionally and sharing my craft with King's Trace.

But here I sit, still baking only for myself.

116

"Cranberry-orange," I tell her, watching as she plucks a muffin from one of eight tins, tearing off a piece of the top and stuffing it in her mouth. "Allergies?"

She waves me off. "Don't worry about that; I have an EpiPen. I'd have to eat like twenty of these for it to really flare up."

"Fine, but don't expect me to dig around in your car for the pen."

Laughing, she plops down on one of the barstools at the island, chewing idly. She glances around the kitchen with its marble counters and vast cabinetry, her dark eyes flickering between me and the muffins. I quirk an eyebrow, daring her to comment.

The thing about Olivia is that she's never, ever, afraid to speak up, especially for something she believes in. She's the stronger of us two, willing to go toe-to-toe with anyone standing in the way of her getting what she wants.

Unfortunately, she's also always been vocal about my choices, and the fact that I don't appear to have a backbone.

That's what all the major news outlets in Maine report on me, anyway; that I'm spineless. A jellyfish, willing to do my father's bidding and suck whatever cock he needs me to. A vessel to help dig him out of debt and look good for his campaigns.

Liv sees it and hates it. Always has. So it doesn't exactly come as a surprise that she's against my marriage, especially knowing how close it seemed I was to getting out from under my father's thumb.

I wasn't, though. She just doesn't know what else he had planned for me.

She doesn't know that marrying Elia was strategic. My

father's not willing to cross the most dangerous man in a town as small as ours, not yet.

Liv sighs, pressing her lips together. "Honestly, Care, what's going on here?"

"I'm baking, same as usual."

"You have *ninety-six* muffins here. How long have you even been up? It's ten in the morning."

"Uh, are you unaware that bakers get up early? Like, middle-of-the-night early?"

"You're not a baker, though. You're, officially, a housewife that enjoys dessert."

I turn on my heel and inhale a deep, cleansing breath. Flipping the light on to the double convection oven, I inspect the muffin-tops for signs of overcooking, but there are none. These are perfect, golden brown and fluffy. Baker quality. *Checkmate, bitch.*

"Did you just stop by to reiterate your disappointment in my life decisions?" I toss her a dirty look over my shoulder as she finishes her last bite. "You could've done that over the phone."

"No." She dusts her hands off on her pant legs, leaning her elbows onto the counter. "I came to check on my best friend, to see for myself that she's still alive. Apparently, Elia gave Luca quite the beating last week." An elegant eyebrow raises in question, prompting me.

"You think he'd beat me?"

"I think you married a made man, and he's capable of anything. And I know about you and Luca, just like I know what jealousy sometimes does to a person."

An image of Elia standing over Luca's bloodied body, then turning and crossing the room to take me into his arms flashes across my vision, startling me with its intensity. It's probably extremely fucked up that I so willingly went to him after, but God, no one's *ever* cared enough about me to do something like that.

Nobody other than my father, who shouldn't care like *that* in the first place.

"Well, I'm fine." I pull on two black oven mitts and throw open the appliance, reaching in for the last tin. The hot, fruity scent assaults me as I set the tray on the stove, shucking off the mitts.

"How can you really be sure, though? When's the last time you left the house?" Her big, brown eyes scan my body, and I know what she sees; sweats, unwashed hair, and a splotch of muffin batter dried to my chin. "You don't look like yourself, Caroline."

How fitting, then, that I don't seem to feel like myself, either.

"I just want my friend back." Liv's voice is soft, almost inaudible, and it makes my heart clench. "Don't get me wrong; I'm happy if you're happy, even if I don't trust the guy. But I didn't think you getting married meant I had to lose you, too."

Turning to face her, I lean back against the counter, tilting my head toward the ceiling. "You didn't lose me. I'm still here. I'm just... doing something different."

Her eyebrows draw inward, and the overhead light casts her deeply bronzed skin in shadows. "Juliet made it seem like you and Elia were soulmates that couldn't stand to be apart any longer. If that's true, I can live with this whole... arrangement. Your response just now doesn't feel like that, though."

"Come on, Liv, you know me better than anyone. Do I ever tell my sister anything of consequence?"

"I know, but she seemed so certain." She reaches for

another muffin, extracting it from its pan and tearing off the top, eating the bottom half first. My stomach lurches at the absolute disrespect, but I remain silent. "So if that's not the case—and, for the record, *duh*, like I wouldn't know if you'd found your soulmate—what's going on?"

I chew on the corner of my lip, contemplating the necessary details. I don't want to involve Liv in anything that could get her into trouble, but I feel bad lying to her, too. She doesn't exactly know everything that's gone on at home in the last decade, but she knows my father is a piece of shit, which is more than I can say for my mom and sister.

"If I said it was time to get out from under my father's reign, would you be able to just leave it at that?"

She frowns. "Uh, no. I definitely need more details."

"Liv, I don't think you *want* the details."

"I think I do."

"*Olivia Taylor*. No."

She swallows, dropping the other half of her muffin onto the countertop in front of her. "Okay. Tell me this: are you in trouble?"

"No." *Not yet, anyway.*

"A promising start. Do I need to ask my dad to be available for counsel, if you *do* get into trouble?"

"No."

"Okay." Wiping her hands on her suit jacket, she shrugs. "All I need to know then. Keep the rest to yourself, but Jesus Christ, Care, don't shut me out completely. I'm still your friend, right, secrets aside?"

"Of course, you are." I shoot her a wide-mouthed grin; it stretches painfully across my face, nearly splitting it in two.

"Good, because I need a date to the birthday shindig I'm throwing myself."

I groan, any hope that her work would keep her from wanting to do birthday stuff shattered. "I don't really feel like partying."

"Oh, come on! You say that every year, and every year we go out and get plastered, and you have a great time."

"A great time throwing up, you mean."

She giggles, her hand coming up to cover the small gap in her front teeth. "Vomit is an indication of a good time, yes. I'm not taking no for an answer, Caroline. Think of it as a bachelorette-party-birthday extravaganza, something to make up for that honeymoon you guys didn't take." Glancing around, she nods, eyes lingering on the tall, white walls that stretch into paneled, coffered ceilings and the grand staircase leading to the second floor. "Why didn't you have one again?"

"We had to reschedule, something about a conflict with Elia's work. *But,* I'll go out with you this time, especially if it means I get to ditch the warden." Hooking my thumb over my shoulder, I point toward Leo, who hasn't moved a single muscle the entire time we've been standing here.

Glancing down the counter at an envelope I discarded— the precursor to baking today—she scans the page from the King's Trace DMV, acknowledging a name change request I never submitted. Because, apparently, my husband is a crazy person.

Sitting up and ignoring the paper, she claps her hands together, already pulling her iPhone from her jacket pocket and typing something out on it. "I'm telling your sister to meet us there for drinks. I had a friend at Jupiter hook me up with exclusive VIP tickets, which cost an absolute fortune. Honestly, knowing who you married, I don't know why we can't get in for free."

Eyes narrowing, I reach for my own muffin, taking a bite right off the top. "Where are we going?"

"Crimson."

As I take a second bite, the tangy fruit flavor exploding against my tongue like a tiny orgasm, my stomach flutters. Many of my father's men frequent the club, known for its high-caliber cocaine and high-security presence. It's the perfect place to get my hands a little dirty, but with Elia on the hunt and looking for insight into my past, it'll be impossible to get in without being noticed.

Maybe with the help of these tickets, bought under someone else's name, I'll have a fighting chance.

WHEN ELIA finally comes home that night, long after Liv has eaten an entire tin of my muffins and made plans to pick me up Friday at midnight, I'm lounging on the sofa in the living room, scrolling through what's available on Netflix.

He stumbles inside, suit jacket and shirt askew, hair tousled, and reeking of stale whiskey and cigars. Leo assists him over the threshold and through the front room, settling him down in the overstuffed armchair across from me.

I see a quick flash of Benito's bald head as the front door shuts, making me miss the crusty bastard. At least he sometimes smiled.

Elia's head lolls to the back of the chair, and he plants his feet pointedly on the floor, the soles of his shoes loud as they smack against the hardwood.

Ignoring his apparent drunken state, I continue looking for some show to lift my spirits, the weight of my life seeping into my bones, trying to drag me into a deep depression.

Elia's heated gaze bores into my skin, setting my soul aflame, but I don't give in and look. No matter how my body yearns for him.

"*Cara mia.*" His voice is breathy and weightless as it drifts across the room to me.

Still, I ignore him, unwilling to acknowledge the desire and concern lurking in his eyes.

We're practically enemies at this point because of my father and stubbornness, yet we're bound by a singular purpose: duty and loyalty.

He wants to protect me. Wants to appear noble and powerful to his men and this town, and I want to free myself of the bondage that's kept me broken for so long. Caged. Fighting. My loyalty lies with me, and that's why I'm here.

The way my husband looks at me, though, makes me wish things were different. Makes me forget that I want revenge. And he may think he's using me, protecting me, but he has no fucking clue that I'm the predator. That I'm using him, waiting for the chance to strike.

"Christ, you're beautiful." His head flops back onto the chair, chin pointing toward the ceiling. His eyes trace the circular motion of the fan mounted in the middle. "What's a pure, innocent soul doing with someone as wretched as me?"

I purse my lips but keep my eyes on the television. "Maybe I'm not so pure and innocent."

Snapping his head back, I see a smile grace his perfect features for a moment. A shiver skitters along my skin, scattering goose bumps in its wake. "Oh, don't I fucking know it."

Ignoring that comment, I settle on a British baking show, watching the contestants go through the motions and trying not to focus on Elia unbuttoning his dress shirt from the corner of my eye. His movements are slow and lazy, and the warmth from his stare sears into me like a cattle prod trying to brand me.

"Do you believe in fate, Caroline? Destiny?"

Sighing, I sit back against the sofa, refusing to turn my head. "We already discussed that the day we met. Luca's party, remember?"

Elia scoffs, shoving his shirt open. "*Luca*, right." He's quiet for a moment, and I try to focus on the contestant attempting to make fondant. They're failing, miserably, but I'll give them props for trying. "Do you ever think about what it was that brought you to me?"

"No."

"Never?"

"I know what brought me to you, Elia. My bastard father. Not fate, or God, or any other sort of universal intervention." Crossing my arms, I finally steal a glance, and when I do, the breath is knocked from my body.

Sitting there with his hair mussed and his clothes haphazardly hanging to his frame, he looks like some sort of god. The picture of practiced ease, though his eyes burn with a heat I feel in my core. His eyes give him away.

He frowns, shaking his head. "I think it was something else. Something *grand*. Spectacular. Earth-shattering, like you."

"What are you talking about?"

"Caroline, I can't get you out of my head. I don't know what it means, especially since we still hardly know each other, but I know these thoughts aren't normal."

I swallow, twiddling my thumbs, unsure of what to say to that.

"Does that scare you?"

"Nothing scares me."

He watches me, eyes narrowed. "Nothing? Not even the fact that you might be developing feelings for me?"

"I *barely* know you."

"We all have to start somewhere." He sighs. "You remind me of my mother. Not in a creepy way, but with how strong you are. How proud and resilient. I know you've seen some bad shit, but it's clear to me that you're still good despite all that. Your innocence might be stained, but it's not missing."

Not waiting for a response, he shrugs the rest of the way out of his shirt, then stretches and fits his head back against the chair. His eyes close, and his breathing evens out, allowing me time to peruse him.

Raking my eyes over his naked torso feels like being punched in the throat and then getting kicked in the vagina. He's cut, the lines of his chest and abs so deep and defined, I think he'd draw blood if I traced my fingertips along them.

And God, do I want to.

But that's not what's so shocking. Honestly, having felt his body against mine a few times at this point, it'd be more shocking to see an ounce of fat on him.

No, the sight that steals the breath from my lungs, razes the walls around my heart, are the scars lining his forearms; jagged pieces of white, raised flesh dotting the corded muscles—like fulfilled destinations on a map, telling me of his sordid past.

A source of vulnerability, as the king of King's Trace rarely allows himself to be seen without a shirt on. And I've not been paying close enough attention otherwise to have noticed the scars before.

A flock of birds swirls around his left rib cage, as big as my head, a tattoo I'm certain no other woman in town is aware of. The linework is intricate, done by someone he trusted, which is not an easy thing to come by when you're born into the world we were.

My heart flutters as I compare the two. His is a world ripe with criminal activity and power; mine thrives on the same things, but it veils them in a much more sinister way—manifests that power and activity differently.

Elia's world needs strong, viable people; mine needs cowards. Bastards like my father.

"What happened to you?" I find myself asking, my mouth moving before my brain can catch up.

His gray eyes flip open and find mine, a sea of emotion I can't—or won't—decipher. "What happened to *you*?"

Pressing my lips together, I shake my head slightly, already giving up the fight. "It doesn't matter."

"Who the hell ingrained in your head that the stuff that happened to you doesn't matter, Caroline? Tell me right now, and I'll go bash their goddamn skull in." He slides off the chair, onto his knees on the floor, and crawls over to where I'm sitting. His eyes are glassy, reminding me that he's wasted, but that doesn't stop my breath from catching in my throat at having him so near. "If it still hurts, it *matters*."

My mouth falls open, a soft gasp escaping my lips as his fingers wrap around my calf. His touch burns me, a hot knife to my cold skin, but I steel myself against leaning into it. "Can you just leave it alone? I don't want to talk about it, especially not with you."

"And why not with me? What's so bad about me, huh? What the fuck have I done to deserve this rage except bail you out of a complete shitstorm that your father got you wrapped up in?"

"I didn't ask you to do that." Not really. Not like this.

He offered, and I didn't refuse.

"No, you didn't, but I wanted to help you." He swears under his breath, the sound garbled. "Christ, I still do. Fuck me, right? I must be the dumbest, weakest *capo* of all time."

I watch his face for a few beats as his mind wars with his emotions, recognizing the agony. Trying to change the subject, I aim for humor. "If I didn't know any better, I'd think you're starting to catch feelings for me."

His eyes harden, mouth forming a thin line. "Would that be such a bad thing? We are married, after all."

"Barely."

I regret the word before it even leaves my lips, but I can't put a finger on why, exactly—why it bothers me that I'm clearly hurting this man, who's done nothing but show me kindness since we met.

Why, deep down, part of me wants this marriage to be more. How I wish things were different.

Snapping his hand back like I've burned him—and not the other way around—he staggers to his feet, mouth puckering. It spreads after a moment into a sinister smile, all teeth and no lips, and a strange sensation I've yet to feel around him until this moment grips my heart, making it beat hard against my chest.

"All right, Caroline. You want barely married; I'll show you exactly that."

As he turns away from me and stumbles to the stairs, he grips the rail like a man with sea legs. I crumple silently, wondering what the hell I've gotten myself into.

I didn't plan on making new enemies, yet I feel like my husband just circled himself on my list in dark bloodred ink.

14

ELIA

FUCKING BITCH.

Blood splatters against my face as my fist rams into the junkie's nose, his cartilage splitting at the impact. He's already a purpled, ragged mess, but the anger coursing through me refuses to stop tonight.

Marco's hand clutches my shoulder, stilling the next blow. "Boss, I don't think beating the shit out of him is doing us any favors."

"No?" I shake him off me, staring down at the pissant. A couple of my men happened to see him trying to break into the back of Crimson with a crowbar, so we dragged him to the cellar for a quick chat.

Usually, that's all I would do. My father was the one known for his inability to show mercy, and I've always tried to prove myself a better man. If not to those I rule, then definitely to the ghost of my mother, who never wanted this life for me.

Why she married a mob boss in the first place is beyond

me. I guess she thought she could take him out of it—that a family would change things.

And they did. She's dead, and now I'm the boss.

Still, I try to keep a level head during interrogations. I like to think rationally, address major concerns, and get as much information as possible before resorting to torture or beatings.

The Montaltos usually leave the former to Kal Anderson, who many refer to as *Dr. Death*, although that doesn't stop them from utilizing his medical services when in need. The man is officially on Ricci payroll as an in-house physician, and unofficially as Death incarnate.

Though a touch younger than me, his medical expertise gives him an edge unheard of among other fixers. Makes him indispensable. Not even Kieran Ivers holds a flame to the cold, calculated doctor.

But Kal is out of town, doing fuck-knows-what in Boston or across the country. Lately, he's been coming around less. Like he thinks he can run from the skeletons with his name etched on their bones.

None of us can.

Men like us don't get peace. We don't get to leave.

Once you're in it, that's it.

You're in, or you're dead.

Today, I've stepped in temporarily as the interrogator, and while typically that would just mean a few dark threats that'd have the perp pissing their pants—my reputation isn't far off from my father's, even if it's not exactly accurate—I'm on a roll today.

To be fair, this coupled with our missing product and lack of answers has everyone on edge. And I don't put it past Kieran or his employers in Stonemore to enter and mess with Montalto-Ricci territory. Especially if Kieran is still upset that I stole Caroline away from him.

Still, the lanky trespasser hasn't been conscious for minutes, and I continue wailing on him, adrenaline pumping my fist like it has a mind of its own.

Because unfortunately, I'm still seething from my conversation with Caroline the other day, and I'm not myself.

I can feel it. Marco can tell, and so can Gia, who's put a wide berth between us this afternoon, perhaps afraid that one of his snarky-ass comments might be his last.

Whirling on Marco, I knock my shoulder into his chest, causing him to stumble. Annoyed with his intervention. "You have a better way to send Kieran Ivers a message?"

"You could actually go and talk to him." Regaining his footing, Marco crosses his arms over his chest and shrugs. "I don't give a shit if you kill this guy, but if he's really working for Ivers, you're just exacerbating a war you don't have any information about. That's reckless, and it puts all of us in danger."

"Fucking hell. When did you grow a damn pussy?"

He isn't wrong, though. Acting on my emotions jeopardizes the entire operation. And if I can't get a handle on things, Rafe is liable to halt traffic to us entirely and cut our portion of the business, which would severely limit my abilities in town. Drugs, as shitty a trade as they may be, make money, and money is God in King's Trace.

Hell, in the entire country.

Without it, I can't guarantee Caroline's safety, and everything else is for naught.

On a harsh exhale, I scrub a dirty hand through my hair, scratching my scalp. Blood cakes my forearms up to my elbows, where I cuffed my white shirt, the edges splattered with the red fluid. "I need a drink."

Gia meets me by the door, hands stuffed in his pockets. I pick up my jacket from one of the dilapidated wooden tables in this near dungeon and push open the metal door, not stopping to see if he makes it through in time.

The door swinging shut echoes through the damp, dim hallway as I head for the hidden staircase, shoving past a guard with my shoulder even though I don't need to touch him at all.

"E, I think you should head home."

Approaching the indoor entrance to the main floor of the club, I glance over my shoulder at the sound of Gia's voice. It breaks through the violent flood rushing between my ears, hot blood making it difficult to see straight.

My knuckles are sore, but that might not stop me from laying into him for insubordination.

"I didn't ask what you think." I push through the double doors, eyes homing in on the bar where Phoebe attempts to fill orders as quickly as they come up. It's a Thursday night, and Crimson is a hotbed for college students from Stonemore. Usually, I try to avoid the area on nights like this, but I need something a little stronger than the scotch in my office.

Gia follows close as I make my way to the front of the line. Phoebe's doe eyes relax slightly at my appearance, one of the few people who seem to take comfort in my presence.

I thought Caroline might be one of them, especially after everything we've gone through at this point, but I suppose I was wrong. She still considers me collateral, a vessel she's using to get her to another space in time.

For some unknown reason, the fact that she's using me

pisses me off, even though that's what this marriage was based on. What kind of a fucking king lets that happen?

"Maybe that's your problem," Gia says, his voice loud in my ear. "You do whatever the hell you want, damn the consequences. Can't you, for once, think ahead and see how your recent decisions are affecting those around you?"

Lifting one hand in a half wave to Phoebe, I cut my gaze to Gia. His eyes are hard, jaw set. I can tell he's angry, probably about the fact that I'm pulling away from his counsel, but I can't find it in me to give a shit right now. "I'm *capo* of the Montalto outfit, G. I *can* do whatever the fuck I want. If I wanted to turn and blow your goddamn brains out right here, right now, I could. And the cops would buy that it was an accident, or self-defense, or any other lame excuse I came up with because I bankroll their asses. So no, I *don't* care how my life is affecting my men. You shouldn't, either."

He rolls his eyes as Phoebe traipses over, dark brown hair pulled off her neck in a neat bun, a pencil tucked behind her ear. "What can I do for you boys?" A couple of frat brothers to my right groan in protest, and she shrugs her tiny shoulders. "Sorry, kids, gotta serve the boss first on his rare appearances down here."

Gia frowns. "Any chance you'd cut him off instead?"

Phoebe pulls the pencil from behind her ear and taps it against the bar, eyes dancing back and forth between him and me. "I don't know..."

"Don't pay attention to him. I'm completely sober and need something strong, *stat*."

"We just got some absinthe and spiced rum in a shipment last week."

"Pheebs." Pressing my palms into the counter, I lean

forward, locking my gaze onto hers. "What's the strongest stuff you've got?"

She chews on her bottom lip. "We have some lemonade moonshine that Marco is experimenting with. I think it's got Everclear in it."

"Perfect. I'll have one."

"He wants me to serve them in Mason jars."

"I don't give a shit if you spit it in my mouth. Just go get the fucking drink." I'm not exactly sure when Marco took over duties behind the bar, but whatever. I'll deal with that later.

As she scurries away, disappearing into the storage closet, I shrug into my jacket, turning and leaning against the bar to survey the crowd. It's mostly young people who reek of stale perfume and have more money than they should carry in their pockets.

About half of them are buzzed—probably from the routine coke sale we conducted just before we opened for the night—and thrashing around on the dance floor like fish out of water. Sweaty bodies line the walls, looking for others to connect with, for someone to share in their misery.

If only for a small, minuscule moment in time.

Gia leans too, following my stare. "Seriously, Elia, what the hell's gotten into you?"

"Don't act like you aren't fully aware."

"I've never seen you this worked up over a girl."

I huff. "She's not just some *girl*, G. For all intents and purposes, she's my wife, and she's made it very obvious she doesn't even want to be." Shaking my head, I tilt my chin toward the strobe lights throbbing on the ceiling. "Why the hell did she agree to marry me if she's this against the union?"

"You think she's using you for something?"

"I know she is; that was the whole point of this. It just... feels like something more is going on, and I can't figure out what the fuck she has to gain. If we divorce too soon, it voids the prenup, and she literally gets nothing. Even less than she'd get if we divorce after six months. I don't think she's got a hand in whoever's stealing from us because she seems to pretty much disdain the entire Montalto name and all it encompasses. What's her angle?"

"Maybe she wants to kill you." He chuckles, the sound loud against the music bleeding from the walls.

My heart stutters, chest tightening until it's damn near impossible to breathe. "But *why*?"

"I don't know."

Phoebe comes back with a chilled Mason jar in hand and slides it across the counter. I take a big gulp, letting the cool, clean liquid relieve some of the heat from my body. It tastes vaguely of citrus and burns on the way down, a scalding reminder of everything I'm trying to forget.

"Well, you said her dad was trying to sell her off, right?"

"He wasn't trying. He *did* sell her—to me. It was the only way he'd let her go without any trouble." The image of a hand-shaped bruise wrapped around Caroline's throat fills my mind, indicating that the money I transferred to him did little to protect her.

"Does she know you bought her?"

I'm certain she's aware that a deal had to be brokered, but I've not explained the full scope of the measures I took. "Why would I tell her that?"

"Are you *sure* she doesn't know? That we don't personally know anyone she's particularly close to? A family member we employ, perhaps, who might take some joy in painting you in a poor light?"

I take another swig of my drink, considering. "Luca wouldn't be that fucking stupid." Gia remains silent, and I curse under my breath. "Fuck, who am I kidding? Luca *is* stupid."

But not disloyal. At least, he hasn't been in the past. I can't imagine he'd offer such information to her.

Phoebe slams a beer bottle and a glass of water on the counter behind us, shoving the bottle in Gia's direction. "If he drinks too much, give him that water. It won't sober him up, but it might keep him from dehydrating."

I smirk, temporarily pulled from the issue at hand. "Phoebe, Phoebe. What would I do without you?"

"You'd have to find another bartender, for starters." She winks, flitting back to the other end of the bar, where she's met with debit cards and demands.

Gia tips the mouth of his beer up, pressing it to his lips. Bringing it back down, he dangles the neck between his thick fingers. "In any case, I think you should keep an eye on both Luca and your wife."

"Maybe." I point a finger at him, detaching it from the side of my jar. "Speaking of eyes and family members, how's your investigation on Angelo going? Figure out if he's stealing for Stonemore yet?"

"Nothing conclusive. I think he might be aware that I'm watching him. He's staying away from the apartment more." Gia shrugs, casting a wary glance over the crowd. "But he's also getting more paranoid, so he's due for a slipup. I'm just biding my time."

A swatch of golden-blond hair captures my attention, though it's likely wishful thinking since I've specifically instructed Caroline not to step foot in this place. I can't stop my heart from lurching into my throat at the prospect of her defying me, of the things I would do to her, how I'd punish her disobedience.

My eyes scan the crowd of bodies, trying to find the elusive hair color that I only attribute to her, and when I see it, I lock on, pushing off the bar before I even realize what the hell I'm doing.

Shoving my half-empty mason jar into Gia's free hand, I shoulder my way through the throng of people toward the VIP area, where a woman who looks an awful lot like my wife sits. She's wearing damn near nothing, watching two dancers make out on top of a guy at the end of her booth.

Blood boiling, cock hard as a fucking rock, I sprint up the metal stairs, jumping over the last one. My feet connect with the platform, a guard pulling the velvet rope aside just in time for me to pass through. By the time I reach the figure in the corner, head tipped back and laughing hysterically, I'm clutching her shoulders and dragging her to her feet before either of us has a chance to recognize the other.

Ignoring the squeals and protests coming from behind me, I pull her through the crowd and toward the stairs leading to my office. Her tiny fists beat into my back, and one of my hands leaves her wrist to fist in her hair, keeping her plastered to my side to weaken her blows.

She stumbles, but I don't slow my pace, something hot and evil pulsing through my veins at her presence.

Barely married, my fucking ass.

Caroline Harrison is my *wife*, and it's time she realizes what that means—that I'm not the kind of guy who shares or is okay with her keeping secrets.

Benny unlocks my office door and pushes it open as we

approach, offering a curt nod as I pull Caroline in behind me. I push her body against the door as it clicks shut, my hand immediately forming a vise around her delicate throat. I'm prepared to kiss the fight from her when the haze of vexation finally clears, and I get a good look at the girl I've just manhandled upstairs.

A girl who is most certainly *not* my wife.

15

ELIA

REALIZATION DAWNS on me that this is, in fact, Juliet Harrison —my reckless, wanton sister-in-law. Stories of her escapades, which include fucking priests and drinking until she blacks out at any and all public functions, run rampant in King's Trace.

Her name is as much a household one as mine. But this is the first time I'm getting a good look at her. Even at our wedding ceremony, I only had eyes for one person.

Where Caroline is often front and center, the prim and proper daughter Dominic is proud to parade around, Juliet gets hidden from the spotlight—her life the *King's Trace Gazette's* wet dream. Something the vultures in this town are dying to exploit.

It strikes me that although she looks like a carbon copy of her sister, she also looks incredibly young. More innocent. There aren't soft lines gracing the corners of her blue eyes, and the frown that seems etched into Caroline's very being is absent with her sister.

There's a distance in her blue eyes, but it's a different

kind than that in Caroline's. A harrowing wall carved, perhaps, by happenstance, whereas her sister's was erected purposefully.

I'm also certain she's not old enough to be here.

Juliet's fingers scratch at my hand still wrapped around her neck, acrylic nails cutting into my skin. "God, was the bouncer at the door pawing through my belongings not enough for the night?"

Relaxing my hold, I take a long step backward. "What are you talking about?"

Curling her hand around mine, she yanks me off her, rubbing at the flushed skin. "I'm like half your size. Did you really have to be so fucking rough?" Inhaling slowly, she presses on, answering me. "My ID, right? I had trouble getting in tonight, something about it not wanting to scan, but I swear, it's legit. I've never had that happen before."

Digging her hands into the front of her top, a strapless tube made of silk, she pulls out crumpled cash and a worn driver's license. She hands it over, and my eyes narrow as I scan the name. "Caroline Harrison, huh? The senator's daughter?"

I know she knows who I am, and yet not a flicker of recognition dawns on her. Either she's drunk or stupid because she just purses her lips and shrugs. "That's me."

"Twenty-three years old, five feet and three inches tall." I glance down at her, studying her frame. She could pass for Caroline if you'd only ever seen my wife from the neck up. Juliet's curves are no match for her sister's.

Her chin tilts up, a fire sparking beneath her baby blues. A definite indication that she's a Harrison. "*Yep.*" Lips popping on the *p*, a fight brewing in her bones. I can tell from the offensive stance she takes, hip jutted, arms akimbo.

She really thinks she has a chance against a fucking capo. "Look, I know my rights. You can't just keep me in here."

"I suppose not." Dropping her license into my jacket pocket, I turn and walk around to the other side of my desk. Settling into the leather chair, I fold my hands together on top of the wood. "Tell me, *Caroline*, what does your husband think of you dropping by his club unannounced?"

Her elbows slacken, gaze darting toward the floor. Clearing her throat, she brings her eyes back to mine, unyielding in her effort to maintain this charade.

Young, indeed.

"He's totally fine with it. I mean, jeez, this place is guarded, right? I'm probably safer here than anywhere else in the world."

"Safe isn't the exact word I'd use." Pushing back from the desk, I cross one leg over the other, hooking my ankle over my knee. "Especially considering I asked my wife not to come here under any circumstances."

Juliet's face pales, her leg snapping back beside the other. A small, victorious smile splays at the corner of my lips, but I bite down on my tongue to keep it in check.

"Elia."

"I'm a little offended you seem to have no idea what your brother-in-law looks like."

She shakes her head, and the movement rattles her whole body. Reaching up, she digs the heels of her hands into her eye sockets, scrubbing with an intensity I can almost feel across the room. When she lets her hands fall to her sides, she breathes out a soft laugh. "Jesus. I know what you look like. At least, I thought I did. But I only saw your profile in the courthouse, and I'm also very tipsy."

"And underage, I'm guessing."

"Guessing?" Her mouth twists, the bright-pink lipstick painted on her face rubbing off with each move. "You're married to my sister, but don't know how old I am? Now, who should be offended?"

Holding my palms out, I nod once, relenting. "Fair enough. That doesn't change the fact that you've illegally gained access to an exclusive club with a strict twenty-one and up policy. Using my wife's name, no less."

She snorts. "I think a fake ID should be the least of your worries on the scale of illegal activity going on at Crimson."

"That's my decision, isn't it? As club owner?"

A shrug.

Carding a hand through my hair, I exhale slowly, the slight buzz caused by the moonshine that convinced me she was my wife beginning to wear off. "How do you think your sister would feel if she knew you were here right now?"

"Please. I've been using Caroline's name and face my whole life. It's the only way I ever got anyone to look at me twice."

I shift, uncomfortable with the emotion in her voice. Drunk girls are prone to tears, and I've never been good at dealing with them. Maybe I should text Gia and ask him to bring me a box of tissues. "Surely, that's not true."

"Would you have given me a second glance if you didn't think I was her?"

Interesting. Though Caroline doesn't talk much about her family at all, I suppose I've assumed she and her sister would be close, especially considering her presence at our ceremony.

Yet it seems as though there's a hidden animosity here.

"Probably not, but that's because I seem to only have eyes for your sister." This last part comes out a little begrudgingly, and I rake my hand through my hair to offset the tone. Make it sound nonchalant like I want feelings for my wife. I make a sweeping gesture toward one of the wingback chairs in front of me, and she stares, an air of caution about her. "Why don't you have a seat?"

Maybe she isn't as stupid as she seems. She crosses her arms over her chest and obeys me. Pulling down the hem of her miniskirt, she sits, glaring holes into the wood of my desk.

"Look, I don't want any trouble, and I don't want Caroline worrying about me. She's always trying to protect me and keep me from making mistakes. But I'm not like her, okay? No one cares about me, not like they do her."

Sadness ebbs from her in silent, invisible waves. It thickens the air around us, and I watch her carefully, wondering just how badly the Harrisons screwed their daughters up.

"I think your sister cares about you greatly."

"That's not always enough, though, is it?"

She stares at me, eyes full of an incomprehensible misery, and I find myself struggling to look away. Hers are like a black hole, a chasm with no end in sight, and it physically pains me to observe the suffering.

Especially when it's clear she doesn't understand it—doesn't know how her own sister suffers. And fuck, neither do I, but I know *something* is off.

Juliet continues, evidently spurred on by the alcohol in her system, or maybe adrenaline. Whatever the case, the words don't cease.

"It's hard being completely invisible to your parents. Mom, at least, ignores both of us. She's a real bitch. But

Daddy, he always, *always* favored Caroline. Said she outranked me in beauty and brains. All of it."

What kind of a father would say that to his kid?

Probably the same that would compliment the other, so he could abuse her and keep her silent about it.

"So what? You think because you're ignored by your parents, that gives you the right to disregard rules and do whatever you want?"

Her jaw clenches. "You can sit and think of me as a spoiled brat like everyone else for sneaking in here, but I don't care. I just wanted to have a good night."

Silence ensues, neither of us breaking eye contact for several minutes.

She continues, gripping the gold locket around her neck. "Care used to say he abused her, and no one ever... they acted like she was a ghost. Like what she said didn't matter. And I always thought if they could ignore something like that, what would they do if they knew the truth about me?"

Tapping my index finger along the toe of my loafer, I wait. Wait for a confession, an admission of guilt, for derisive laughter that often accompanies sadness in her generation. But the gaze staring back at me no longer holds anything; her blue eyes look almost empty, devoid of everything.

Like she got tired of waiting for people to notice and turned it all off instead.

"What's the truth about you, Juliet?"

For a moment, I think she might tell me. Her nostrils flare, and her fingers curl into fists in her lap. She inhales, and a beat passes along between us, as if she's savoring the moments before her confession.

But then, she rolls her eyes, brushing a strand of golden hair from her face. "I don't know why I'm even spilling all of this to you, a complete stranger. I must have had way too much to drink."

"Strangers often make the best therapists." *Made men do not.* I don't mention how her speech isn't slurred in the slightest, how her pupils seem to have relaxed like she's coming down from whatever high she was on. It's not my place to point out or to ask why she's pretending to be drunker than she actually is.

"It's just been weird having Caroline out of the house. I've been back from school officially since last week, and usually, we hang out all summer because she's never doing anything else. Other than stupid shit for Daddy."

A heavy pressure rankles in my chest, squeezing my heart. "She never does anything? No work, charity, nothing like that?"

"Caroline's a homebody. She doesn't *like* the attention she gets from being Daddy's princess, so she stays home, baking until she loses her mind."

I process that, coupling it with the surveillance I've seen since we've been married of her spending all her time in my kitchen, rolling dough and using whatever's available in the pantry. A natural chef, just like my mother, and it feels like that potential goes to waste with each passing day she spends at home.

"If you ever want to surprise her, and I only suggest this because I know you could do it, you should get her a bakery. Like one to own and operate. She's had the name picked out since we were kids: Care's Crazy Cakes."

A smile ghosts over my lips as I observe the wistful expression on Juliet's face. "I'll keep that in mind."

"Daddy always said that she wasn't business-savvy

enough to own one. Said us Harrisons were bred just to serve men."

"That's a dick thing to tell your daughters."

She shrugs, picking at a loose thread on her skirt, trying to pretend it doesn't bother her. But I can tell by the downcast eyes and the flush of her cheeks that it does.

My throat constricts, words barely able to pass through. I can't help wondering how far the abuse extends from Dominic, how badly he's broken these girls. "What kind of stuff are you interested in?"

"I don't know. I'm in school for marine biology, but... we'll see, I guess. I've not put a lot of thought into it." She eyes me, lifting her chin. "But that doesn't mean I'm stupid."

"I wasn't implying otherwise."

"Well, you'd be the first." Pushing a stray hair out of her face, she slumps back in the chair, smacking her lips together. "I hope you don't tell Caroline about any of this. She'll just worry and probably hate you for not calling her immediately."

"Why would I call her?"

"Everyone always calls Caroline when I'm in trouble like she's my mother or something. Like I'm a child in need of supervision."

I cock an eyebrow. "And that's not the case."

She glares at me through half-lidded eyes. "No, it's not. I can take care of myself. Whatever Caroline thinks she's protecting me from, I guarantee I can handle it."

The way she hurls words at me, accusations laced with venom, makes me think she might already know *something* is up with her sister. But it's clear she doesn't know *what*, and it irks her.

Same as it does me.

Watching her, I take note of the exact moment her chest begins rising and falling more slowly. Her breathing evens out as the fight leaves her. We sit in silence for a few minutes before I page Benny into the room, instructing him to send her to my house in a cab and make sure she gets inside okay.

It feels as if I have fewer answers to the mysteries of my life than I started the week with.

I plan to get to the very bottom of my wife's true history soon and figure out what she's hiding, but for now, I'll sit in the shadows, watching and keeping her safe.

Hopefully, Kieran and her father will lose interest.

Because the only way I'm letting her go now is if they pry her from my rotten corpse.

~

"JULIET? ARE YOU OKAY?"

The younger Harrison slurs something sleepy and unintelligible, and I slink back farther into the shadows, not wanting Caroline to see me just yet. Pressing into the shrubbery surrounding our back patio, I try my best to blend in as Benny helps my sister-in-law inside. As they lead Juliet to a couch, I make my way to the door, which they leave open, and lean my ear against the jamb to listen. "She passed out, and you just happened to find her?"

"Yep. I called the boss, and he said to drop her off here."

"Okay, well... thank you, I guess. I'll take care of her from here."

Benito walks out, fist-bumping Leo on his way through the door, and stops to look at me for his next order. I hold out my hand for the tablet he keeps on him, strapped to his side next to his gun.

He sighs, handing it over. "You're real creepy; you know that?"

I roll my eyes and wave him away, then set up camp on a chaise lounge outside slightly obscured from Caroline's direct line of vision. Pulling up the security footage app, I let the camera load as I stretch out, dialing up the volume.

Caroline kneels beside her sister on the couch, pressing a damp rag to the young girl's forehead. She stirs, trying to brush her away. "Ugh, where am I?"

"My house. One of Elia's men dropped you off."

"Oh." Juliet blinks, a blush spreading over her cheeks. "Well, this is just like old times, isn't it? You trying to keep me from a massive hangover."

"I thought you stopped doing this, Jules."

"And *I* thought you weren't gonna cut me out of your life anymore. Why haven't I heard from you since you got married? Did your heart shrivel up and die or something?"

Caroline sighs, sitting back on her haunches. She reaches behind her and picks up a muffin from the tray on the coffee table. "Here, eat this. Maybe it'll absorb some of the bitterness in your gut."

"I'm not bitter. I just miss you."

"And I'm not actively trying to cut you out. Married life is hard, and it's taking more of an adjustment than I anticipated."

"Well, what am I supposed to do when I need you? Sometimes I do, Caroline, even if I don't want to admit it. Mom and Daddy can be so... cold, sometimes."

They're silent for several beats, and then Caroline's voice filters through, her tone icy. "Has Dad said or done anything to you?"

"Like what?" Caroline doesn't answer, so Juliet shrugs,

rubbing her forehead. "No, he just acts like I'm not there. As usual."

Caroline bends down, dropping the untouched muffin back to its pan, and shoves herself under Juliet's legs. She hugs her knees to her chest, and they just sit there, not talking, just existing.

A love I can't comprehend—a protectiveness that rivals my own.

After a while, Caroline pats her sister's knee, and I can hear the faintest whisper drop from her lips. "I see you, Jules. You're not invisible. You never have been."

My heart feels oddly full, watching Caroline dote on and care for her sister. It's clear that she's looking for an outlet, something to channel the goodness within her and distract her from the evil vying for her soul.

She's caring and considerate. Warm and soft, all the things I can't imagine ever being, and it makes me want to walk inside, scoop her into my arms, and never let her go.

Fuck, I'm gone for this little nymph.

16

ELIA

"You may be interested to know that I caught your sister at Crimson the other night using a fake driver's license."

Caroline tucks her hair behind her ears, turning from her bathroom sink to look at me. She has on a sleek, thin pink robe tied loosely at the waist. The curve of her tits strains against the part in the middle, begging me to take a step forward and untie the knot, but I hold back.

There's a storm in my wife's blue eyes like she's jonesing for a fight.

And what I'm about to tell her is sure to start one.

She has no idea I sent Juliet here that night, no idea that we've been in constant contact since.

"I think you need to reevaluate what topics you find interesting."

"What about the fact that she used *your* name and picture?"

She rolls her eyes. "Please. Juliet's been using me since I turned twenty-one, and she's not exactly slick about it."

Pushing past me in the doorway, she continues into her bedroom.

Since moving in, she's transformed the place from its basic pristine whites and added splashes of color here and there. The sheets and curtains are a satin material and bloodred, which feels more fitting here than anything else. Her makeup decorates the built-in vanity against one wall, while clothes are splayed in piles on the bed and draped over the back of the vanity chair. A smirk tugs at my lips; who'd have thought this proper, uptight woman would be messy?

"I like what you've done with the place." Walking in behind her, I situate myself on the window seat across the room, folding my legs so the soles of my shoes press against the wall.

She glances around, picking up a pair of sleep shorts from the bed and running her fingers over the soft material. "I'm going through my things. Getting rid of stuff I don't need or wear."

"Less to pack when you run, right?"

Her eyes widen, face flushing. "No, I just have too much shit. My... *dad* bought me new outfits for every occasion he forced me to go to."

I don't miss the way she swallows over the word *dad* like it physically pains her to even mention him. That makes my announcement harder. "Right, well. If you're planning on sending them as hand-me-downs to that brash sister of yours, you're in luck."

"What do you mean?"

Reaching around to the back of my neck, I scratch at the skin just beneath the collar of my dress shirt. "I, uh, invited our families over for dinner."

Dropping the shorts to the floor, she whirls on me, eyes blazing. "Are you serious?"

"Sure am, *cara mia*."

"Oh *God*." A low groan comes from her throat, and she glares at me. "Don't fucking call me that. I can't believe you did this. Jesus, you're an idiot."

Raking her hands through her hair, she begins pacing back and forth, short little steps that match the way breaths stagger from her nose. I watch her, curious over whether she's panicking because she doesn't want to see them or if it's because she doesn't think we're prepared to entertain.

Even though I'm sure it's the former, I focus on the latter, tucking my arms behind my head and gazing out the window. My lawn care maintenance men stand outside, clipping the hedges lining the fence with the summer heat blaring down on them. One guy wipes at his brow, waving to me once he notices me watching.

I lift a hand in response, then turn to Caroline. "Don't worry about the food or anything. I have Benito and Leo bringing takeout from Portland, and my grandmother's sending her world-famous Italian wedding soup."

She pauses, cocking an eyebrow. "First of all, they're bringing food from Portland? That's three hours away."

"I mean, that's where the closest authentic Italian market is. The food will be cooked here."

"By who?"

"Benito and Leo." I tilt my head, studying her. "What's confusing you?"

"Those guys know how to cook?"

"Oh, Christ, yes. It's in our blood."

She waves me off, returning to her pacing once again.

"Okay, well, whatever. Food's taken care of. But why would you invite my family?"

"I don't know. Consider it a delayed wedding reception since ours was interrupted. And I haven't gotten to know my in-laws yet. I feel like it's time."

"Did Juliet put you up to this?"

"No, although she did help get your parents on board. Your mother does *not* like me."

She scoffs. "My mother doesn't like anyone."

"Well, I plan on winning her over."

Perching on the edge of the bed, Caroline exhales slowly, pinching the bridge of her nose. "This is not going to end well."

"Why do you think that?"

"I just know my family, okay? They won't behave themselves. My mom will continue asking if I'm pregnant because she was really convinced before the wedding. My dad will try to push his weight around like I'm still his property, and Juliet will probably rifle through your things, looking for something valuable to steal. Or drink all your hard liquor."

Pulling my suit jacket together, I remove my feet from the wall and push upward, making my way over to where she sits. She brushes the neckline of her robe, absently exposing more of her skin.

I crouch in front of her, placing my palms on either side of her body, flush against the mattress. So close, I can smell that fruity, floral scent that lives in her pores. "I can remedy all of those problems."

Her eyes lift, meeting mine, hand stilling. "How?"

My hand glides up, caressing her thigh on the ascent to her hip and over her rib cage. Grazing the underside of her breast, I stop when I reach the valley between them. I drag my thumb slowly over the flesh not covered by her robe, reveling in how she shivers beneath my touch.

Breath hitching in my throat, my cock comes alive, pushing against my pants. I lick my lips, dragging my gaze from her nipples, puckered under her clothing, and let my thumb travel higher. "I'll put Benito on Juliet duty; no one's ever stolen a thing from me, and I've had lots of guests."

"Lots?" she asks, her voice barely audible. Breathy. Needy. Her chest rises and falls, deliberate in its attempt to remain calm.

I nod, passing the column of her throat, smoothing my calloused hand over the soft expanse. "*Lots.* None as important as you, though."

She closes her eyes as my thumb reaches her pretty pink mouth, rubbing gently over her bottom lip. "And my father?"

"That fucker won't even be allowed to look at you if you don't want him to."

"I don't," she answers quickly. I cock a brow, and she clears her throat, adding, "Want him to look at me, I mean. The less interaction I have with him, the better."

Every fiber of my being screams at me to push her on this, but the guarded look in her eyes stops me.

Instead, I concede. "Done."

Her tongue darts out, swiping at the tip of my thumb, and I follow its retreat, pushing into her mouth. She swallows, laving around the digit as her warm, wet mouth encases it, and I swear I almost come in my slacks right then. Sucking softly, pulling me into the knuckle, she flutters her eyelashes, waiting.

"As for your mother," I growl as I push my thumb farther inside, pressing down on the flat of her tongue. The organ struggles to break free, her cheeks hollowing out as her body wars with logic and pleasure. Defiance flares in her irises, darkening them, and my cock swells to the point that it feels like it might fucking explode. "We can get started on that. Prove her right. Give her a reason to stop speculating."

She freezes, eyebrows drawing in. Jerking back, she releases me with a shove, and I get to my feet, letting her. I don't know what it is about her fire that gets me, but each time she pushes me away or slices me open with her mouth, my heart turns to putty, aching for her to give in.

"You can't say shit like that to me."

"Is it so crazy to want an heir from my beautiful, intelligent wife?"

"Kids are not in the cards for us, Elia."

I can't stop the frown that pulls at my lips. "Do you not want children?"

She gapes at me in silence for a moment, eyes wide. Lost in some sort of internal battle that she has no desire to let me in on.

Finally, she just shakes her head. "Our marriage isn't like that, and you know it. We've been over this." She gets to her feet, pulling her robe tight against her body, and walks to the door, standing beside the frame. "You need to leave."

"And if I don't want to?"

Her jaw clenches as she crosses her arms. "You don't want the answer to that."

We stare at each other, breath still struggling to return to normal, blood still draining from certain body parts, but she doesn't budge. She's unwavering, and it makes me want to take her even more, to conquer her, body and soul.

Make her mine for real.

But I don't. Not tonight, anyway. That would only scare her away, and frankly, I need to calm down regardless. I'm quickly spiraling beyond control, wanting things I've never even considered before and threatening the fabric of our relationship. If you can even call it that.

I push past her and head downstairs, calling over my shoulder, "Be ready in half an hour."

17

CAROLINE

My mother sips from her spoon as Leo refills her wineglass
—*Screaming Eagle Cabernet Napa, 1995*, which she brought as
a wedding present and decided to open without asking
permission. Her hair sits twisted in a tight bun on top of her
head, a string of pearls clasped around her thin neck.

Elia's stayed true to his word, at least about two of the
issues with having my family in our home; my father hasn't
spared me a single glance, instead opting to talk to my
father-in-law about the state of Maine's pension fund. Benito
flanks my sister, even as she sits at the table eating like the
rest of us, his eyes trained on her.

It won't surprise me if she ends up dragging him off to an
empty bathroom before the night's over. For all the sadness
she seems to collect, she's never been one to turn down a
quickie. I don't let myself think about that being her coping
mechanism.

So far, we've broached the subject of my future, which is
nonexistent at this point; it's hard to make plans when you
have no idea what will happen in the next few months. Still,

I've expressed my love of baking to Orlando, Elia's father, who regaled me with a story about Elia's mother and the scones she used to make for them.

The story very clearly made Elia uncomfortable, so when my father requested the elder Montalto's attention, I let him have it.

Even if I do want to know more about his mother, I shouldn't.

I push my soup around with the butt of my garlic bread, unable to eat. My stomach churns in a violent storm I'm trying to tame.

Elia reaches for a saltshaker, his hand brushing mine as he leans over. "Doing okay over there?"

Nodding, I switch to my spoon, ladling soup broth and then dumping it back into the bowl. "Feeling a little sick is all."

"Do you need something? Anti-nausea medicine? Water?" He waves to Leo, requesting a glass with ice.

"Why are you being so nice to me?" Our conversation is hushed so as not to draw attention. "I was rude to you upstairs."

"I'm a Montalto; we have thick skin, *carina*."

Leo returns with a glass, a blank expression on his face as he pours from the stainless-steel pitcher at the center of the massive dining table. I take it, bowing my head gratefully as he returns to the other side of the room, and gulp down a big sip. It glides down, icy and shocking to my core, and I welcome the distraction.

"And," Elia continues, his lips curving against my ear, "I won't lie and say I don't like it when you're rude to me. I told you long ago; your mouth is my favorite part about you. I'm excited to see what else you're capable of."

The water stills in my throat, choking me, and I sputter some of it up into my hand. He reaches over and rubs my back in a fluid, soothing gesture while my father glances over at me for the first time since he's been here.

"Don't mind my wife." I can practically hear the smile in Elia's voice, and as I work to clear my throat of the liquid obstruction, it pisses me off. "She can be so overeager sometimes, is all. Isn't that right, love?"

I nod, silent, pulling my napkin from my lap to wipe my mouth. Returning the glass to the table, I swallow, straightening up against the scrutiny I'm suddenly receiving.

"Caroline, eager?" My father snorts into his wineglass. "You must be getting her confused with someone else. Caroline isn't excitable in the least. I had to drag her to every one of my galas when she was younger. She doesn't like public affairs."

Untrue. I just didn't like them with him.

"That's odd. She was entirely too excited to marry me."

"She's probably out for your money," my father mutters, cutting into his lasagna.

"Or pregnant," my mother adds, swirling the wine in her glass. "I swear, don't you think she looks a little plumper since she left us?"

Juliet frowns, lifting a shoulder. "I don't know, Mom. If she says she's not pregnant, then I think we should believe her."

Catching her eye, I send her a soft smile. She's never really been on my side, too absorbed and sheltered in her own life to see beyond. But I'm glad for this, at least, that she might try to protect me in her own way, the way I've always tried to with her.

"I'm just saying." My mother shrugs, diving back into her soup. When she comes up for air, she points her spoon at Elia. "I blame you for corrupting her, regardless. Look at this house— where's the character, the personality? According to the *Gazette*, Caroline never even leaves. When she was with us, she went to all of Dominic's functions and helped with everything. Are you keeping her tied up here all day as some kind of sex slave?"

"Mrs. Harrison, with all due respect, I'm not going to discuss my sex life with you. Certainly, you get enough from your husband that you don't need to sniff around other couples' bedrooms."

She huffs, tossing her spoon down. "This town talks, you know. We know what goes on at that little club of yours, and we know what girls have reported about what you like sexually. The stuff of deviants, honestly. I can only assume you've drawn my Caroline into some kind of demonic sex cult, and that's why she was so willing to jump into a loveless marriage with you."

"Now, hold on a minute—" Elia's dad tries to cut in, but my mother starts back up, apparently releasing a month's worth of pent-up anger.

"If that's not the case, then explain it to us. Tell me why my daughter suddenly felt the need to marry you, to tie herself to a *murderer*, when she's lived her life thus far without a single ripple in the water." She inhales, cutting her gaze to me. "This isn't you, honey. You're not spontaneous or irresponsible. If you're in trouble, just tell me. I can help you."

Not anymore, you can't.

She plays her role well; I'll give her that. Sitting here listening to her drone on, it's almost possible to believe she actually cares that I left, rather than the fact that I can't be controlled any longer.

Elia's hand curls around the back of my chair, fingers tangling in the ends of my hair. "Maybe someone broke her spirit."

My father scowls at Elia's tone and drops his fork to his plate. "If you have something to say, son, by all means. Let's hash it out at the fucking dinner table. I'm sure the princess has filled your brain with her lies about me."

Elia leans back in his seat, smoothing his free hand over his tie. His father cocks an eyebrow at us on his other side. "I'm sure I don't know what lies you're talking about."

"No?" Reaching into the pocket of his khaki pants, he pulls out a folded sheet of paper, tossing it in our direction. "How about that list of names, then? You see that shit? Notice whose name's circled at the bottom?"

The air in my lungs empties out of me. Ceases to exist as the paper falls to the table. I hear my heart between my ears, roaring like a river, and my eyes glue themselves to the sheet, terror gripping me in its cold claws.

I don't turn my head when my husband tosses me a glance, then swipes the paper, unfolding it and scanning the page. It's a list I know by heart, one I was sure I'd deleted from every hard drive at the old house and purposely never printed out.

The names of all the men who ever involved themselves with my father sit there, some worse than others. Some simple groomers, like him, and others full-on creeps. Elia's is one of the few there just because of association, scribbled at the bottom and outlined in bright red ink.

"Tell him what it is, Caroline. What you're planning to do to these men."

Everyone waits for an answer, but he speaks before I can. Not that I have anything to say.

"She wants to fucking kill us, all because of her misunderstandings about how things operate in this world. How we have to network and conduct business in very specific ways. She's claimed I abused her for years, that I let my men touch her when they shouldn't have, that I prepped her for pedophiles, but there's never been any substance to her allegations. She's just a dumb little girl in way over her head."

My mouth dries up, and my palms grow sweaty. The bread in my hand falls to the table, forgotten, and I try to talk through the desert forming on my tongue. "I don't know—"

My father's fist comes down on the table, causing the dinnerware to rattle with the impact. I flinch out of habit. "Stop fucking lying, whore." I glance at Elia from the corner of my eye, watching his nostrils flare, eyes darkening.

"Get the *fuck* out of here." His voice is a calm, cool tone I've never heard before. It feels powerful. Threatening.

We all fall silent.

My father falters, mouth dropping. "Excuse me?"

Elia stands abruptly, his chair sliding into the wall with the force of his departure. "You heard me. I shouldn't have invited you in the first place. Caroline was right."

"She was right? Son, I hate to break it to you, but your wife's a lying little—"

Rounding the table with a ferocity that makes the walls shake, he stops in front of my father, gripping his collar, and hauls him from his seat, slamming him back against the wall.

His elbow pushes against my father's windpipe, cutting off his air supply; the older man's eyes bulge, face reddening, and a sick wave of satisfaction washes over me, thinking this might be the night my nightmares come to an end.

That everything I've been working toward culminates here.

"If you keep talking about her like that, I swear on my mother's grave that I will gut you right here in front of your family. And I'll let the Mrs. mop up your blood afterward."

I press my thighs together, trying to relieve the inappropriate ache between them. *Jesus, I'm a mess.*

My father's hands raise in sweet surrender, and Elia moves back, shoving him in Benito's direction. The guard comes over and grips my father's bicep, dragging him behind as he makes his way to the living room and through the front door.

Juliet and my mother sit frozen at the table, the latter's eyes wide as saucers. My appetite seems to have renewed itself, and while they watch me, incredulous, I finally dig into my pasta. "This pesto is delicious," I say to Leo even though I know he won't respond.

Elia's father clears his throat, getting to his feet. "Son, can I talk to you in private?"

He nods, following him from the room and avoiding my gaze, leaving the three of us with Leo.

My mother pushes her dish back, gathers her sheer scarf around her shoulders, and stands up. "Well, it seems you've won over a very dangerous man. Congratulations, dear. I hope he doesn't kill you in your sleep."

I kind of hope he does.

She exits the house the same way Benito and my father did, heels clicking against the marble floors and echoing through the house.

Juliet takes a drink of her wine, not fazed in the slightest.

"That was super hot."

"Which part? When Dad called me a whore, or when Mom told everyone I look fat?"

"You know how Mom is." She sets her glass down, leaning forward. "What was that list about, though?"

I lift a shoulder, shrugging. "No clue."

Her eyes narrow, studying me. "What aren't you telling me?"

Everything. "Nothing."

"Caroline."

"Juliet. It was a bogus list that Dad brought to stir shit up. He probably falsified the whole thing, thinking he could turn Elia against me."

She scoffs, raising her eyebrows. "Trust me, no one in this world could turn that man against you."

I ignore the way her words make my heart fill with blood, how it feels like my veins constrict and swell all at once.

She chews on her lip, adjusting the spaghetti strap on her minidress. "Well, this was still fun, in any case. King's Trace is *boring* this summer. Lonely, even. I needed some entertainment."

"Fucked your way through town, huh?"

A smirk tugs at the corner of her mouth. "Besides your husband and his family, there's only one man in town I've not been with. I'm just waiting for him to come down out of that creepy mansion."

My eyebrows shoot up. "Wait, *what*? You want to fuck Kieran?"

"God, yes. Haven't you seen those pictures of him online from before he went into hiding? Sex on legs, Care, I'm telling you." She tilts her head with a dreamy look in her eyes. "I mean, I know you were supposed to be promised to him or whatever, but I figured since you're married now, you wouldn't mind?"

"I don't, but I know someone who will."

"Who, Elia?"

"They're rivals, you know. He stole me away from him, and from what Luca's told me, he's not exactly happy about it."

"I bet I could make him forget all about you."

I hesitate, remembering Elia's warnings. "I don't think he's a good man, Jules. I think he could hurt you."

She gives me a wry smile. "What man can't?"

Relenting, I push back from the table and stand, figuring that Elia and his father won't be returning for a while. Walking to the front door, I peek out one of the large windows, pushing aside a curtain; there are no cars outside, indicating Benito took our parents home.

Turning on my heel, I smile at Juliet, who downs the remainder of her wine like a woman who isn't sure when she'll get her next taste. I pull her up and hook my arm in hers, starting up the stairs to my room. "Let's remedy the loneliness, shall we?"

We settle under the comforter on my bed, eating chocolate I have stashed in my nightstand and giggling at reruns of *Friends*. It's not until much later, after I've heard the front door open and close a few times and Juliet's head lolls on my shoulder, that I think back to the questions about the state of my uterus, wondering where the hell my period is.

I glare at Jennifer Aniston's nipples, trying to dispel the thought from my brain. I don't exactly have time for this.

Besides, Elia and I only half did it once. He didn't even finish.

I'm sure it's just stress.

Slipping lower beneath the comforter, careful not to jostle Juliet, I pull her limp body into mine, hoping I can keep her safe a little while longer and this night didn't ruin everything for us.

Elia pokes his head in after I've just started to fall asleep; he perches on the edge of the bed, a hand reaching out and running down over my shoulder. I crack one eye open, peering at him in the darkness, and he stills. "I can feel you looking at me."

"That's creepy," I whisper, mindful of my sister's sleeping form beside me.

"Not as creepy as that list you had."

I bite my lip. "Are you... what are you going to do?"

He stays quiet for a long time; the only sound between us Juliet's light snores. Finally, he sighs, cupping my knee through my comforter. "I don't know. What was that, Caroline? Did... those men hurt you?"

No response. I don't even know what to say. How to begin to explain.

"Do you want to talk about it?" he asks, his voice impossibly soft.

"No," I whisper.

His fingers squeeze me. "I'm gonna fucking kill them."

"Elia, no, you can't just adopt my problems for yourself. This is *my* pain, my fight to be had."

"I don't care. I'm gonna make every man who ever laid a finger on you regret it."

A trench opens up inside me, a foreign feeling taking root. He pats my knee once, standing and leaving the room. Burrowing further beneath the covers, I stare outside the window at the night sky, a devious smile sliding over my lips.

That's exactly what I'd hoped he'd say.

18

CAROLINE

Luca scans the sheet of paper again, arching his eyebrows. The underside of his jaw still sports light bruising from the beating Elia gave him, and I'm starting to wonder if his split lip will ever heal. "This is *the* list?"

I bristle, annoyance prickling at the bottom of my stomach. "That's what I said, isn't it?"

"You always answer questions with more questions?"

"Do you always talk out of your ass when conducting business?"

He smirks, letting the sheet fall to his desk. Luca's apartment sits above a law office-slash-laundromat at the heart of downtown—which, compared to the downtowns of other cities, is not all that impressive. Inconsequential, with its dated brick and stone buildings and small businesses barely keeping afloat. It's that anonymity that allows the local mafias to run things, and what paints my father as a senator coming from "humble beginnings."

"Considering your generous little husband doesn't give

me much opportunity to actually conduct business, no, I can't say talking out of my ass is a common occurrence." Reaching into his shirt, a crisp black button-down, Luca pulls a pack of cigarettes from the interior pocket and flips open the top. "Smoke?"

My fingers itch to take one, just to calm my nerves, but I don't want to arouse suspicion when I go home. Elia's already on high alert since our dinner the other night, and finding out I ditched Leo to get here will only make matters worse.

But since Liv's forcing me to attend her birthday bash tonight at Crimson, I couldn't pass up the opportunity to take a shot at a few of the men on my list.

Besides, by the time I'm supposed to leave for the club, Elia will be forty-five minutes away in Stonemore, trying to figure out his own problems; I should be the least of his worries.

And if not, well, that's what I'm counting on.

I wave Luca off, leaning forward to point at the paper between us. "Sheldon McCarty and Todd Davis are known to hang out in the VIP section on Friday nights when college kids clear out, and they get their pick of the dancers."

My chest constricts, a massive weight pressing down like a knee into my breastbone, as I utter these names. I try to shake it off, but the images of them circling me in my old kitchen, predatory and evil, flash in my mind. Memories of hands fixing themselves to whatever body part was in reach while my father left me to fend for myself cause a thick wave of nausea to spread through my abdomen.

It's a nightmare I can't escape. A hole in my soul I've tried filling a dozen different ways, always with the same result.

Nothingness. An empty rattle I've come to loathe.

Right now, the scenes give me renewed strength, the chills tickling my skin at the memories reinforcing my resolve to go through with this plan.

I clear my throat, swallowing the bile that's risen there. "Friday nights are also when the dancers who offer... *extra* services at Crimson look for weekend work."

Luca pulls a cigarette from the pack and slips it between his lips, lighting it with a red *Bic* swiped from the desk drawer. Tossing it back in place, he takes a long drag, studying me. "So your plan is just to expose them for being perverts?"

"Illegal perverts." *In more ways than one.* "These are men running electoral campaigns based on Christian values. Who wants to elect a hypocrite? I take a few pictures, email them to the *Gazette*, and their careers are over."

"Right, but half of King's Trace is ensconced in illegal activity. Maybe even more than that. I don't think morality is all that high on the priority scale."

"Okay, but it's still illegal. So even if the citizens don't give a shit, the police officers will." He doesn't respond, just inhales on the butt of his cigarette, and my heart sinks a little further into my stomach. "Or... not?"

"It's a good plan, but not one you could conduct *at* Crimson. Elia has law enforcement on his payroll, and he won't allow any bad publicity to surround the club. Meaning phones are checked into lockers, and those let into the VIP area are typically well-vetted."

I chew on the inside of my cheek, the soft flesh wilting through my bite. "What am I supposed to do, then?"

He shrugs, pushing a plume of smoke from his mouth.

"What do you *want* to do? When you first came up with this revenge plot, didn't you have something different in mind? Something... taboo?"

My nostrils flare, fingers tap on the edge of the desk. *He knows.* Knows why I picked Elia Montalto of all people. "I didn't want to lead with that."

"Why not?" Gripping the cigarette between two fingers, he leans in, gesturing wildly with his hand. "These men hurt you, abused you. They *stole* your innocence. Your *life*, Caroline. You and I both know there's only one way you can get that back."

"There are no refunds on innocence, Luc. It's not a tree limb or an octopus tentacle. Once it's gone, that's it."

"That's not true if it's not something you wanted to give up in the first place."

I shake my head, tucking my hair behind my ears. "I just didn't want to be like them."

"How badly did these men hurt you? How badly do you want them to pay?"

My breathing scatters as I remember the catcalls, the whistling, the leers a fifteen-year-old shouldn't have to fend off from men twice her age. Todd and Sheldon were the worst, with Todd constantly placing his hands on me whenever my father left the room, and Sheldon being the one to take my virginity.

And the fact that I was seventeen when that happened didn't even faze my father. He'd just smiled when he found out and said everything was going according to plan.

Dominic Harrison pimped me out to his friend, a man expected to uphold the values of this country, for clout and cash.

How badly do you want them to pay?

Glancing at the list, I reach over and mark out all but four names: the ones who destroyed me and the one who unwittingly put me back together again. The one avenging me, even if he isn't fully aware of his role yet.

Luca folds his hands and tucks them beneath his chin, elbows propped on the desk, cigarette burning. The butt flickers orange, enticing in the unwavering life it holds despite not being touched. "I'm going to help you, Care, but not if we half ass this. These men deserve worse than what they did to you."

Still. I hesitate, unsure if he's saying what I think he is. "*I* can't very well kill two grown men in a packed club."

"No, *you* can't." Sucking on the cigarette again, he smiles on the exhale, smoke falling from behind his teeth. He looks at that last name and back at me. "You know that wasn't the plan, anyway. There's only one person who can."

I SUPPOSE it should make me nervous when I leave Luca's office building and am met by my husband, leaning against the door of a black SUV I've never seen before. The only cars parked in our driveway are expensive, luxury vehicles that no one ever takes out, almost like they're just for show.

But it doesn't unnerve me. If anything, it sends a wicked tingle down my spine at his protectiveness, along with a shot of annoyance.

Technically, he's just doing his duty within the scope of our arrangement, but still. I don't need a fucking stalker.

He looks delicious standing there; thick arms crossed over the chest of his black suit, a practiced, bored expression on his face. His dark hair swoops over one eyebrow, obscuring the slight quirk there, the strands just begging to be tugged.

Fuck, no. Get a grip, Caroline. You're on a mission, and this man is a target. You can't allow your vagina to reduce you to a quivering puddle every time you see him.

There are plenty of attractive men in the world. Save yourself for one who doesn't have a body count.

The glass door slams closed behind me, and the sunlight bounces off the frames of Elia's Ray-Bans, temporarily stunting my vision. Turning on my heel, I make a left and head down the dilapidated sidewalk, ignoring his presence entirely.

His footsteps thud behind me, trailing close. We pass a few boutiques, trinket shops, and a couple of cafés; tourist traps meant to draw people in from Portland and Augusta, sometimes even Quebec. Folks with too much money and idle hands, itching for something to do.

That's what my father was, decades ago, before he came in from Stonemore to settle down here. Just the heir to an old mining fortune with a degree in public policy and a penchant for depravity. Underage girls, those whose daddies would do anything for association with a Harrison.

I don't know what pushed my father to become one of those men, forcing me to do his networking and clean up messes I had no business even knowing about. But it's the fuel to my internal fire—my need for revenge.

Elia keeps pace just behind me, a shadow I'm not in the mood for. "You know, you could throw your influence around town and ask the mayor to fix some of these sidewalks," I grumble.

"It's not my job to look after the city." Catching up to my

side, he falls into step with me, long legs dwarfing mine. "And anyway, I could say the same regarding your father, the *actual* bureaucrat. Giving his hometown a makeover seems like just the kind of publicity that could launch his campaign into the stratosphere."

I snort. Fat chance of there even being a campaign if I have my way. "Maybe you should mention that at the upcoming fundraiser."

"Maybe we can bring it up together."

I freeze mid step, whirling to face him. He mimics my stance, eyes unreadable through his dark lenses. "I'm not going to that."

"Caroline." He inches closer, mouth turning down at the corners. His ridiculously plush, kissable mouth. My thighs tense of their own accord as he cups my jaw in his rough palm. "If you think I'm letting you out of my sight after I found you with Luca, you can think again."

Jerking away does me little good; he steps in again, barring my body against the storefront we've stopped in front of, gripping the other side of my face in his free hand. He cradles it like precious cargo, and I try to ignore the fluttering in my stomach, the way moisture slickens between my legs.

I don't *want* to mean anything to this man.

Yet I want to mean everything.

The contradicting feelings are frustrating. I don't know what to do with them.

"You can't possibly be with me every second of every day. Besides, what happened to *barely married*?"

"You're the one who assigned us that title. I'm tired of using it." His warm, minty breath washes over me, devoid of any scent of alcohol for the first time since I've known him.

"And it never meant I'd allow you to fuck men behind my back, especially one of my own. You still belong to me."

Defiance bubbles within me. "Does that mean you stopped sleeping with dancers?"

His jaw ticks. "I don't know what you mean."

"Yes, you do. You're just surprised I know about it. Siena, is it? Does she have bigger tits than me? Her mouth sharper, hair brighter?" I lean forward, closing the distance between our chests. His heaves at the contact, nostrils dancing. "Pussy tighter?"

I can feel the resistance thinning, can sense the moment the band bundling his control starts to snap. His hands slide down my jaw, one slipping over my shoulder and skidding along my spine, the other locking around my throat, barely robbing me of air.

Just the way I like it.

The way that makes me forget anyone else ever hurt me.

He doesn't ask how I know his dancer's name. It must be obvious that Luca told me, and a pang of regret stabs at my stomach as I wonder if I'm endangering my cousin even more.

But then Elia leans in, and every thought flees my mind.

"You really think I have use for anyone else after having tasted you? After I've been inside you? There's no pussy tighter than yours, *amore mio*. No mouth that gets my cock harder than the one attached to your beautiful little body." He bends his head, teeth nipping at my earlobe.

My pulse skyrockets, and my heart thrashes against my rib cage. We're standing in the middle of downtown, engaged in a seemingly passionate embrace, not a care as to who might see.

Which, I suppose, for a newlywed couple, public

SAV R. MILLER

displays of affection might be expected. But no one else knows the truth, that our coupling is a war, a fight for power —one that can only end in bloodshed.

"You should be careful what secrets you reveal to me, *carina*," Elia whispers into my ear, lips grazing my skin. "Every kernel of information you give that isn't public knowledge puts your little lover in danger. I'd hate to have to murder your cousin."

I swallow over the knot in my throat, refusing to acknowledge that Luca's not my lover. "If you kill him, I won't forgive you."

"Baby." Straightening to his full height, he grips my waist and pulls my pelvis into him, the length of his erection pressing into my stomach, making me dizzy with desire. It's hard to focus on his words. "I don't need your forgiveness. Don't want it. All I want is your goddamn surrender."

My body curls into his, my fingers splaying themselves on the hard plane of his chest. I give him my most saccharine smile, the one I reserve for times of desperation. "You won't get it."

His lips spread, revealing his straight teeth, blinding against the sun. "Oh, we'll see about that."

The hand on my throat loops around my waist, linking with the other just above the curve of my ass. Without warning, he dips, pressing his shoulder into my stomach and flinging me over it. I squeal as he walks the way we just came, trying to get a grip on the skirt of my dress to maintain a shred of modesty, considering the crowd we've suddenly amassed.

"Oh my God, you're an asshole." I smack at his back, unwilling to acknowledge the tight muscles working there beneath his clothes.

174

"Speaking of assholes, yours is probably showing, so I suggest you stop fighting."

"I hate you." I mumble the words into his back so softly, I almost don't even hear them myself.

But I certainly hear his response. "You just wish you did."

Mortification flushes my skin, and when he sets me down, I can tell he isn't expecting continued retaliation.

I get it. I'm not much of a fighter; for the past decade, I've lain down and taken every beating, all the abuse, as it was given. No contest—to keep my sister safe, to keep our family, however secretly broken, intact.

A sad, delusional form of self-preservation I'm no longer leaning into.

So instead of letting Elia shove me into the car for the second time in our short marriage when his arms snake around me and begin to lift, I channel each lesson of defense Luca taught me last year and throw my body weight into him.

My elbow connects with the side of his jaw at the same time my knee collides with his groin, eliciting a satisfying grunt from his mouth. My joints throb, agony spreading like an oil spill, but I push through, ensuring the hits have as much power behind them as possible.

His sunglasses fall to the ground, breaking on impact. He doubles over, nearly taking a knee, a mixture of shock and utter rage lighting his features. I don't stop to consider the way his pupils seem to dilate ten times their normal size, or for Benito—who I just know is behind the wheel of the SUV —to come out and grab me.

Instead, I whirl on my heel and take off, my feet pounding along the sidewalk to the rapid beat of my heart.

There are no stolen glances over my shoulder. No pause

to consider that I've just assaulted my husband, a very dangerous and powerful criminal.

I just run.

And I don't stop until I'm sure he's not coming after me.

19

ELIA

A CURSE RIPS from my throat as Siena drops the ice pack into my lap, sending pain splintering through my groin. I hiss through my teeth and clutch the arms on my chair, squeezing my eyes shut.

A part of me knows she's acting out because of how I treated her the last time we sat in my office, but she was the only one available when I limped inside. A smarter man wouldn't let yet *another* woman scorned anywhere near him, but this day only proves how stupid I truly am.

"Can you fucking watch where you put that?"

She lifts one shoulder, clad in one of the red silken robes we keep on hand for Crimson's dancers, moving to adjust the gauze strapped to my chin. "That bitch really got you good, huh?"

"Don't fucking call her that." I glare at her from narrowed lids as she dabs at the coagulated blood decorating my lip. "And you don't have to sound so damn smug."

The harsh overhead light enhances the freckles on her

angular face as a soft grin spreads. "Sorry. It's just not often someone puts you in your place."

"She didn't put me in my place."

"The bruise on your jaw begs to differ." She cocks an eyebrow, turning to toss the damp paper towel in her hand into the wastebasket beside us.

"I don't need a reminder, Siena." Especially when my pride's just been wounded.

After Caroline cold-clocked me and left me writhing on the sidewalk, unsure of my ability to produce children in the future, a few people from the *Gazette* trickled out of a café and snapped pictures.

Benny helped me inside the SUV and destroyed as many cameras as he could. But the foreboding sense of dread that someone still has photos settled in my stomach hours ago.

At least, that's what I'm telling myself the dread is about. I don't want to connect it to the fact that I don't know where Caroline disappeared to; she ditched her phone at the house, and I've yet to bug any of her underwear.

I know she has that list memorized; I just haven't figured out what the hell she's doing with it. Part of me wonders if she disappeared to take care of the names on it.

But I don't care. She can get herself butchered doing so, for all the shits I give. Kieran's been quiet lately, but I'm sure he'd be willing to step in if he found her before me.

The fire in my balls agrees, even if the pinch in my heart says otherwise.

"I just can't believe she's still alive." Siena wipes her hands off with an alcohol pad, and I reach down to move the ice pack over an inch. "Imagine if any of your men pulled this stunt."

"My men are trained to kill, not wound. If they did something like this, I wouldn't expect to live to tell the tale."

"So you're letting her off the hook because she's a bad shot?"

"Who said she's off the hook?"

Siena rolls her eyes. "Jesus, I called you by your first name, and you put me in a chokehold."

My jaw ticks, irritation bubbling in my stomach. Her voice is beginning to grate on my nerves like nails dragging down a blackboard. "Siena." She glances over at me as I lift my head. "Shut the fuck up."

She does, mouth clamping together, but I can hear the hurt in her breathing. It's soft, stuttered, like she's actively trying not to annoy me—which, naturally, pisses me off further. *Where's the fight? The fire?*

This is why we'd never have worked out; she's already broken, malleable, and there's no thrill in sculpting her.

Not like there is with my wife, whose fire burns so bright she fucking blinds me just by existing.

The door to my office swings open, my father's bulky form filling the frame. He stalks inside, kicking the door with his heel so hard the glass windows behind me rattle. Stopping just short of where Siena sits perched on the edge of my desk, he slams his phone down, his face turning a deep shade of red.

"Christ, Pops, are you having a heart attack?"

"I fucking must be because what I see on the goddamn front page of the *Stonemore Times* is an abomination. I'm so disgusted with you; I could spit."

Sitting up, I reach and grab the phone as he shoves it toward me. I'm immediately met by a picture of Caroline's knee lodged in my groin, followed by a shot of her running off and leaving me in the fetal position on the sidewalk.

I know exactly what he sees: vulnerability in a *capo*, a man the people in town are supposed to fear—someone supposed to keep our rivals at bay, even if just based on reputation.

Rage boils in my veins, a violence I've never felt before surging ugly and angry, nearly blinding in its presence. My face heats, heart thrashes wildly in my chest. *I'm going to slit the throats of every journalist in a fifty-mile radius.*

Pointing at the door, I motion for Siena to leave; she obeys, pulling it closed behind her, and I work on calming the mounting agitation curdling in my gut.

I'm annoyed with myself for letting my guard down. Again. For not chasing after my wife and shoving her into my vehicle after the humiliation she caused.

For marrying her in the first place and allowing myself to get caught up in her beauty. As if she's not been a viper all along, waiting for the chance to strike.

Still, I try to play it off, shrugging as I hand the phone back to my father. "So they caught a lovers' quarrel on camera. Certainly, this isn't the first of its kind. Must be a slow news day."

"You call that a quarrel? Son, she laid you out to dry like wet fucking laundry." He runs a hand through his graying hair, pulling at the roots. "What the hell were you thinking?"

"Between the time I had my hands on her and when she maimed me? Honestly, I didn't have time to think much of anything."

"Exactly. You're becoming too soft, and she's only been in your life a little while. Have you made *any* progress on the thief we have in our midst?"

"Gia's working on the investigation—"

"And what are *you* doing besides playing house and getting your ass handed to you?"

Inhaling deeply, I clench my jaw against the tightness gripping my chest. I'm beginning to regret coming to the office at all; if I'd nutted up and gone home, I'd be relaxing in my pool with a crossword puzzle in hand. Maybe Caroline would even be there.

"So where is she?"

"Who?"

My father's nostrils flare. "*Elia.*"

"Pops. My wife has a name, you know."

"Your wife." Shaking his head, he drops into the seat across from me. "I told you not to marry that girl. Said she'd be trouble. First that dinner, now this. You know how many emails I've gotten from Ivers this week, asking when I'm returning his stolen property?"

"He's emailing you?"

"Yes. I don't respond, naturally, since email is a hotbed for government tracking." He scoffs, loosening the tie around his neck and scrubbing a hand over his face. "You'd think Kieran would know better."

"He's probably purposely leaving a trail, trying to get Dominic in trouble. Or trying to set us up."

Or maybe he's just fucking with us. The bastard does have a notoriously sick sense of humor.

Maybe he doesn't want Caroline at all but keeps the charade going because he can.

"Perhaps." Leaning back in his chair, he steeples his index fingers and studies me a few minutes in silence. "In any case, I want you to pay him a visit. Try to put this feud behind you."

"Fat chance of that happening, Pops."

"Son, honestly—"

A knock on the door cuts him off, and Benny sticks his head in, requesting my father's presence. "Kal Anderson is here to see you, sir."

"He doesn't want to deal with Elia?"

Benny shrugs. "Elia said he's not to be bothered, except for emergencies."

I grin at the crimson flush spreading across the tips of my father's ears, letting my head drop back again. But I don't feel the curve of my mouth in my heart.

My eyes stare up at the ceiling, unseeing. All I can think about is where the fuck my wife is and what I might do when I get my hands on her.

My father points a finger at me as he stands, adjusting his coat. "I meant what I said about Ivers. Put this to bed, and get that girl of yours under control. I don't want to have to call Rafe up in Boston and tell him you're unfit to lead this outfit any longer."

I roll my eyes as he leaves, pressing a fingertip to the cut on my lip. Siena re-enters the room, crossing her arms. She blows a strand of red hair out of her face like she's trying to distract herself from speaking.

"Something to say?" I ask, careful to keep my expression tame and my voice bored, disinterested, so as not to give her any ideas. Siena's always been rather forthcoming when it comes to her feelings about me, but I thought she'd take the hint by now that I don't reciprocate.

This black heart lies elsewhere, with a girl who wants nothing to do with me.

Caroline's made it perfectly clear where we stand—

married for convenience and nothing more. Clearly, if this afternoon is any indication.

That doesn't stop me from wanting her. My brain knows how my heart feels. Knows how early it is, how sudden and inappropriate.

I'm just not ready to accept it. Not willing to give myself over entirely.

But that doesn't mean the feelings disappear.

"Nope." Siena cleans up the bandages and gauze, packing them into the first-aid kit Phoebe keeps under the bar. After several beats of silence, she shrugs and leaves, a cloud of perfume standing in the room in her wake. It's nauseating.

The office door swings open again, revealing both Gia and Marco with matching expressions of stoicism.

"Boss, we've got a problem." Marco hesitates, glancing at Gia before sliding his gaze back to mine. "Make that two problems, actually."

I stare at a bullet hole in the floor, caused by an altercation with a former employee years ago, trying to calm my racing pulse. Sweat beads along my skin as I rip myself from my thoughts. "I told you I didn't want to be bothered tonight."

"We have a concrete lead on the stolen product."

Sitting up straight, I wait for them to continue.

Gia sighs, walking over and dropping a photocopy of the list Dominic Harrison gave me onto my desk. "We cross-referenced every name on that list; most of those guys have connections to flesh auctions all around Maine, the majority of which specialize in stolen minors."

"Okay..."

"Well, you know how Dom owes just about everyone

money, right?" I nod, and Gia continues. "We think he's using his network to source young girls and has an inside guy in our warehouse crew skimming blow in an attempt to pay off his debt now that Caroline isn't a viable option."

Anxiety spikes in my stomach, my chest tightening like an overblown balloon. *I'm going to kill that fucker.* "How is this going on right under our noses?"

"The blow goes missing at some point after leaving the warehouse. It passes through so many hands after that, it's difficult to determine who's taking a cut."

"So what are we doing about it?"

Gia swallows. "Angelo's already admitted to helping, and he's agreed to assist with the investigation in exchange for a simple exile."

I nod, folding my hands together. "And we're *sure* Kieran Ivers isn't involved?"

"There's not been a report of activity from his home in weeks, but obviously, we can't be absolute. My gut says no, though."

"Well, I'm not paying you to fucking guess. Figure it the fuck out, and don't let my father catch wind of this." Leaning back, I rub my temples. "What was the other thing?"

Marco and Gia share an uneasy look, and Gia leans back on his heels, discomfort radiating from his posture. His shoulders slump inward, mouth flattening, and a second wave of bile rises in my throat, making me gag.

"Jesus Christ, what is it?" My fingers cut into the leather on my chair, nails splintering at the pressure.

Marco reaches behind his neck, scratching. "Well, you said to come get you if anyone with Caroline's ID showed up tonight."

Fucking Juliet. "Where is she?"

"In the VIP lounge, causing a scene with a male patron. People are starting to get uncomfortable." Gia frowns. "But, Elia, you should know... it's not the sister."

My stomach flips, and I push to my feet despite the pain in my groin. Buttoning my suit jacket and ripping the bandage from my chin, I tilt my neck from side to side, reveling in the way my bones crack. I move between my soldiers and head out into the hall.

Gia catches up first, stalling me with his hand on my shoulder. "Elia. She's drunk."

"Yeah?" I swipe my thumb across my lip, the sting a now-welcome reminder of this afternoon. A balm to my mounting feelings, fuel for the punishment I'm about to serve downstairs. "She's about to be fucking dead."

20

CAROLINE

I FEEL Elia's presence before I even see him; his soul radiates toward mine like a heatwave in July, hazy and thick and suffocating. I know he's down here, hunting, looking for me.

But I've had too many drinks to care—to consider the repercussions of my earlier actions.

Liv's celebratory flaming tequila shots turned into Vegas Bombs, and then some weird moonshine drink served in a small barrel. My legs have felt like jelly for the past twenty minutes since I "tripped" and landed in the lap of Todd Davis.

Lucky me.

Todd's arms tighten around my waist, as though he can sense something terrible is about to happen, and I lean back, fitting my ass more firmly into his groin, preparing for the show. The oversized Hawaiian button-down he has on brushes against my bare arms, itchy and reeking of cigar smoke.

We're seated in a sticky booth at the back of the VIP lounge, entertaining ourselves while the dancers change shifts. Liv's been off to the side chatting up the female bartender, a tiny girl with a brown ponytail, who looks so out of place here I had to do a double take when she dropped off our drinks.

A grossly moist pair of lips graze the shell of my ear, and a shiver skates over my body, prickling my skin in the worst way. I cringe, trying to pull away from the middle-aged man's fried pickle breath. *Who orders food at a club known for luxury cocaine and hookers?*

"What's the matter, sweetheart?" Todd's fingers squeeze my side, dancing along the exposed skin, making me regret borrowing this outfit from Juliet, who was nursing another hangover and couldn't come out tonight.

The seductive red dress is short, with crisscrossed ties holding the tight bodice together on the sides. Seemed like a good idea an hour and a half ago, but now I just feel exposed.

Somehow, despite the amount of flesh on display, my face is hot and sweaty. I feel disconnected, like my soul is floating outside of my body and having a hard time making its way back.

"I need to go to the bathroom." Wriggling around on Todd's lap, I try to ignore the hardness beneath my ass, focusing on disentangling myself from him. Luca was right —a *little* flirting goes a long way with these men, and here I am, upping the ante. Like Todd wasn't absolute putty in my hands the second he saw me here.

"I'll go with you."

"To the ladies' room?"

"Sure, sweetheart. You and I have *loads* of unfinished business, so why not take care of it really quick?"

"I'd prefer we not do that here." I bat my eyelashes,

trying to appear innocent. The way his puffy eyes darken makes me think I'm doing it right. "We should get a cab or something."

"I think we should just stay right here. Makes it more exciting that way, don't you think?" His hand splays across my belly, pinkie finger caressing my pubic bone. I swallow down the knot rising in my throat, unease settling deep in my bones like a lead balloon dropping to the floor. "Besides, you owe me. Your daddy owes me."

"I didn't agree to anything like that."

"Doesn't matter. This between us is a long time coming, and you know it, *babe.*"

I grit my teeth against the nickname, wishing I could bleach it from my memory. "I'm married."

"Never stopped me before."

I'm starting to get pissed; this isn't how this interaction is supposed to go, and here I've fucked everything up because I let Liv convince me to indulge a little. One drink is never just *one drink.*

I push against Todd and aim for my footing, heels slipping along the slick hardwood as I stand.

Todd moves with me, keeping my ass pressed fully against him, preventing my departure.

Dread floods my stomach, panic sluicing through my blood. "Let *go* of me."

"Why should I? You're the one who's been dancing up on me and flirting with me all night. Don't act like you don't want this."

I did want this, or at least the illusion of it, but things are progressing too quickly for me to keep up. My head swims, and I'm lost at sea, trying to remember what my plan was here in the first place.

My heartbeat kicks up, a thunderous pounding in my ears I can't shake. Not that it keeps me from trying; moving my head side to side, my hand slips off Todd's lap with the movement, and I fall out of his grasp, crashing to the floor.

Except I never quite hit it.

A pair of strong arms wrap around me, keeping me from face-planting on the ground. They right me, yanking the hem of my dress down farther along my thighs, pulling my back into his front.

Right on time.

At the same time he catches me, Elia's fist whips out across Todd's cheek, causing him to stumble backward and flatten against the booth. He cradles his face, a crowd forming quietly around us. I see two Montalto men off to the side, dressed in all black with their arms crossed, poised to join in at the drop of a hat.

Elia's clean, whiskey and chlorine scent assaults my senses, making me feel fuzzy. I straighten my spine, pulling away gently while his hands grip my biceps, keeping me close. "Are you okay?"

Liv rushes to the edge of the crowd, trying to elbow her way in, but no one moves for her. She watches, eyes narrowed, and I try to look confident. Like I'm okay. Inside, my stomach battles a million different emotions, unable to settle and focus on just one.

"Never better, Captain." I try to salute him, but it's damn near impossible with his iron-clad hold surrounding me. His gray eyes flash, something unfamiliar and terrifying in their depths, and this time when I shiver, it's in an oddly good way. I feel the tingle all the way to my toes, vibrating between my legs.

Blinking down at me like he's trying to erase a spell, Elia

moves one hand to smooth it over my hair. "What the hell is going on here?" He asks the question without moving his gaze from my face, but I can tell by the volume and edge cutting his voice that he doesn't mean for me to respond.

For some reason, probably Everclear-related, the fact that he isn't immediately blaming me makes my heart swell painfully, like it's trying to launch itself from my chest and into his throat.

"Just trying to show the little lady a good time." Todd shrugs one shoulder, still holding his face, as if unaware of who he's speaking too. He must've had more to drink than I realized. Or maybe patrons just aren't used to Crimson's owner coming down for visits.

"Oh, good, you do speak English." Elia's arm slips around my waist, tugging me into his side. *Christ, he's warm.* I can't stop myself from leaning into him, using him as support. "So when the *little lady* says she wants you to let go of her and you use her clearly drunken state as an excuse to manhandle her, you're just being an asshole."

Todd bristles, eyes flickering to me. Mine slide to the floor, zeroing in on Elia's expensive Italian shoes. *Why's he always so polished? What's he hiding beneath that suit?*

The memory of scars decorating his forearms flashes in my mind, a reminder that he may claim he doesn't like secrets, but it's clear he has many. He has to; all made men carry things to their graves.

Some end up there because of them.

"Look, man, I didn't mean anything by it." Todd holds his hands up, palms out, gesturing toward me. "She came onto me."

"I find it hard to believe my wife would come onto a pig like you. Especially with me just upstairs."

"Wife?" Todd's eyes bug out, jaw dropping. He scrambles to his feet, adjusting the way his ugly shirt lays against his chest. "She didn't say anything about being married to a Montalto. I never would've—"

"You're Dom Harrison's friend, right?"

Todd nods, and Elia's fingers stroke my side, a strange surge of comfort blasting through me at the movement. I shouldn't feel this way, especially as this situation escalates toward my goal, but I can't seem to help it. "Are you really trying to tell me you're unaware that his eldest, highly publicized daughter got married to the owner of a club you frequent? *Cristo*, Todd, if I'd known you were this much of a fucking dumbass, I'd never have given you access to my VIP lounge in the first place."

"Elia, I—"

"You put your hands on my wife. I think we're done talking."

"Can't I even defend myself at this point? Jesus, your father was way easier to fucking deal with. It's not my fault you married a slut; why don't you ask her about the services she provides for the rest of her daddy's friends."

Elia's eyes slide to me, his chin dipping down. I stare up at him, pleading silently with him not to take that bait. I don't want to explain that I never serviced anyone; not willingly. Not because I wanted to. Don't want to travel down the rabbit hole I've spent the last few years crawling out of.

My husband's brow furrows, a war brewing in his gaze. Something seems to click, relaxing the strain on his face; he exhales, bending to press a kiss to the top of my head. "I want you to go upstairs with Gia and Marco."

I shake my head even though all I want to do right now is

lie down and take a nap. "Elia, I don't need you to fight my battles."

Lie. That's been the whole point of this marriage.

That was the whole point of me coming here tonight, even knowing he might still be angry with me for this afternoon.

"*Amore mio*," he murmurs, the music blaring from the speakers nearly drowning him out, "I've stopped caring about what you think you need. Go upstairs and try to sober up. Your friend Olivia can join you."

Casting a glance at Todd, who seems to be scanning the area for an exit, I take a step closer, tilting my head up. "What're you going to do with him?"

"You don't need to worry about that. Let me take care of him." He offers me a soft smile, cupping the sides of my face, and I can't reconcile this man with the one I assaulted earlier today, with the dominant alpha I've come to know; the man I'm supposed to want to leave once this is all over. The tenderness he's showing causes something to crack in me, a levee bursting open with uninhibited waters. "Let me take care of *you*."

"There's a line she's heard before, pal." Todd chuckles to himself, and my body tenses.

Why is he still talking?

Elia stiffens, straightening his spine, and when one hand drops from my face and slips beneath the flap of his suit jacket, I already know what's coming. He pushes me behind him as if to shield me from the situation unraveling before a hundred pairs of eyes, but I grip his waist, rooting myself in place.

The .22 glints in the strobe lights flickering above our heads, sleek and black, looking right at home wrapped in my husband's massive palm. His finger curls around the trigger, flexing. Baiting Todd.

"Caroline." Elia's voice is low, gravelly, and meant only for me. My body buzzes, high from his attention. "Go, *now*, or so help me God in heaven I will shoot you, too."

I fit myself into him, trying to erase our seam. "I don't want to go with anyone except you."

"I came down here to kill you for stepping foot in this place. For disobeying me, again. What am I gonna do with you?"

"Anything you want," I breathe, alcohol going straight to my groin. How badly he wants to protect me has me practically drooling. "Just *please*, don't make me leave."

He exhales harshly through his nose, glaring at me. After a moment, he squeezes his eyes shut; they pop back open, and he gives an almost imperceptible nod. Turning his attention back to Todd, he adjusts his hold on the gun and cocks it.

Gasps fill the air around us, people scattering and scrambling to get as far away from the weapon as possible. Liv finally breaks through the throng and glues herself to my side, trying to pull me away. But I don't budge. Don't want to.

This is exactly what I came here to see.

Todd scowls, taking a step back. "What the fuck, man? You gonna just shoot me in public? I *told* you she came onto me. Why aren't you dealing with her?"

"Gia, Marco." The two men from before rush over to Elia's side, ready to take orders. "Get these people out of here. We're closing early."

The VIP lounge is already pretty empty at this point, with people not looking to get caught in the crossfire. The music overhead silences, the lights dimming and then shining fluorescent, illuminating the entire club. We watch, frozen in time, as bouncers filter people out of the front doors. One of the men from before—Gia or Marco, whoever has the tattoos—drags the female bartender out from where she's doing inventory and toward the back of the club, disappearing with her through a side door.

"What the hell is happening?" Liv whispers into my ear, arms winding around my waist. She buries her face into my neck, burrowing like she would when we were kids watching scary movies. Like monsters go away if you stop looking at them.

"Nothing good."

"I wanted tonight to be fun. Stuff like this wasn't supposed to happen. I'm sorry, Care."

I pat her back, sure it's the alcohol talking, unable to voice my true feelings—that this is the best night out I've ever had, that my pussy clenches and throbs with each passing second of Elia pointing his gun in Todd's face.

Jesus, I'm fucked up.

"You're a businessman, Elia. Surely, we can come up with some kind of deal here." Todd swallows, wiping his palms on his cargo shorts. His gaze shifts around the room, still searching, as if he thinks he might actually be able to run. "I really didn't mean anything by it."

"We probably could've settled this civilly, except for the fact that you keep disrespecting me by calling me *Elia*, and not only were your hands on my fucking wife but when she told you to release her, you didn't. Tell me, *Todd*, how many other girls have been in her position? How many am I avenging by killing you right here, right fucking now?"

Todd's eyebrows shoot up, and he opens his mouth to speak again, but before he has a chance, Elia's shoving himself forward while one of the men from before wraps their arms around Liv and me, dragging us away from the scene. Liv's body faces the other way as she complies, but I keep my head turned, trained on my husband's lithe form.

He grips the back of Todd's graying hair, right at the base of his neck, and tilts it back until it's parallel to the ceiling. I watch, keeping in step as the men pull us to the stairs; Todd's eyes widen impossibly, mouth going slack.

Elia takes the barrel of his gun and pushes it inside the man's mouth, forcing it in until the trigger resists against his chin. He's saying something to him, a menacing look on his face that I can almost *feel* from where I'm retreating.

There's a muffled popping sound, though I can't tell if it's muffled through the drunken haze waxing and waning against my brain, or if there's some kind of silencer on the pistol.

I recoil out of reflex, pulling my hand from the Montalto man's grip, and lean against the balcony. Todd's eyes are stuck open, unseeing, as Elia lets him fall to the floor. His mouth gapes, but I can't see the wound. As my husband turns and tucks the gun into the waistband of his slacks, he glances up at me, pausing.

There's bright red blood staining his hands and splattered across his face. It pools beneath where Todd's head has landed, face turned, hiding the mess.

But I can imagine it. Can sense it, smell its smoky, metallic existence. *One down, still more to go.*

My head swims the longer I stare at Todd's lifeless form, and just as I turn on my heel to find Liv again, my knees buckle, snapping like measly twigs. I go down, my vision blurring and fading to black as my body collides with the floor.

21

ELIA

SHIT, shit, shit.

I bolt up the stairs, ignoring the shouts from Benny and Gia, racing to catch my wife before she collapses entirely. The fact that I've just killed a man in my own club doesn't even register, a complete afterthought the moment I see her falling.

Her head bounces off the hardwood, blond hair splaying limply around her like an explosion. Dropping to my knees and wiping my hands on my pants, I curse under my breath. "*Caroline*," I whisper, a futile attempt to lure her back to consciousness, my palms drifting to cradle her face. She's clammy, feverish, and it makes my heart ache.

I shouldn't give a shit. In fact, I should be pissed about everything that's happened today: her assault earlier and then her disappearance, and then that pervert having his hands on what's *mine*.

But none of that mattered once I saw the vulnerability in her blue eyes, a need lurking like a ship lost at sea.

The fear I could smell sweating from her pores when she

realized he wasn't letting her go. The way she leaned into my touch, my body like she needed an anchor—needed my support.

Needed me the way I'm beginning to need her, an automatic response derived from being two halves of a whole picture.

I can't deny how good that felt; everything else be damned. I might be way in over my head here, but my brain is starting to catch up with my stupid black heart, wondering what it'd be like if this marriage between us was real. Wondering what it might feel like not to have to let her go, after all.

The scene playing out before me is too similar to a memory I haven't allowed myself to think about in years, and it sets my bones on fire that I find myself once again unable to do anything.

Couldn't save my mother when I was seven, can't save my wife now.

I'm stroking her cheek and beginning to move her head into my lap when a deep, dark voice calls over my shoulder. "You're not supposed to move head injuries."

Recognition flickers before I even turn my head, and when I do, I'm met by a flash of black—the Grim Reaper in the flesh.

Doctor Death.

Kal Anderson stares down at me with dark, soulless eyes, the sharp angles of his face highlighted in the club's shadows. He shoves his hands in the pockets of his black trench coat, rocking back on his heels. "So this is the infamous Caroline Harrison?"

"Montalto," I correct even though she hasn't changed her

name yet. And why should she, when she thinks this is all over after our prenup expires?

"Hm. She know that?"

"Does she know she's married to me? Yes, dick."

Kal chuckles, crouching down to his knees beside me. "That's not what it looked like when she flung herself onto the lap of that man you just murdered. Looked like she was trying to take him for a ride. And not on the River Styx, if you catch my drift."

"*Gesù Cristo.*" I huff out a breath, running a hand through my hair. "You looking to join that fucker?"

Shrugging, he presses his palm to Caroline's forehead. "You couldn't kill me even if you really wanted to."

He's not wrong, and it only pisses me off further. With several inches of height and pounds of muscle on me, there's no doubt in my mind that an attempt on Kal's life would end poorly, as they have for so many others. He's too large, too calculated, to be taken advantage of.

Not to mention the eyes. Hard and unwavering like darkened storm clouds.

Evil ripples off him in waves, like an iridescent mist following him around, and a single look in someone's direction might send them scurrying with their tail tucked between their legs.

It's a part of the reason the Riccis have him on their payroll in the first place; there isn't a man on the East Coast with a higher body count or who's more skilled in torture.

Then again, legend says the Riccis made him this way. Not that anyone can ask Kal for confirmation.

"I'm just saying, something fishy was going on here." Pulling back, he reaches into his pocket for a handheld flashlight and uses his opposite hand to peel Caroline's eyelids back, checking her pupils. "I don't give a shit who you kill, but have you ever seen someone sit around and watch while you did it?"

"We all do that. New recruits, especially." That way we make them accomplices, and if they rat us out, they implicate themselves in the process.

"A civilian, though? She couldn't tear her eyes away."

He pockets the light, hand dropping to her right ankle. My fingers itch to dig into his skin and pull him away—to keep him from touching her. But a sliver of metal catches my attention as he rolls her limb, turning her heel so it faces me.

Tucked into the strap of the stilettos she has on is a tiny pocketknife, folded shut and clipped on for safekeeping.

"That's the same one she had in her underwear when we met." I run a finger over it, remembering how she'd acted like it wasn't an unusual accessory.

"Know many girls who carry?"

"Around here? Just about all of them."

"Yeah, women employed at a club known for its high-quality blow." He rolls his eyes. "What's your overprotected, sheltered wife doing with this? How'd she get in here with it?"

I scrub a hand over my jaw, the stubble rubbing me raw —irritation spikes in me at his presence, at his logic. More now than ever, it's clear to me that Caroline was being abused behind the scenes by her father, but I still don't know exactly what she's doing *now*.

Did she come here knowing her father's friend would be here? Is that why she brought the knife?

And if this is a plan for revenge, why not go straight to the source?

Why involve me at all?

Exhaling, I give the doctor an irritated look. "What are you doing here, Kal?"

"Just finished up a meeting with your dad since I was told you weren't taking calls." He stands, brushing a piece of fuzz from his black slacks. "Now, I see why."

"Why did you meet at all?"

Again, he shrugs. "Because Kieran Ivers owes me a favor, and your dad wants to collect."

"Of fucking course, he does. Save the favor, Kal." I glance over my shoulder at the body lying on the ground, then slide my gaze back to our fixer. "Can you handle that?"

He scoffs. "Don't insult me." Gripping the balcony in one bony hand, he sweeps past me, coattails swishing behind him. Pausing at the top of the stairs, he turns his head. "She probably has a concussion, so when she comes to, don't let her go to sleep for a few hours. Try to keep her from vomiting and exerting herself."

I nod in response, and then he bounds downstairs, immediately moving to inspect the dead body. In a matter of minutes, he'll have disposed of it so well that no one will ever be able to trace it back here.

Shucking off my suit jacket, I wrap it around Caroline's front and slip my arms beneath her limp body, settling the curve of her neck and the bend of her knees in the crook of my elbows. Lifting her, I turn and head downstairs for the back exit, stopping briefly when Gia appears beside me.

"Boss."

"*What?*"

"What do I do with the friend?"

"Drug her. I don't want her remembering any of this. With any luck, she'll just think she drank too much."

He nods, and then hesitates, scraping over his bottom lip

with his teeth, jerking his chin toward Caroline. "Do... do you want anything for *her*?"

"No. I need her to remember everything."

SETTLING Caroline's unconscious body on my bed is a lot more difficult than I'd anticipated. Not because she's heavy or particularly inflexible, but because each movement of her limbs causes her dress to ride up or loosen at the sides, exposing more of her creamy skin to me.

And fuck, it's been far too long since I've felt it beneath my fingertips.

Still, I don't want to scare her, so I refrain from copping a feel. She can think I'm an asshole, but I won't let her lump me into the same category as her father and his associates.

When I touch her again, I want her to be aware. I want her to want it.

Her dress slides down her shoulders easily, and I retrieve a T-shirt from my dresser and work it over her head, tugging her arms through the sleeves and covering her to the tops of her thighs. Without her assistance, it'll have to do.

The dress stays on beneath, waiting for when she wakes up and can remove it herself.

I reach down and unbuckle her shoes, tossing them to the floor, and stick the knife in my pocket, where she'll have to violate me to get it back.

A stab of guilt prods my brain, knowing I'm taking away her only defense, but I ignore it.

Stripping slowly, I keep my eyes trained on her sleeping form; her chest rises slowly with each breath, her face a peaceful mask I've not had the pleasure to experience thus far in our relationship. She's always guarded and on edge—a caged tiger waiting for her chance to strike. *To run.*

My chest aches with the realization that I don't want her to.

Resisting the primal urge to curl my body around hers, to keep her safe from whatever it is she's trying to escape, I perch on the edge of the bed and pick up my phone, thumbing through my messages while I wait.

Two from my father asking if I've had a sudden lobotomy that caused me to kill a government official. One from Kal, saying everything at Crimson is under control, and one from Gia, letting me know he's headed to Stonemore to interrogate his brother and taking Kal with him.

Good. Kal's presence will certainly get him talking, and if it doesn't, his tools will.

Heaving a sigh of relief, I drop back on the bed and let my phone clatter to the side, staring up at the ceiling. The white sheets are fresh thanks to the housekeeper, Francis, who makes it a point not to be around when I am. They're soft, plush, and inviting, and sleep overtakes me before I have the chance to fight it.

I welcome the darkness that typically envelops me in this plane of subconsciousness, but it never comes; instead, I'm encased in bright light, surrounded by a sky of soft watercolors and more starlings than I've ever imagined existing. They soar above me, higher and higher, an endless stream of flight that mesmerizes me.

My mother's there, waiting for me, a warm smile on her still-young face. It's a dream I haven't had in ages, and it causes a cavern to crack open inside me, spewing my evil traits for her to see.

But she doesn't recoil or even seem to acknowledge all

the bad things I've done or all the cruel things I am. Her arms open, calling me to her embrace; I'm seven years old again, a boy needing his mother.

When I reach her, everything in me seems to soften, to lighten. Like she's the water for this long-dead soul I drag around.

"*Elia.*" Her lilted voice whispers in the wind around me, wafting through my hair and skimming my skin. Goose bumps pop up; it's been so long since I've heard her—since I've felt like she was still with me.

I squeeze around her waist as tight as I can, unwilling to let her go this time.

She hugs me back just as tightly—like she's been waiting for this moment.

But it doesn't last.

It never does.

When I tilt my head back up to get another look at her face, it's already morphing into something vile; blood seeps from her eye sockets, which have blackened and swollen, and a bright red splotch spreads on her white dress, soaking through. I feel it on my chest, tainting me the way it did when she died the first time.

Fuck. Wake up, Elia.

Her hand reaches out and grips my throat, applying pressure until I can't breathe at all. My esophagus crumples, and I can't help thinking I deserve this. That I'd carry it over into real life if I had the chance. That I'd go with her if I could go back.

She shakes me, releasing my throat to clutch my shoulders, thrusting my body back and forth until she starts to blur and fade. The starlings overhead swarm above us until they block the sun, the *sort sol* she always admired; a Danish phenomenon in nature, a nightmare in this dream.

Her body seems to evaporate into thin air right at the moment my eyes fly open, my body jerking upward with adrenaline, nearly knocking over the person gripping my shoulders in real life.

Caroline's face hovers close to mine, blue eyes dilated, and our breaths match in harshness and frequency. Her fingernails bite into my bare shoulders, and I welcome the pain.

It's a reminder that I'm awake. Alive.

Here, with her.

That I have questions she needs to answer.

She licks her plump lips, teeth sinking into the bottom one. Desire for her courses through my veins; she's a fresh rain after a long drought, her innocence a magnet I can't tear myself from. The fire in her soul something I want to consume me. Make me whole. Redeem me.

All this time, I thought she'd be the one surrendering—giving in. *Jesus Christ, was I wrong.*

"You were having a bad dream, I think." She blinks at me.

"Yeah," I breathe, mesmerized by her proximity. "I was."

Shifting slightly to put an inch between us, she clears her throat, eyes locked on mine. God, I don't ever want her to look away. "Are you okay?"

"No."

"Oh." She blinks again, her chest inflating and concaving with each increasingly labored breath.

My shoulders warm under her touch, pleasure slithering down my spine, and I can't help but wonder if she feels it too.

But instead of addressing that, or our altercation earlier,

or the fact that she's injured, or that I just had a fucking nightmare for the first time in years, I lash out.

Gripping the back of her neck, I drag her lips down to mine, sealing her fate, entwining it with my own. *Sort sol* be damned; Caroline obliterates the sun all on her own.

22

CAROLINE

It's hard to think with Elia's tongue in my mouth; he's a diver on an expedition to the seafloor, searching for buried treasure.

His large hands tangle in my hair, and he fuses our mouths before I have a chance to ask about the sounds he was just making in his sleep. Pitiful moans woke me from the blackout slumber I'd fallen into, and even though my vision swam when I sat up, searching for the source, I still found myself reaching for him.

That would've been the perfect time to sneak into my room and lock myself inside, but his groans grew in pitch with every shuddering breath wrenched from his chest, and it freaked me out. Made him seem too human.

My head pounded, pain ebbing from a single spot on my temple, and I hadn't been able to think clearly. I was reaching for him before I realized what was happening, drawn to him by some invisible force.

He kisses me with a voraciousness that steals the air from my lungs. One of my hands brushes over the tattoo on his side as it falls to his stomach. The other winds up his chest, wrapping around his neck.

My fingers press into the rock-hard muscles, making him shiver. I'm straddling his lap as he strains upward, forcing us closer like he's trying to sew our bodies together, erase the evidence that we're two separate entities.

Stroking his side, I wrestle his tongue with my own, lapping and licking and sucking until the sounds of our sloppy kisses fill my ears, heating my cheeks and making my thighs clench.

His hand leaves my hair and makes the slow, agonizing descent down my back, leaving a trail of molten lava in its wake. I pull back, tearing my lips from his. He moves forward again, trying to reconnect us, but I retreat, keeping the distance.

"Elia." My voice comes out breathless. *Husky.*

"*Amore mio*," he whispers, rolling his hips beneath me.

The shirt I'm wearing—*did he put this on me?*—slides up at our contact, allowing better access between us, and my clit presses against the bulge in his boxers.

It hits me that this is only the second time I've seen him this undressed outside of the pool. Since that day he came home drunk and took off his shirt, he's been more cautious around me like he suspects I feed off his vulnerability. Yet here he lays clad only in his underwear, body on full display.

"We have to stop."

"Why?" He leans forward, lips grazing my neck, and the heat flaring in my pussy nearly makes me cave.

"Don't you think we have stuff to talk about?"

"We have the rest of our lives to talk, Caroline."

The throbbing in my head intensifies. An ache so powerful that my vision blurs around the edges like a vignette filter. My palm covers the spot, applying pressure, and Elia slides me from his lap, concern marring his features.

"Fuck, did I hurt you?"

"No. I think I hit my head earlier."

He curses under his breath, getting to his feet and scooping his dress pants up off the floor. "Kal said you probably had a concussion. Jesus, I completely forgot." He turns, raking a hand through his messy locks. "Do you feel okay, otherwise?"

"I guess?"

"Nausea, blurred vision, fatigue?" He rubs his palms over his face like Lady Macbeth washes her hands. "Shit, I let you stay asleep. You've probably got brain damage by now."

My eyes widen, and I sit up straight despite the pain flaring. "Whoa, whoa, I think I'm okay. This isn't my first concussion, you know."

"Well, that makes it worse."

"The only thing making it worse is you freaking out right now. Seriously, I'm okay."

He turns, staring a hole through my soul, and my breath catches. Taking a step forward, he exhales, cupping my cheek. "Sorry, I just... this is familiar territory, and it didn't exactly end well the last time."

My brain jolts, desperate for another sliver of his personal life even though I shouldn't care—shouldn't want to know anything else about him. But I do. *God help me, I do.*

"What other time?" My eyes flicker to the scars on his arms, another question on the tip of my tongue.

Shaking his head, he drops his hand to his side. "It doesn't matter."

"Where have I heard that before?"

"This is different. Something that happened more than twenty years ago. It really *doesn't* matter."

I cock my head to the side, settling back against his headboard. "Didn't you once say that if it still hurts, it matters?"

"Again, this is different."

"Why?" I can't stop myself from pressing, from trying to figure him out. We've been at this charade for a while now, and it feels like he knows more about me than I do him. The imbalance makes me uncomfortable and gives him an edge I swore no man would ever have on me again. "Because I'm just a little girl who needs saving? Who needs some kind of trauma for my life to be meaningful enough for you to give me a second glance?"

"*Cristo.* No, Caroline, it's because your situation is still happening, and you won't let anyone help you."

"Someone *is* helping me."

He stares at me for a long moment, a flicker there that looks a bit like pain. But when he blinks, it's gone, replaced by a coldness I don't understand.

Doesn't he know I'm talking about him?

"Right. Well, I'd hate to stand in their way, but for the time being, you're *my* wife, and I think I should be the one avenging your soul."

"I'm not asking you to do that." I don't know why I say it. Why I deny him, even though he *is* that person. I can't make myself stop.

Again, he just stares at me, his gaze so intense it sparks a low heat in my belly. I ward it off, trying to maintain a semblance of dignity. He stuffs his hands in his pockets, not dropping his eyes, and slowly pulls out the pocketknife I had strapped in my high heel.

"What was your plan tonight, Caroline?"

"I—"

He moves, his gait slow and lithe, a hunter approaching his trapped prey. My thigh muscles clench as he flicks the blade open, knees knocking against the edge of the mattress. "Don't lie to me."

Lashing his hand out, he grips the hem of the T-shirt I'm wearing—his shirt, I'm realizing—and yanks it up, exposing my dress. A few of the ties have loosened, making it sag away from my skin, but it's still plastered against my chest, pushing my breasts together obscenely.

Elia's eyes darken, pools of unbidden desire, and he presses the tip of the blade to the middle of my chest, applying the slightest pressure. It's a pinprick, light and barely there, and it sets an inferno ablaze in my heart.

Something is seriously wrong with me.

He pulls back, the knife ghosting over my skin, and pauses with it poised at the seam of the dress. "Were you going to kill Todd Davis?"

I shake my head, and he pauses, tilting his, studying me. My nostrils flare at the proximity of the knife, an awareness that he quite literally holds my life in his hands flooding through me, scattering goose bumps over my flesh.

Kneeling on the bed, he uses his free hand to tug the T-shirt up and over my head, tossing it to the ground. His palm flattens against my breasts, pressing me back into the mattress.

He hikes his leg over me, straddling my thighs on his knees, and my eyes close against the sensations swarming in my stomach. Hot, heady need flashes through my body, a fever I'm not going to be able to sweat out.

The back of the blade glides across my collarbone,

smooth as silk. I swallow over the lump in my throat, hoping he can't see just how affected I am by this.

Hell, who am I kidding? The stuttered breaths falling from my parted lips are a dead giveaway.

"Do you like this?"

My tongue sticks to the roof of my mouth, and my fingertips tingle, but I remain quiet.

"Answer the question, *amore mio*." Elia's tongue joins the fray, licking up the trail of fire the knife leaves behind. He laves around the base of my throat, teeth scraping against the spots the blade explores, and my body jerks beneath his. "Keep your eyes closed and answer me."

"Which question?" I'm hoarse, my throat clogged with want.

I feel him shift, feel the knife strain against my dress, and when I peek through hooded lids, I watch as he slices through the material, splitting it down my middle. The cool air brushes my newly exposed skin, heightening my arousal.

Pushing the dress from my breasts, he cups one in his large hand, rubbing the pad of his thumb over my hardened nipple.

"The first one. I can tell by the way you're squirming beneath me that you fucking love this."

My back bows, arching away from the mattress, but he moves again, holding me in place. "No panties," he growls, a slight quiver in his voice that sends electricity singing in my veins. "Naughty girl."

Feathering kisses on the inside of my thighs, one hand still massaging my breast, I feel the knife slide along my side, cool against my heated flesh. The whole situation feels dirty, depraved, and I'm starting to see stars.

Elia Montalto isn't a king; he's a *god*.

He licks up my seam, the tip of his tongue delving between my slick folds, and presses the dull edge of the blade into my belly button, dragging his hand down. Metal accompanies his tongue, the juxtaposition of the two temperatures making my thighs quake.

Blowing on my clit, he probes my entrance with the handle, and a soft whimper escapes me at the intrusion. "Answer me."

"I don't remember the question."

"Yes, you do." My eyes start to open, exasperated, but he tsks. A light jab at my pussy wracks a shiver down my spine, fear heating my blood. "Eyes closed, *amore mio*."

I clench my jaw. "No, I wasn't going to kill him."

"But you wanted him dead. His name was on that list."

My walls crumble, the barrier between us stretching thin; it snaps as the knife comes up and rounds my ear, nicking the shell. A soft gasp escapes me; I go to open my eyes and retreat, but Elia's free hand clamps over me, keeping me in darkness.

"I'm not going to hurt you, Caroline."

I scoff, feeling shaky. "I've heard that before."

"Baby, the difference here is that I actually mean it."

"You hurt me just by being nice to me."

I can't see him, but I feel the moment his body tenses, muscles seizing up. He shifts, pelvis digging into mine, and moves his hand. But I don't open my eyes.

His lips find my pussy again, kissing and caressing like a man on a mission. He sucks at the skin, rolling his tongue around my clit, all while keeping the knife poised at my entrance. When his teeth sink into my silken flesh and tug harshly, I cry out, waves of pleasure ebbing through me.

Using the heel of his hand to stimulate me more, his hot

breath echoes over my wet, flushed skin. One of my hands comes down and palms my breast, squeezing tight as he edges the knife into me.

I'm so turned on that I can't tell if it's the sharp or dull side. All I feel is excitement and a slight bite of pain. "Oh fuck," I moan, the sound almost primal and not at all like me. None of this is like me.

What would Mommy and Daddy say?

He withdraws, flicking my hip. I don't understand how his hands can feel like they're everywhere on my body, all at once, but it certainly intensifies the ecstasy coursing through me. Fire builds in my abdomen, pressure pushing up and down simultaneously, and my hands grip the bed sheets until my knuckles ache.

"Jesus Christ, *bella*. You're fucking perfect." With an inhuman growl, he buries his head between my thighs, sucking and lapping like a man getting his last drink for all of eternity. Like he can't get enough. I writhe, pumping my hips up and pushing my pussy further into his mouth, riding the high he's giving me.

The knife is back, swirling at my opening, but this time I don't clam up. He doesn't relent, devouring my clit while the blade begins its inward ascent.

The *blade.*

Fear and thrill constrict my throat, and my entire body tenses to the point of exhaustion, waiting for him to flay me open.

Right at the moment he presses in completely, the instrument disappearing inside my pussy, I realize there's no pain. I open my eyes and see the knife, closed, beside my body, while he stares up at me with those impossible gray eyes, fingers pumping into me.

"I'm not going to hurt you."

The sounds of my arousal, crude and sopping, fill the room. Just as his pinkie probes the hole no one's ever been in, fingering the tight ring of muscle, a sharp stab of euphoria washes over me. Like a tide being released from the pull of the moon, I come harder than ever before.

My toes curl, my back bows, and my mouth opens on a silent scream as fireworks explode in my mind, blacking out everything else—no pain, no shame. Nothing except the absolute ecstasy zinging to my extremities.

It's so powerful that as soon as I've come down, I shift over the side of the bed and promptly vomit on the floor.

23

ELIA

THE SMELL of charred flesh permeates the air as I walk into Crimson's basement. Inhaling deeply, I round one of the makeshift tables made of discarded milk crates, meeting Kal at his toolbox.

He's wiping blood from a meat cleaver; hands gloved, as usual, black hair pinned back with a shower cap. A plastic smock drapes over his clothes, but a smidge of red still managed to splatter onto his neck.

I clear my throat, nodding at the slumped figure across the room. Sheldon McCarty's behemoth form droops in a chair, wrists and ankles chained down, head lolling forward. Thick, red liquid pools on the tarp around his feet and at least three fingers are missing from his right hand. And he's completely naked.

"Get anything out of him?"

Kal slides his dark gaze in my direction. "Doubting me?"

Shrugging, I shove my hands into my pants pockets and watch as he tucks his toolbox into a structured duffel bag. "You know how important this is."

"Every job is important; otherwise I wouldn't be here." He mutters something about the Hippocratic oath, turning from me as he adjusts the smock around his neck, tossing his bloody rag into a nearby biohazard bin. "In any case, I'm not done. He's one tough son of a bitch."

Pulling a pair of rusty pliers from his back pocket, Kal shoves his sleeves up past his elbows and makes his way back over to Sheldon. He kicks the man's shin with the tip of his boot until a bruise starts to coagulate, and the congressman returns to consciousness.

Kal rips the gag from Sheldon's mouth and grips the hair at the base of his neck, jerking his head up toward the ceiling. There's a severe amount of detachment in Kal's eyes as if this is the most normal thing in the world. That makes him the best damn fixer on the East Coast. Highest paid, too, which I suspect is the reason he's still at it. Helps him fund free clinic hours and vacation homes, or whatever else he does in his top-secret free time.

"Ready to tell Montalto here what your relationship with Caroline Harrison is?"

Sheldon's breathing is sporadic, black eyes wide and disconnected—in shock, I'd guess, from what he's endured thus far. Upon closer inspection, I see Kal left one mutilated finger on his right hand still partially intact; the skin completely removed. Only bone remains with the tip ground down.

Instead of complying, the wheezing sack of shit spits at us, launching stringy blood and saliva in our direction. I'm too far for it to land, but it hits Kal's exposed forearm, and he lifts his chin as the temperature in the room seems to drop.

He doesn't lash out, but his hand flexes, drawing the pliers closer to Sheldon's mouth. "I suggest you decide now how important this information is because I'm three seconds away from ripping out his tongue."

Shifting my weight from foot to foot, I contemplate the situation. Sheldon likely has information on how many government officials in King's Trace are involved in Dominic's depravity. As days pass by, more of my blow goes missing, and Caroline shrinks from me, hiding her heart and soul as though I haven't already staked my claim on them.

I want all of those men dead, for her. For whatever they did to her.

That they're also stealing from me is just a fucking bonus.

We've yet to fully interrogate Angelo, however, and he's the most likely to cooperate. It's just a matter of getting him to come in; he got spooked the day Gia and Kal went to see him, and Gia says he's afraid that if my father catches wind of his hand in the matter, Angelo's semi-immunity will disappear.

It might, whether my father finds out or not. I haven't decided yet.

Making my way to the chair Sheldon's strapped to, I stroke the stubble lining my jaw, imagining this asshole's hands on my wife. Touching her without her consent, just because her daddy said he could. Offered her as payment for debts that he accumulated for his own personal gain.

She hasn't exactly admitted that's what happened, but it's not a difficult situation to piece together. It helps that Luca's been on board with my assistance, secretly passing me details while Caroline sits at home on bedrest, recuperating from her concussion. I'm just glad to see he didn't take that beating from a few weeks ago to heart.

A week's passed since the night I killed Todd Davis, and

Caroline puked in my room. We've avoided one another ever since.

Each night I come home, it takes everything in me not to slide into her bed and wrap her in my arms, the only place I feel I can adequately keep her safe, but I know she's not ready for that.

She's also a horrible patient; when I'm not hanging out in Crimson's basement or tracking shipments so Marco can guard them better, I sit in my office and watch her on surveillance. She spends most of her time baking; her favorite thing to bake seems to be scones—blueberry and orange—and she always makes more than she can eat. Not that it stops her from trying. I've watched her eat a dozen pastries in the last two days.

Though she's putting her culinary arts degree to use at the house, I can tell she's antsy, occasionally watching the news and constantly making phone calls to Olivia and Juliet. Anything she can use to distract herself from the control that slips further from her grasp every single day.

In any case, I've taken over her apparent quest for revenge, aiming to eliminate these fuckers before she has a chance to get hurt. Hopefully, one day, she'll thank me.

"McCarty, all you have to do is tell us how well you know Caroline," I grunt, eyeing the slimy fucker.

"Why? So you two can get off to the image of me forcing my cock inside her?" Sheldon smirks at the same time that my eyes narrow, making my blood boil. I tuck my hands behind my back, exercising restraint. For now.

Kal doesn't, though. His nostrils flare, pulling the pliers apart to wedge Sheldon's lip between the instrument head. He pulls and twists the pink flesh, smiling as the congressman begins writhing, trying to break his restraints.

"Fuck, okay, okay. Jesus. I'm fucking talking, aren't I?"

"Say something worth listening to," Kal snaps.

I cross my arms over my chest. "Are you saying you had sex with her?"

"If that's what you want to call it, sure."

I glance at Kal, who raises his eyebrows and yanks on Sheldon's hair. He squeaks, but it doesn't wipe the smug look off his dumb fucking face. "What would *you* call it?"

"Getting what I paid for. Dominic promised we could all take turns on the broad if we forgave his debts. I was first in line; she went with me, thinking I'd be gentle."

"You weren't?" My heart pounds in my ears.

He scoffs. "Gentle or not, it didn't matter. She didn't want me, didn't want any of us. She was seventeen, and my fetishes are... not for the faint of heart. Not for virgins."

"You had sex with a child," Kal deadpans. His spine is rigid, and I don't think I've ever seen such a heavy rage in his gaze.

An eyebrow raises, surprise flooding Sheldon's features. "Now wait a damn minute. She was above the age of—"

"If you say consent, I swear to God, I'll blow your brains out right now." I fold my arms over my chest, disgust crawling across my skin. "You, a man who at the time was at least forty, had sex with a *minor*. A child. Consent doesn't fucking mean anything when someone can't fully understand what—or who—they're consenting to. She didn't have a fucking choice."

Kal's breathing grows shallow.

Sheldon shakes his head. "She chose me—"

"*The lesser of many evils.*" The words explode on my tongue, outrage shooting through me like white-hot lightning. "You're a pedophile. What the fuck is wrong with you?"

My heart beats rapidly, a pang ripping through the organ as I consider Caroline's inherent need to fight—to deny her feelings, her sadness, and anger; how she clams up at the mention of her past, how she doesn't seem to have spoken about it with anyone.

I fucking *hate* that I'm finding out about it all like this, but I can't fault her for how she copes.

We all do what we can to survive. Who we are and how we get through this life are not one and the same.

Trying to reconcile the girl with so much hate and pain etched into her very being with the warm, feisty, caring woman I call my wife is difficult; I can't imagine how long it took to get there. The need to somehow correct this nightmare for her resurges in me.

Clenching my jaw, I stare at the blood on the floor beneath my shoes, trying to find a focal point to center my rage on. Sinister darkness passes through me, lighting my nerve-endings on fire, and I exhale slowly, snapping my head back up.

My head is foggy as I move, my brain on autopilot while my senses take over; red splashes across my vision, painting my insides with fury. Kal steps aside after a long moment, holding the pliers in his palm, and I snatch them away, positioning myself in front of Sheldon, legs spread, feet planted on either side of his chair.

One hand seizes his throat, and I feel his windpipe shift under my hold, trying to adjust to the pressure. His breathing scatters, eyes bulging like Todd's the other night, and excitement sings in my veins at the sight.

I smell the exact moment his smugness turns to unadulterated fear, glancing down as his cock leaks, piss dripping down the chair.

"You'd better be sure you don't need anything else from him," Kal says, voice unwavering as I work the head of the pliers between Sheldon's top left canine.

"I don't think I fucking care anymore."

Kal shrugs, holding his hands up in surrender. He disappears behind me, and the smell of bleach hits my nostrils seconds later, indicating that he's cleaning.

Sheldon sputters against me, jerking in the chair. "Hey, I didn't mean anything by it—"

"I'm sick of people saying that where Caroline is concerned." Closing the pliers around the tooth, I ground my palm into the handle and begin pulling; canines and their bulbous roots make extraction tricky, but it also makes the agony in a victim's eyes so much sweeter.

My only hope is that my mother isn't looking down from wherever the hell the afterlife is—that she doesn't visit me later when I'm asleep.

"I hope this hurts," I spit into Sheldon's face, my grip tightening and increasing in pressure. "I want you to know I'm putting that girl back together if it's the last fucking thing I do. Her scars are not permanent; they're erasable. *Just. Like. You.*"

Hiking my foot up, I suck in a deep breath and shove the sole of my loafer right into his dick. His stomach spasms, a gurgling sound ripping from the back of his throat. As I grind my shoe into him, feeling the muscles in his flaccid cock mush together, he throws his head back, assisting me in removing the tooth.

I feel the root pop out from his gum as he lets out an ear-piercing scream. Blood drips from the wound, his chest heaving, sweat pouring down his forehead.

But I don't give him time to writhe or cry out again;

tossing the pliers and tooth onto the floor, I pick up the discarded rag, ball it in my fist, and force it between his bloody lips until he gags.

Not bothering to stay and watch him seize up, I wipe my hands on my pants, turn on my heel, and leave the rest for Kal.

~

Caroline

"Did you get it?"

Juliet shimmies her way into the stall, holding the grocery bag up in her hand. "Yeah, I got it, weirdo. I don't know why this couldn't wait till we got back to your house, though."

"This is the only place I can do it in private."

She shrugs, untying the bag handles, and pulls out the rectangle box. "I don't get why you're hiding this from your husband, but whatever."

"You should be grateful you're even involved in this," I snap, nerves getting the best of me. If I hadn't already scheduled sister-bonding time with her this afternoon, she'd be out of the loop entirely.

But I can't fucking stand the not knowing any longer. Bedrest left me with too much time to overthink and overeat. And each time Elia comes home and tries to act like a normal husband, a fresh wave of anxiety further cripples my already-battered heart.

Given the stress of the last few weeks, being late shouldn't be all that surprising; still, I need to know for sure. It only takes one time, after all, and even though Elia didn't finish weeks ago, he also didn't use a condom.

This is the first time Leo's taken me out of the house since my night at Crimson; we picked Juliet up on the way to the mall in Stonemore, far enough away from my husband's overprotectiveness and the gossip rags that seem to camp out in our front yard.

Juliet rolls her eyes, turning away as I hike my skirt up and pull my panties down. "Jesus, you're gonna be a fun pregnant lady."

I inhale through my nose, peeling the little plastic stick from its box and positioning it between my legs, trying to concentrate. When I'm done, I stick the cap back on and set the test on the metal toilet paper dispenser, double-checking the directions and then my phone to make sure I get the results right. Because there is no room for a fuckup here. Not one like this.

Still, something deep in my soul tells me I don't even need confirmation.

Reaching out, I grip Juliet's shoulder and turn her toward me. She swipes at smudged eyeliner beneath her lid, eyes watery, and I feel a pang of guilt for being so short with her. "I can't imagine doing this without you, Juliet. As badly as I wish I just didn't have to. I shouldn't have said that."

She sniffs, shrugging my hand away. "Gross. You just peed on that and then touched me."

I laugh, pulling a handheld sanitizer from the front pocket of my purse on the floor. I squirt some into my palm and rub my hands together, both a hygiene ritual and silent prayer.

"You know what would make me feel more appreciated?"
"What?"

"If you just told me what the hell is going on here. You acted like you and Elia were so in love just before you got married, and then at dinner that one night it was pretty clear how he feels about you. And here we are, hiding some pretty life-changing shit. Why the secrecy?"

I chew on my bottom lip, glancing at the pink stick. "Not everything is as it seems, Jules."

"Well, duh. But what, specifically, is going on here?"

Running a hand over the side of my face, I shake my head. "You don't need to know. The less you know, the safer you are."

"Safe from what? Daddy?" I don't say anything, and she frowns. "What did he do to you?"

Swallowing, I level her with a stony look. "You already know the answer to that."

She starts to say something else, to dispute my claims, I'm sure, but the clock on my phone changes. I twist around, checking the little result window as butterflies somersault in my stomach, bile churning close to the base of my throat.

My heart sinks to my feet, and without another word, I wrap the test in toilet paper and drop it into the hanging trash receptacle.

I grab Juliet's hand and push the stall door open, resigning myself to a fate that, once again, I didn't fucking ask for.

24

CAROLINE

RESTING my chin in my palm, I stare at the amber liquid in my martini glass, aware that the two don't go together. Like Elia and me, two materials cut from a different cloth, brought together because I'm an idiot.

I raided his office liquor cabinet half an hour ago, trying to work out in my brain my next move. The glass sits on the edge of the pool, completely untouched, but I can't stop glaring at it.

"I'm so stupid," I say out loud, the sound echoing off the pool water around me, falling on closed ears.

Leo sits on a chaise lounge with his feet flat on the floor, posture rigid and alert. Ready for an attack that never comes. His head turns slightly, a silent acknowledgment, but that's all I get. I'm sure he thinks I'm a crazy person.

Juliet pushes open the French doors at the back of the house, carrying a tray of store-bought chocolate chip cookies on her hip. "Here, I brought you this, courtesy of Liv. I don't know why she couldn't bring them herself, but whatever. When I pointed that out, she asked if I wanted to single-handedly run a social media font launch. I had no idea what that even meant, so I got the hell out of there." Plucking two out of the container, she shrugs. "Anyway, she said *Focaccia's* makes the best emergency dessert in Maine."

I nod, catching the two cookies she tosses to me, working hard to maintain balance while stretched out on the float. "They add a pinch of salt to most of their dishes; the combination of the sweetness and saltiness adds a deliciousness that is unparalleled."

She raises an eyebrow, glancing at Leo, and then drops to her butt, hooking her legs over the edge of the pool and letting them dangle in the water. Leo gets up and heads inside. "How're you holding up?"

"Well," I say, plopping a bite of cookie into my mouth and gesturing around us, "I'm sitting in the middle of an eight-foot-deep pool, and I don't know how to swim. How do you think I'm holding up?"

"I'm pretty sure even newborn babies know how to swim, Care. You can't even doggy paddle?"

"Nope. And can we ix-nay the baby talk?"

She kicks her feet, slicing against the water. "If you fell in, maybe the baby would send information to your brain for survival, and the ability to swim would just kind of kick in. Like a shot of adrenaline, from your peanut."

I groan, throwing my free hand over my eyes and shielding myself from the sun. *It'd be a great day for the star to implode and kill us all.* "Jules, shut up."

Shrugging, she tilts her chin up toward the sky, and I can't help but wonder if she's uttering her own silent prayer, and what that might entail. The realization that I've spent my whole life just trying to protect my sister without actually getting to know her hits me hard, like a sucker punch to the gut, and tears prick behind my eyes.

"This is the twenty-first century, you know."

"I'm aware. Your point?"

"I don't know. You don't *have* to keep it if you don't want to. If it causes more problems than it solves."

"It doesn't really solve anything."

"*Well...*" she draws the word out, trailing off. Sliding my hand from my eyes and settling the remaining cookie on my stomach, I cock my head at her, waiting for more. Her toes point forward as her head drops, chin grazing the locket around her neck. "Take care of it, then, before it gets you into trouble."

Unease settles on the floor of my belly like a poison spreading through my body, rotting me from the inside. "Can we talk about something else?"

"Like what?"

"Like... how's school?"

She makes a face, puckering her lips together. "It's school, Caroline. Boring and uneventful."

"There's nothing wrong with boring. God, I'd welcome some of that at this point."

"Of course, you would."

My eyebrows raise, my cookie leaving chocolate residue on my skin. "What's that supposed to mean?"

"No offense, Caroline, but you're not really looking for an adventure."

There's a pinch in my heart, and I let out a soft, surprised laugh. "Now, why would that offend me?"

"It shouldn't. I don't mean it to, anyway. I just..." She reaches up, sweeping blonde hair off her shoulders, and leans back on the concrete on her palms. "This is almost the exact life you had planned out for yourself, and you're not even sure if you want to continue it, because it might not be easy."

"That's not—"

She holds her hands up, cutting me off. "I know, that's not what you *think* the problem is. But you need to seriously take a step back and look at your life and see if it's not fear holding you back. Clouding your decisions. Before you do something you can't take back."

Crossing my arms over my chest, I focus my gaze on the highest point of the mansion, the white brick chimney that shines bright against the blue backdrop of the sky. "There's so much more going on, Jules. Stuff you can't understand."

"That I *can't* understand, or that you *won't* explain to me?" She withdraws her legs from the water, hiking her jean shorts up, and shakes the water from each limb. Her blue gaze is steely, annoyance flickering there, and an ache flares in my temple. "I get that I've not been the best sister, that I haven't always believed you when I should have. And I get that there's not a lot I can do to make up for it all. But I'm trying here, Caroline, and you're not giving me anything. Who are you even trying to protect? Me, which has been your self-imposed calling card since I was born, or yourself?"

My mouth drops open, tongue poised on a retort, but nothing ever comes. The back door opens, my husband's suited form appearing on the patio and effectively ending our heart-to-heart.

"Ah, the only in-law still speaking to me." Elia smiles, clapping Juliet's shoulder and shaking her with the impact.

She doesn't move her gaze from mine, though. "I was just leaving. Think about what I said, okay? I'll see you at the gala next week."

Stealing a few cookies from the tray on the ground, she stuffs them into her pocket and leaves, letting herself out through the French doors. Elia watches them drift closed, and then walks to the edge of the pool, hands in his pockets, Ray-Bans perched low on his nose.

Jesus, how does he get more attractive every time I see him?

He clears his throat, Adam's apple bobbing in a way that makes my pussy pulse. "I've never seen you in this pool."

"You won't be seeing me get out of it, either."

An eyebrow perks up, intrigued, lighting my body like a three-wick candle. I shove my extra cookie into my mouth, buying time. The reaction my body has to him doesn't have to mean anything, right?

It doesn't matter that having him home makes me feel safe, that him standing near me makes me want to climb him like a fucking tree.

Some of that is just hormones... right?

"I don't know how to swim," I admit. Better than the alternative word vomit, which I'm not sure I should bring up. Sure, he has a right to know, but if I don't want to keep it... does it even matter? You can't mourn something you don't know exists, right?

Yet there's a hollowness in my thoughts, ripping apart my insides with indecision.

"No one ever taught you?"

I shrug. "Guess they didn't think it was important. Weird, considering we're a lake town, and we spent a lot of time fundraising on Koselomal when I was a kid."

He shakes his head, glancing down at the dessert tray by his foot. "Juliet brought cookies? You didn't bake anything today?"

"I wasn't really feeling up to it."

Alarm flashes behind his eyes, and he's discarding his jacket and rushing into the pool before I have a chance to amend my sentence. He swims over in record time, his strokes clean and lithe, and my mouth actually fucking waters watching his back muscles ripple in the water.

Coming up beside my float, he grasps the corner by my feet with his palms, steadying himself. I smile, poking his chest with my toe—bad move, because his dress shirt sticks to the hard planes of his chest, dark nipples puckering beneath the material. My toe seems to have a direct line of communication to my core because the second I make contact with the material, a jolt of electricity shoots through me.

I bite my cheek to repress the moan threatening to escape. "You know I wasn't in any danger, right?"

He breathes heavy, his eyes alight with a mixture of emotions I can't quite decipher. "*Amore mio*, I wish that were the truth." Swimming around to where the top half of my body is, he presses the palm of his hand to my forehead. I pray he can't see how my own nipples have stiffened under my bikini top. "Are you okay? You've only just been released from brain rest."

"I'm *fine*. Seriously, you didn't need to ruin a good suit just to jump in here, you insane person."

Laughing lightly, he brushes a few strands of hair from my face and presses a soft kiss to my nose, swimming backward and putting space between us. As soon as he hauls himself from the pool, I let out a long breath of relief.

"Would you do something with me tonight?"

I blink, swirling my hand around in the water beside my float. "Like what?"

"I thought I could cook you dinner. Show you my mom's favorite recipe."

A heavy weight lands on my chest, squeezing the air from my lungs at his hopeful tone. Standing there dripping wet, a boyish grin on his face, he looks vulnerable again. It's so startling and sudden, I have a hard time catching up with the emotion, allowing too much time to pass before answering.

His face falls, and he mashes his lips together, looking uncertain. "I can just bring it to you in bed, too, if you'd prefer."

Something shifts between us, the chasm from before shrinking exponentially, and even though I know I should run and hide, shelter myself from the disaster I'm welcoming, I find that I don't want to.

Revenge be damned, I want to welcome the hurricane that is my husband. At this moment, if never again and never before, nothing else matters.

"No." Paddling with my hands to the underwater steps, I slide from the float and climb out of the pool, offering him a small smile. "Dinner sounds great."

Elia

I don't have a clue what the fuck is going on; Caroline sashays into the house in that small-as-shit red bikini, suddenly agreeable and shocking the hell out of me.

My heart beats against my ribs, on the precipice of losing total control.

Strolling in after her, I race upstairs and change into a pair of jeans and a light T-shirt. My palms are clammy as I pad back down, seeing she's yet to return and feeling like a teenage boy going on his first date.

Heading to the kitchen, I dig in the junk drawer where I've buried the memories of my mother. I find the little index card with her chicken scratch stamped on it and stare at it for a few beats, before slapping it down on the counter and retiring to the living room to wait.

Nerves course through me, jitters rattling me to my core, at the prospect of finally getting to wine and dine my wife. To explore our connection, see how she feels beyond the obvious sexual compatibility.

And to relieve myself of the guilt I feel from murdering yet another man in her honor.

Not that I feel bad about Sheldon being dead, but every second I spend in Caroline's presence reminds me that all of this is worth it—that defying my mother's last wishes might not have been in total vain.

I switch on the television, flipping through the local news channels until landing on one the *Gazette* runs. The headline stops me dead, nerves turning to ice and stalling my heart in my chest.

Local Congressman and lawyer found dead at vacation home in Stonemore; foul play suspected. Suspects at large.

What the fuck?

This wasn't supposed to be leaked yet. And there certainly wasn't supposed to be evidence involved.

Just as I begin pulling my phone from my pocket, I feel someone standing behind me. Turning my head, I expect to see Leo. I don't expect to be staring down the barrel of a gun.

"What did you *do*?"

25

CAROLINE

THE LOOK on Elia's face presses at the cracks inside my chest, searching for a way inside. For a way to rip open the sutures barely holding me together and replace them with the venom in his eyes.

I swallow as my thumb brushes against the safety of my dad's gun, the weight heavy against my palms. I have both hands wrapped around it, keeping the weapon steady despite the tremors wracking my soul.

Todd and Sheldon's names flash across the television screen in bold, unmistakable print, but they flashed on my phone first while I was still upstairs, alerting me. I knew about Todd. Orchestrated that. But Sheldon is new. Unexpected.

Despair simmers in my gut, reinforcing my stance, wrath cycling within me, propelling me into motion. Taking a step forward, I jut my chin toward the screen, cocking an eyebrow.

"Answer me, Elia."

His eyes darken, the clear gray morphing into a charcoal

I've never seen before, and his hand grips the back of the sofa, fingers leaving welts on the fabric. "I don't answer to you, *cara mia*. I don't fucking answer to anyone."

My thumb slides back, pulling the safety with it. "I told you to stop calling me that."

"What am I supposed to call you, Caroline?"

"Nothing. Stop referring to me as anything. Stop acting like this is a real marriage, and like you want more from me. Just stop everything. *Please*. It makes me—" My voice breaks on the last syllable, and I clear my throat, trying to force some of the hoarseness from it. Pressing my lips together, I inhale a deep breath, refocusing on the problem at hand.

Bringing his hand to his lap, he stays silent, watching me for several beats. I shift my weight around on my feet as numbness settles in my calves, uncomfortable under his scrutiny. It feels like that's all he's done since we met, and I can't stand what he's seen—how he peers into my eyes and sees right to my dirty, blackened soul.

"What does it make you, Caroline?"

"What?"

"When I call you pet names. Terms of *endearment*. What happens to you when I do that?"

I shake my head. "Stop trying to distract me."

Getting to his feet, he takes a singular step toward me; he's slow and deliberate, hands spread in front of him, the way you might approach a rabid raccoon. My palms grow sweaty, though I can't tell if it's from the nerves bouncing around my brain or his stupid, delicious scent.

"When I call you *amore mio* and *carina*, how does that make you feel?" He takes another step, and I shift, pointing the gun right at his chest. It doesn't deter him the way I hoped it would. "Does it make your chest swell, make your heart inflate with implied affection? Do you feel dizzy when I look at you and wish you could explain away your reaction as simple sexual attraction? Does it anger you, realizing it's more than that?"

My lips part as he stalks even closer, the mouth of the gun a hair away from the fabric of his T-shirt. *Jesus.*

"Or do my words make you feel dirty because they've been tainted by men who never had permission to call you anything in the first place? So you focus on the evil within, use it to fuel your hatred toward me, hoping it expels the truth lying dormant inside you."

I lift my gaze to his, defiance bleeding through my every pore. "Take another step, and I'll put a bullet in you."

He chuckles, ignoring me, stepping *into* the gun. The grip I have on the metal slips as my heartbeat skyrockets inside my chest, pounding against my ears like arrhythmic cymbals. A bubble lodges in my throat, and I swallow over it, hating all of this.

Him, the effect he has on me, my entire situation. He's ruining everything.

My entire life.

"Tell me *why* you hate me so much, and maybe I'll return to the couch." His chest heaves with each breath as we stare at each other, like we're two separate halves of one soul being kept apart by invisible force fields. "Talk to me, and I won't rip that gun from your hands and hold it against your temple until your secrets pour out of you."

I lick my lips, unable to tear my eyes from his. "I don't hate you."

"I know." His fingers wrap around the barrel, but he doesn't push or pull. It's almost as if he's trying to connect us, keep us together somehow. "*Talk* to me."

Something inside me deflates, an anchor sinking to the bottom of the ocean. "I-I can't."

"You need to."

"No, I don't. Stop talking to me like you've got me figured out, and like you know me. Tell me what you did with Sheldon, or I swear I'll kill you right here."

"Do it. Save me the fucking trouble of having to sit around the next few months while you pathetically attempt to exact revenge on men from a world you're completely unprepared to go up against—of watching you leave when you've gotten what you need from me."

"I'm *supposed* to go when this arrangement is over, Elia. That was the plan all along."

"Plans *change*, Caroline. People, feelings, and circumstances change all the time. The universe gives and takes away, and our job is just to try to keep up."

"*Mine* didn't change. That's the whole problem."

"You're a liar." His grip on the gun tightens, jaw clenching. The anger sparking in his eyes sends heat through my core, but I press it down. Ignore it, like everything else. "If you would just take a second and open up to me, you'd—"

"I'd what?" The words come out louder, harsher than I mean for them to, but once they've been spit into the air between us, I can't suck them back inside. The blood whooshing in my ears doesn't stop me; the fire licking down my spine doesn't hold me back. I shove the gun against his chest, knocking his hand from it, and let my index finger hover over the trigger. "What would talking to *you* do for me, Elia? Ease my pain, erase my memories? You think a conversation will fix me, make me whole again?"

His lips part, a response already curling on his tongue, but I move forward instead, knocking him back toward the couch. Dropping to his ass, he releases the gun, and I raise it, letting the cool metal line up with the middle of his forehead.

"I just want to help."

A million different thoughts run on repeat in my mind, like tiny forest fires no one ever quite extinguished that kept rekindling and spreading. *Tell him about his baby. Tell him how he really makes you feel. Tell him you* want *his help, want* him, *for more than just six months.*

Tell him something. *Make all of this mean something.*

"*News flash*: I'm not some broken little girl in need of fixing. Those men didn't *break* me. I don't need to be saved."

Tapping his forehead, I bend and straddle his thighs, my pussy on high alert, my brain firing on empty cylinders. This is too close—too intimate—for a gun to be in the middle. But I don't even care.

He doesn't seem to, either; his hands come up and cup my thighs, slipping under the fabric of the dress I have on. Our breath mingles, joining as one until it's impossible to differentiate between the two vapors.

"I know, baby. I'm not trying to fix you or save you."

"Then what the hell did you do to Sheldon McCarty?"

I slide the gun from his forehead and down the side of his face. His eyes follow the movement, snapping back to mine as I force the barrel under his chin, pushing his head back.

"*Amore mio.*" His cock hardens beneath me, thickening against my ass.

Grinding myself down a little, I revel in the hiss that comes from his teeth. "It's sick, isn't it? How much we love this violence? How our bodies crave it from one another, ache for it in the cruelest way?"

"This is not how I planned this evening ending." At my sides, his hands tremble against me.

I reach up with my free hand and undo the buttons on my dress, allowing the tops of my breasts to pop out; though he can't move his head, his gaze locks on, fingers squeezing my thighs until I'm sure bruises will bloom under his touch.

"Fuck. Me."

Smirking, I press my chest into his, my nipples puckering at the contact. "Answer my question, and maybe I will."

"Baby, everything that's happening right now is only because I'm letting it. You have no real control here."

Shifting my hips forward, I rock once into him, eliciting a strangled grunt as his body buckles to meet mine. "We both know that's not true."

He exhales, teeth peeking out and sinking into his bottom lip. "You already know what I did."

"I want you to say it."

"*Why*?" His eyes blaze, anger contorting his features. The grip on my thighs turns punishing, and I whimper at the slight bite of pain. But I don't falter. "Does it turn you on knowing I'd kill for you?"

My stomach hollows out, and my lungs expand until it's hard to breathe. I swallow, the dryness in my throat making it difficult, my tongue swelling. Moisture pools between my thighs, revealing the truth, and I clench, hoping he doesn't figure it out.

"That's not a battle I asked you to fight," I say, but my voice is small. Unsure. Because even though I didn't ask explicitly, he *knew*—what I wanted, what I needed—that he'd be the only one truly able to offer me peace.

"You don't have to ask, *amore mio*. At this point, I'd do

anything for you. Spoken, unspoken, I don't care. I want all the responsibility."

I shake my head, pulling the gun away. He knocks it from my hand, reaching to re-lock the safety before tossing it to the floor and grasping my face in his hands. "Why?" I squeak, terrified that I already know that it's already over.

"Because you're worth it."

The blood in my body seems to evaporate, the weight lifting from me and settling elsewhere. "You killed Sheldon. For me."

"I did. And I'd do it a thousand times over if it meant I get to keep you."

My forehead drops to his, our sweat combining. I don't want to dwell on hidden meanings, because I know deep down that there's nothing good waiting for me there. A pit opens up in my stomach, a cavity trying to suck in my soul, but as I bend and connect our mouths, igniting a fire we've been dancing around for too long, it can't get a good grip.

The pit falters, its opening webbing together, threatening to close all on its own. To go to bed hungry for once and leave my soul alone.

Fire rages on, the flames building in our bodies as our lips continue their voracious assault.

And as he shifts, hauling my ass into his hands while he stands and takes me up the stairs, I allow myself to melt.

26

ELIA

LIKE SHE WEIGHS NOTHING, I toss Caroline onto my bed, watching her breasts bounce against the material of her dress as she lands on the mattress. We're skipping a few of the steps I'd had planned, but having her spread out, a delectable buffet of creamy, pinkened flesh, chases every other thought away.

All my brain can focus on is how badly I want her; body, mind, soul. I want to drink from the fountain of her youth, use it to keep me effervescent, and worship her for all of eternity.

I scramble on top of her, using both hands to peel the straps off her shoulders, then down her arms until I can slip her from their confines. Gripping the bodice, I yank and free her gorgeous tits; I squeeze one in my palm, plucking at the nipple.

She squirms against me, blue eyes heating with all the passion I've wanted since the moment I met her. Dipping my head to her chest, I run my tongue along one swollen peak, sucking it into my mouth without breaking eye contact.

And I can't stop feeling fucking dizzy, like I'm three seconds from passing out from the sheer pleasure of getting to have her like this. *Finally.*

Her fingers curl in my hair as I work to fit more of her tit in my mouth, scraping my teeth along the soft tissue of her skin. Pulling back, I feather kisses over to the opposite side, laving around the other nipple in the same quick, circular motions, and glide my mouth up to her collarbone.

My balls are heavy as I suck on her throat, my mouth pulling at the delicate column with abandon. I'm definitely leaving bruises on her tonight, and the thought of branding her with my mouth—and my cock—has excitement coursing through me, stuttering my movements.

"Kiss me," she whispers, breathless.

I chuckle at the desperation coating her words. "What does it look like I'm doing?"

Her fingers flex in my hair, using the roots to haul me toward her face. "Like *this*." Before she's even finished the sentence, she pulls me down and fuses our lips, and I swear to God I've never fucking felt anything close to this.

She's heaven.

Her calves wrap around my waist, dragging me into her. Stars dance across the backs of my eyelids, expanding and exploding in my chest like supernovas.

Shoving my tongue in her mouth, I lick along the edges of her teeth, flicking against her tongue and tasting every secret and repressed comment that's ever formed here.

Hooking her fingers in the hem of my shirt, she yanks up, and I pull back just in time for her to tug it over my head, exposing my body to her. It's not the first time she's seen me without a shirt, but there's still a shiver that runs through me at the way it makes her eyes soften.

She trails her hands over the scars on my forearms, pressing a gentle kiss to my chin. "Will you ever tell me how you got these?"

My palm falls to her chest, the valley between her breasts, pushing her down into the mattress. "After tonight, I'll tell you absolutely anything you want."

Licking her lips, she silently raises her hips, the friction between us increasing. I grunt, moving to shove her dress down over her hips and then onto the floor. Taking a moment to discard my pants and boxers, I climb back on top of her, my eyes soaking up every single inch of her skin.

She's an untouched canvas, all pink and white hues despite what disaster others tried to paint on her flesh, and here she's offering herself to me. On a fucking platter, bare and ripe for the picking.

Every single part of me aches to devour her, to indulge fully in sin and fuck her until she can't remember her own name. I run my hands up her thighs, and as my fingers dip, twisting between them, I realize how badly I don't want to ruin the masterpiece.

I want to own her; for our souls to be so entwined, there's no way they can ever be separated, but not at the expense of her goodness. Her innocence.

Fuck me; I want to love her.

I think I might already.

My breath stutters, chest tightening, as I stare down at her, settling my knees on either side of her hips. She peers up at me, eyes hooded and awestruck, and I fist my cock, running it through her seam, gathering her juices. "Christ, baby, you're *soaked* for me."

"Always," she breathes, eyeing my movements with an expression of curiosity and lust. She licks her bottom lip, sexy as hell without even trying, and I'm getting too close to coming without much stimulation. No fucking way am I about to shoot my load before I've sunk balls-deep inside her.

Her palm wraps around my length, pumping in short, shallow strokes that send jolts of electricity straight down my spine. It collects in my balls, making them feel dense as I continue to suppress my climax.

"I've, um, never done this before."

I quirk an eyebrow, one of my hands falling to the head-board as she continues massaging me. My skin stretches as tight as it can possibly get, and sweat beads along my fore-head at the sensation of her small, smooth palm on my shaft. "Done what, baby?"

"Given a full-on hand job."

"Not even with Luca?"

"No. That wasn't... that was just so I could forget... the other time. It wasn't like this." She blinks up at me, a shyness I've never seen shading her features.

I reach down and grasp her wrist, stilling her motions. "And what *is* this, Caroline? What does this feel like?"

"It feels right," she whispers, and all my resistance seems to snap in one single move, the last rock holding together the levy of emotion threatening to flood my heart breaking off.

My body flattens on top of hers, once again connecting our mouths like an unnavigable impulse. Frisson coils low in my abdomen as my hands sweep over her luscious body, and she bites my bottom lip, drawing the flesh into her mouth and sucking like a vacuum.

Bucking against her as she releases me, my cock slips between her slick folds, probing against her entrance as if it has a mind of its own. She seems to undulate under the pressure, rocking forward in an attempt to capture me and bring me inside, where I fucking belong.

Pumping once, I grip her chin in my free hand and force eye contact, making sure that she knows everything happening is her choice. That I won't ever take anything she isn't a hundred percent willing to hand over.

"*Amore mio*. I need to know what you want. I don't know how much longer I can handle not being inside you."

Her fingernail meets my chest, scraping down the center until she reaches my pubic bone, ghosting over my skin in quick flicks of her finger. My thighs twitch in restraint, and I squeeze her chin harder, loving the way her jaw drops and her eyes blaze.

"You know what I want."

I shake my head. "I need to hear you say it. Need to know I'm not alone in this."

For a moment, a flicker of defiance seems to flash across her face; her mouth clamps shut, nostrils flaring, and she closes her eyes, cutting me off from those baby blues that have become my drug.

But then they reopen, heady and intoxicating, and without another word, she grabs my cock, pulling me down and guiding me into her entrance. She pushes off the bed, lips grazing against my ear as I allow myself to sink deeper. "*Fuck* me, Elia. Fuck everyone else into oblivion, so that it's only ever you for me for the rest of our lives."

"Do I need a condom?" I ask quickly, my neck straining from not pushing all the way inside her glorious pussy. But I don't want a repeat of how she got upset last time, and if that's what she needs to feel safe, I want to give it to her.

Her legs lock around my waist again, slowly pulling me

in inch by delightful fucking inch, heels pressing into my ass. "I'm good if you are."

And with that, I give myself over entirely; the last shred of my resistance collapses, defenses and rationale deflating as I sink as deep into her pussy as I can get.

She's soaked, a wet spot darkening the comforter beneath her ass, so I manage to slip inside with ease. Still, she pinches her eyes closed as I root myself into the hilt, balls flush against her ass cheeks, and I can't help but wonder if my size causes her a bite of pain.

"Are you okay?" I swallow, working to control the hysteria rising in my stomach. *She feels so fucking good. Too fucking good.* I want to set up camp inside her and never fucking leave.

Her eyes flutter open, a deep pink flush working its way over her tits. Unable to resist, I take one in my free palm, gripping her hip with the other, and roll a puckered nipple beneath the pads of my fingers. She arches her back into me, her pussy swallowing more of my cock. "I'm perfect. *We're* perfect. Fuck me, *please*, Elia."

So I do.

Jesus Christ, I do. My hips piston against hers in fast, punishing thrusts, not giving her time to adjust to the bodily intrusion. But I don't have the luxury of waiting for her to catch up; my cock and my heart know where they want to be, and they'll stop at nothing to get us there.

"You like that? You like it when I fuck you? When I shove my cock so deep inside you, it's impossible to feel anything else?

"*God*, yes."

"I'm gonna fucking ruin you, baby. Gonna come in you and brand you with my semen. Maybe lick that pretty pussy clean when we're done, just so I can flip you over and mount you all over again."

She clamps down around my cock as I pump in and out. My vision blurs at the edges as I ram into her, pleasure licking up and down my spine at the little moans falling from her lips.

"*Fuck*, baby. You're so goddamn tight, I don't think I can last."

I grit out the words, doing my best to stave off the impending orgasm swelling my balls; she reaches up to cup her own tits, pressing them upward in a way that makes them seem completely obscene. As I continue fucking her, my eyes stay glued to her breasts, hips swiveling, and I can't help but wonder if they look bigger than before.

Must be the withheld climax talking.

She meets me thrust for thrust, raising her hips and riding me right back.

My cock pulses, edging toward heaven. "*Amore mio...*"

"Oh, Jesus. Right there, Elia. Oh—oh my *God, yes...*" Her pussy walls quiver around my dick, the first official signs of her own release, and I can't stop mine from shooting straight up through my balls.

I come as soon as she does, blacking out as I unload my cum deep inside her, coating her pussy with warm, sticky fluid. She milks me, whimpering and grinding herself against me, fingers gripping the bedsheets so hard her knuckles turn purple.

A low groan rips from my chest as I collapse on top of her, my cock still somehow dripping cum as the aftershocks of her orgasm drink it up.

"Holy shit." Her shoulder muffles my words, and my

entire body feels like jelly, as if she's reduced me to an unmovable mass of muscle and flesh.

Her legs wrap tighter around me like she can't get me close enough. "That was... *wow*."

I smirk, pushing up and planting a kiss to her nose. Disentangling myself from her limbs, I pull out slowly, careful of any soreness she might have at the motion. Dropping to my side, I wrap an arm around her and yank her tiny body into mine.

"That was worth the wait."

We lay in silence for a long time, and I'm very aware that we're still sweaty and covered in each other's juices, but I don't want to move. Don't want to disconnect from the warmth of her body or face the repercussions that might come from not having admitted how I felt before potentially knocking her up.

Fuck. Even though the idea of her stomach swelling with my child makes the blood rush to my dick all over again, I can't help wondering how she'd feel about that, how it might feel like I'm trapping her, trying to stifle her dreams the way her father did. I don't want her to associate me with him.

Still, my hand slides down over her abdomen, tracing tiny hearts around her belly button. She tenses beneath my touch, shifting so she's facing me, eyes wide and fearful.

"What is it, *cara mia*?"

Chewing on her lip, she taps my chest, sucking in a deep breath. "I have to tell you something."

27

ELIA

I'M HAVING AN OUT-OF-BODY EXPERIENCE, my brain floating around in space, looking down at my body wrapped around my wife, struggling to process the words that just came out of her mouth. Tied with "we need to talk," "I need to tell you something" is one of the most anxiety-inducing sentences in the English language.

She worries her bottom lip, dragging her forearm across her breasts, shielding herself from me. Fear laces her features, and I feel her body go rigid as she starts to pull away and sit up.

Using the hand that isn't plastered to the mattress underneath me, I brush some hair off her shoulder, leaning to press an open-mouthed kiss along the curved skin. "You can tell me anything, baby."

Twirling a lock of hair around the tip of her index finger, she tilts her head, turning to study me. Her eyes scan the length of me, resting momentarily on my half-hard cock, bouncing back to my face as soon as she reaches my feet. Instead of offering an answer to a question she's proposed,

248

she dives in with a different one. "Can you tell *me* something?"

"Anything. I told you I would."

"Your mom. What happened to her?"

"She died."

"I—I know that. I mean, how?"

Twisting away from her, I settle on my back, curling my arms behind my head. "Are you sure this is something we need to talk about right now? I can't think of a better way to kill an afterglow."

She shifts to her knees, starting to slide from the bed. "No, you're right. It's none of my business. I'm sorry, I—I'm going to get in the shower, now."

I sit up, hand reaching out for her wrist, and tug her back down into me. "I didn't say you could leave. And I didn't say it's not your business—as my wife, a title I'm hoping you'll want to keep one day, you should know about the woman who shaped me into the man I am now."

Sinking into me, laying her cheek on my chest, she nods. "I... think I want to keep it." She turns her face up, blinking those beautiful baby blues at me, looking so goddamn angelic I can't help but steal a kiss. "The title, that is."

Her body tenses again, spine stiffening, and I knead her bare hip, focusing on my dresser across the room. Its glass knobs reflect our position on the bed, surreal in appearance, a kaleidoscope showcasing the colors of our love.

Love. Jesus, I'm in this deep. No choice now but to keep digging.

"My mother was an immigrant from Denmark. She grew up pretty poor on Staten Island, but she was incredibly smart and managed to snag a scholarship to Vassar in Poughkeepsie. She met my father there; he was being groomed to become an underboss for an outfit in Brooklyn. She stayed away from him at first because rumors lined every sidewalk in New York about him being dangerous and powerful. A force to be reckoned with, although really, she was *his* reckoning. He never even saw her coming."

I chuckle, considering the similarities between them and us, ignoring the slight pang in my chest at how their story ended. *This won't be a repeat.* My arm winds around her waist, my hand settling on her stomach, and her fingers tentatively fit themselves between mine.

Kind of like how she's managed to weave herself into the fabric of my life, an integral sew that, upon removal, would destroy the entire foundation.

"Anyway," I continue, pulling myself out of my inner monologue, "eventually, she gave in to his *many* pleas for a date. 'Just coffee,' he told her, and if she didn't fall head over heels in love with him at the end, he'd disappear and leave her alone forever."

Caroline snorts, her breath skating across my chest hair. "That worked?"

"Montalto men can be very persuasive." One blonde brow quirks, as if in agreement. "Still, she wasn't exactly convinced at the end. She didn't hate him, but she also wasn't in love with him. That didn't come for *months*. They developed a quiet friendship—as much as a non-criminal can with someone in the Mafia."

"*You* have friends."

Hooking my thumb under her chin, I tilt her face up, licking the seam of her lips. "I'm not my father, *amore mio*. Not in the slightest."

Her cheeks darken, hand falling to my pelvis, stroking the skin there with her soft fingertips. "So what happened?"

"They attended a Hans Christen Anderson festival in Boston, and when a *sort sol* occurred up above them just as the sun began to set, my mother took it as an act of fate. Thought it meant she and my father were meant to be."

"A *sort sol*?"

Nodding, I adjust her a bit, so she's not glued to me, sweeping a hand over the tattoo on my rib cage. "This thing she grew up seeing occasionally as a kid. A flock of starlings. One of nature's most beautiful and terrifying phenomena." I tangle a hand in Caroline's hair, working my fingers against her scalp. "Kind of like you."

She doesn't respond, just traces the path of the birds on my skin, causing goose bumps to pop up in her wake.

"It's temporary, almost inconsequential in the grand scheme of things, but the murmuration can sometimes completely block out the sun, cloaking the world in darkness. They do it just before they decide on where to rest for the evening and often resemble a dance-like formation. My mother had never seen any in the United States, so when that happened, she took it as a sign."

"Is that why you believe in fate? Because your mom did?"

I avert my gaze. "I don't believe in it *because* she did. It's almost the opposite. Her belief got her killed; I've spent my life since ensuring I don't leave things up to fate or chance. Making decisions for myself, sometimes because of loyalties and sometimes because I feel like it."

"What was I?"

"Completely unexpected. An absolute fucking miracle."

Her toes flex, and she draws abstract shapes on my hipbone.

"New York Mafia families have stringent rules about culture and ethnicity. They like Italian-made stock,

Catholics with closet drinking problems and violent streaks. Flawed creatures they can mold and use to continue the business. My mother, a Lutheran Dane that liked herbalism and openly supported contraception—even for married couples—became an instant target."

"So your dad's outfit killed her?"

"No. They planned on it. Hired a few different guys to drive her out to the middle of downtown Queens and leave her in an alleyway, frame her as a prostitute and let the police chalk it up to just another day in the city."

My pulse kicks up, pumping blood through me at an erratic rate, and she slides her hand up from my side, covering my heart with her palm. "If this is too hard, you don't have to tell me. I know all about repression. Sometimes, it's a handy tool."

I cover her hand with my own. "Repression just flattens the memories and stuffs away our feelings. But they remain, and the pain associated with them won't ever go away if we don't unpack it all." My chest rises as I draw in a deep breath, dropping down as I blow it out above our heads. "My mother failed to recognize that a *sort sol* can be a bad thing—an omen. I mean, it translates to *black sun*, literally. What good connotations does that actually hold?"

"Maybe she saw black as a clean slate. A chance to pour color into something, make it brand new."

"Maybe, but it still doesn't change the fact that she married my father, had me, despite knowing the world she would involve us in—one she didn't belong in and didn't want me to be a part of. I think the black sun, in this case, completely blocked her ability to reason, to run. Like a stamp on her brain that bled her of all logic.

"They came for her one night, men with ski masks and

machetes. Broke into our crummy apartment when my dad was out of town on business. I heard the commotion, ran out of my bedroom to find her writhing on the ground beneath a man, who had his massive hands wrapped around her neck."

I swallow over the knot in my throat, placated only by the warmth seeping from Caroline's body into mine. Otherwise, it'd be too easy to sink into the memories and recall the cold Brooklyn air drifting in through one of the broken windows, or the way the cool tile on my back felt like being dropped into an ice bath.

"I fought back when they spotted me. That's how I got these." I point at the moon-shaped scars scattered along my arms, the sting of their knives carving into my skin almost palpable.

"How old were you?" Her voice is low, broken, and I grip her tighter, wishing I could shield her from my reality—from her own. From everything.

"Seven."

She rolls her head, burying her face into my chest. "Jesus, Elia."

I lift a shoulder. "Some people are younger than me the first time they experience violence."

"That doesn't make it okay."

"No, it doesn't. But it means I'm not alone. It doesn't matter how old you were; you're never alone in that."

Lifting her face, she meets my gaze with watery eyes; pools of desire and sadness I find myself wanting to drown in.

Blinking, she breaks the spell. And fuck if I don't immediately want to cast it again, pull her into me for all of eternity, stitch her inside my skin where I can keep her safe.

"Who killed your mom?"

I cup her cheek, the truth barreling through me before I have a chance to stop it—to consider the consequences. "I did."

～

Caroline

His dark chuckle makes the muscles in my thighs cramp, clenching far too often in his presence. I should be surprised, maybe even disgusted, at his admission, but I can't help feeling... envious.

Of his strength, the ability to carry on and create a life for himself utterly separate from the demons haunting him. How he somehow created a new soul from the tainted one given to him, becoming one of the most lethal, dangerous, richest men in the entire state.

Because as much as I like to think my life is unaffected by the things my father and his friends did, by this world of crime and evil, I can't deny that I've lost a significant amount of my life to him.

To my father, my plan for revenge, the sleepless nights I spent plotting and healing, only to find someone else to cut me open, make me vulnerable, and pluck the revenge from my hands.

But I don't think Elia wants to see me that way. He likes the fire within me, my passion, and spark, and it somehow eases the canyon in my mind where thoughts of a better life go to die.

I don't feel suffocated, like allowing him to step in somehow puts me in his debt. If anything, that he's aware of my list—and the intent behind it—and refuses to hold it against me, or look at me like I'm a monster, makes me feel like an equal.

Like he loves me.

Absently, I cradle the bottom of my flat stomach.

"For the record," he says after a long, almost painful silence stretches between us. Worry creases his brows like he thinks he's losing me. "I'm not a psychopath. I don't kill indiscriminately, and I didn't kill my mother for the fun of it. They left us there, bleeding out from more stab wounds than I could reasonably attend to, and there was this horrible wheezing sound coming from her."

He sucks in a shuddered breath, and I pull my body from his, hiking a leg up and sliding onto his lap, straddling him. As I let my palms rest on his chest, he continues his story while trailing his fingers up the outside of my thighs.

I feel myself leaking on top of him, a mixture of his cum and arousal, and it makes my stomach clench so hard that I see stars.

"She was seizing, her body locking up, crying out in absolute agony, begging me to finish the job. So I did, because I loved her and couldn't bear to watch her suffer. There was nothing else I could do, and the weight of *that* has followed me like an enraged storm cloud ever since."

I let those words soak in. "That's why you wanted to help me at Luca's party. Some kind of atonement."

"That's what it started as, yeah. But, Caroline, I fucking swear to you, it's become so much more. I'm in lo—"

I bend down, sealing his lips with my own. As I pull back, swiping my thumb along his chin, a soft smile grows on my face. "I know, Elia. I know."

Sitting up, I straighten my back and grab both of his hands, settling them over my stomach, palms flat against my skin. It feels so fucking good to have his hands on me that the fear lurking within is almost nonexistent.

But not entirely.

Like a stalker lying in wait, it sits. Watching. Looking for the first opportunity to fuck everything up.

And as a question dawns on him, eyes flickering between his hands and my face, a tender expression melting his features in a way that makes my heart soar, I roll off him before he has a chance to speak.

"Caroline—"

I struggle to my feet, one leg getting caught on the edge of the mattress, and shimmy into my dress from before, purposely avoiding looking at him. Never mind the fact that his impressive dick is still out and covered in *me*. I know that if I look back, he'll see right through me. And, unfortunately, my anxiety is winning out.

I scrape my teeth over my lip, staring a hole in the floor. "Do you think you could show me?"

"I—show you what?"

"How to kill my father."

28

CAROLINE

THE NIGHT before my father's fundraising gala, Juliet and I stop by Jupiter Media to help Liv stuff invitations for her launch party for some indie artist's upcoming album.

My arms ache and feel heavy from a full week of practicing self-defense with Elia. Apparently, our house has a home gym tucked in the back, and I've lived there all this time completely unaware. We've kept it light, focusing primarily on defensive weapon strategies and stamina, though he still has no idea why we aren't exercising with more vigor.

But he's been wearing me out at night, too, since I've agreed to start sleeping in his bed. And I refuse to give up his energetic dick, so I'm trying to keep all other aspects of physical exertion to a cool minimum.

Liv clucks her tongue when I note I still haven't told him about the baby, licking across one of the lilac envelopes embossed with her company logo. "You're such a chicken."

I snort because that's exactly the role I've purposely cast

myself in. Makes it harder to point at me as a suspect if no one thinks I'm capable of bad things. "It's a big deal."

"Yeah, but I think you're blowing it out of proportion. *Bawk-bawk*," Juliet mocks as she sets a new stack of envelopes at the center of the conference table. "But seriously, most husbands would be ecstatic about this kind of thing."

Liv nods. "Exactly. Didn't you and Elia talk about having kids before you got married?"

"I've told you both; this marriage isn't conventional. We didn't talk about much of anything."

"It wasn't conventional at the start, but you've been together for weeks now. You've spent a lot of time together, and you've still not talked about kids? Birth control? Nothing?"

I shrug. "It hasn't come up."

Liv sighs, pulling a fountain pen from her blouse pocket and signing her name at the bottom of the invitation. She blows on the ink for a moment, and then stuffs it into an envelope, continuing the sealing process. "Okay, let's talk about how *you* feel. Do you want to keep it?"

"I think so."

"Do you want *him* to want to keep it?"

My hand draws invisible circles on the table. "Yes."

"So what's the problem?"

"I don't know what he wants."

"*You*, Caroline." Liv points a manicured finger at me, and Juliet nods her agreement. "We've all seen how that man looks at you. It's enough to make *me* wet, and I haven't been attracted to a man since middle school. Stop pussyfooting around and just tell him."

Feeling simultaneously scorned and empowered, I move

on to the next invitation. We work in silence for a few moments, and as I scan over the artist's name for the millionth time, curiosity wins out. "Okay, who the hell even is Mia Lombardi?"

Liv smirks. "She's only the greatest Irish-Italian indie songwriter in the freaking country. Seriously, you need to get out from that rock you've wedged yourself under."

"Irish-Italian sounds like a great idea for a restaurant," my sister murmurs, fiddling with her pile of invitations.

I glance at Juliet, eyebrows drawn in, before turning back to Liv. "I don't like indie music."

"Well, you're in the minority here. She's mainstream indie, like Lorde and Lana Del Ray, kinda. Does everything herself, from writing to recording and even producing. Moved to LA at eighteen and happened to get lucky."

"Luck of the Irish, am I right?" Juliet snickers, and I watch as she takes a swig from an insulated water bottle, wondering if she honestly thinks I can't smell the alcohol inside.

Liv blinks at her, sliding her gaze back to me with an eyebrow raised. I shake my head slightly. Whatever Juliet needs to get through the summer at home, I can't begrudge her.

God knows a little drinking problem would've helped me. And as long as she isn't blacking out, who is she really hurting?

"Anyway," Liv says, picking up a dozen envelopes and pushing them into a neat stack to her right, "my dad was in Houston during her last tour and happened to meet her at a smaller gig. He mentioned Jupiter, and she said it sounded like a great business model and sound leadership, so she hired us to do her album release. So here I am, almost single-handedly running this fucking show because I gave people the last week of this month off. Because not only am I the boss but I'm also an absolute dumbass."

"I've known you for, like, a decade. I can't imagine you letting your interns help, even if they wanted to."

"I'm letting *you* help, and you have no idea who we're even working for."

"You're letting us help with physical labor. Why haven't you pitched any other part of your launch plan?"

She smirks. "Maybe you have a point."

Laughing, I ball up a torn envelope and toss it at her head. She swipes at it a moment too late, giggling, and for the briefest moment, it's easy to forget everything else outside this conference room—all the pain, the worry, the stuff that keeps me up at night.

I feel normal again. Almost like no one ever broke me in the first place.

LATER THAT NIGHT, I stand at the kitchen sink, watching my husband roll ground pork around in his palm. My face scrunches up at the food. "I've never seen meatballs with milk in them."

He's trying to teach me how to make them, but I keep getting distracted by the way his back muscles strain against his T-shirt. It's black, but still, he gets less and less buttoned-up around me with each passing day. The outline of a gun tucked into the waistband of his jeans sends a ripple of desire through me.

"You've never had mine, *bella*. Americanized meatballs are always so dry and spherical; adding half-and-half makes them a little sticky and wonky, so they don't roll right off your plate." Cocking an eyebrow, he turns up the corner of his mouth when he catches me drooling.

"Uh-huh." I avert my eyes, dropping butter into the skillet, watching it crackle and begin to melt under the heat. "What'd you say this is called?"

"*Frikadeller.* It's not my mom's original recipe, but it's close enough to the ones I can remember her making for me as a kid."

My stomach twists, and I press my thighs together in an attempt to relieve the throb between them. There's something so hot about this made man being domestic that if I weren't already pregnant, I think the sight before me might result in the same predicament.

"Aren't meatballs supposed to be Italian, though? Like, isn't that kinda your thing?"

"Pasta is *kind of* our thing, although that's debatable, too. Meatballs transcend culture, Caroline."

"Maybe all the baking's gone to my head."

"Well, in any case," he says, dropping the pork in his hand into the skillet and reaching for another handful of the mixture, "the main difference is spices. If I were making them with my Italian heritage, I'd add Italian seasoning, parmesan cheese, and maybe even some olive oil. *Frikadeller* uses nutmeg and sage. And I never mix meats because the all-pork method with these makes them more savory, which works really well with the gravy."

He drops more meat clumps into the skillet, pressing the tops down with a fork so they resemble tiny patties. I chew on the inside of my cheek and resist the urge to reach out and slide my arms around his neck, distracting him from the task at hand.

"Does your dad do a lot of cooking?"

Shaking his head, he adjusts the stove heat and moves down the counter to mix the gravy ingredients. "Not since I moved out. I guess with just him in the house he doesn't see the point. But for me, it makes me feel connected to my ancestors. And my mom."

"How come this is the first time I'm seeing you make anything?"

"Baby, you hogged my kitchen for weeks when you moved in. I was scared to ask you to move over; sure you'd chop me up in my sleep and bake me into a batch of banana nut bread."

Laughter bubbles up in my throat, and I move closer to him, seeking out his warmth. Our shoulders brush as he measures flour in a glass cup. My tongue darts out subconsciously, roving over my lip while he works, and he glances at me from the corner of his eye.

"You okay?"

I clear my throat, trying to blink through the fog of need pulsing through my body. "I'm good."

He straightens, dumping the flour into a ceramic bowl. "Okay, well, stop looking at me like you want to eat me. I won't be responsible for my actions, otherwise."

Pulling my lip between my teeth, I rake my eyes over his body the way I want to run my tongue over it. "What if I *do* want to eat you?"

A low growl rips from his throat; he shoves the bowl back on the counter, slipping his arms around my waist and hauling me up. I wrap my legs around him, pulling his erection flush against me through our clothes, and he places my ass on the edge of the counter.

His hands tangle in my hair, tilting my head back so he

can feather kisses along the column of my throat. "Fucking hell, *amore mio*. Why does this just keep getting better?"

My mouth parts as if it has an actual answer to give, but nothing comes out. I don't know how to tell him it's pretty hard to improve what already feels perfect without addressing the secret I'm keeping.

As if on cue, a sharp pain cuts across my stomach, and I hiss against it, my body arching into Elia's. He moans, crashing his lips into mine, and I swallow the sound, wishing I could keep it for myself and play it on repeat any time I need him.

He pulls back after a few minutes of our tongues sparring, cupping my cheeks. "I've been thinking."

"That's dangerous," I quip, my lips curling up.

He rolls his eyes, one hand slipping down to grip my throat. Leaning in, he slides his tongue from my chin to my eyebrow, making my knees quiver. "You said you've never given a hand job before. Does that go for mouth stuff, too?"

"*Yep.*"

His gray eyes flash, fire dancing in their depths, and he drags my face to his again, kissing me harder than before. It feels like being branded—bruising and swelling in the most delicious way possible, and I swear I feel it in my soul.

"The food's gonna burn," I murmur against him.

Teeth latching onto my bottom lip, he gives a wicked grin. "Let the whole goddamn world burn, baby."

And we do.

He takes me to his room, and soon we're a panting, quaking mass of limbs and muscle, sweaty and grunting our pleasure until I'm sure he's fucked my brains out. My head hangs off the side of the mattress as he comes deep inside me, a low warmth filling my stomach.

The smoke detectors sound not long after, and I move to get up and go to the kitchen; he pulls me back, positioning us beneath the covers and pressing his lips into my hairline. He wraps one arm around my shoulders and curls the other over my waist, tugging me into his body, and I settle into it, accepting everything—my feelings, our situation. My *secret*.

I'm keeping it out of fear, but less because I don't think he'll want it and more because I'm sure he will. And it's hard to reconcile that with everything else that's happened, everything he is and what it means for me; I can't imagine he'll allow me to go through with the plan to kill my father.

Still, each second that passes creates a hole in my heart because I want to share this experience. I want to see how it morphs him, how he extends his feelings for me into what we created.

Elia may have blood on his hands, but it's not mine. It's not that of the innocent or the damaged.

And I've never felt safer or more loved than I do at this very moment.

"Shouldn't we be concerned about that?" I ask after a silence plagued by beeping.

"Leo will get it."

I nod, burrowing deeper into his side, wishing I could just climb inside him and live. I'm just starting to drift off to sleep, working out in my brain how drastically everything has changed between us in these short weeks when I hear the softest confession.

"I love you, Caroline."

Panic seizes my chest, causing muscles to tighten as my eyes spring open. I sit up, holding the comforter against my chest, and blurt out the first thing that comes to my brain. "I'm pregnant."

His face remains still for several beats. So long, I'm not even sure he heard me. He just stares, mouth in a firm line; I start to pull away, anxiety edging its way into me all over again, when he breaks into a wide smile, grips my shoulders, and flips me onto my back.

"Are you serious?" He hovers above me, eyes bright and hopeful. I swallow, nodding, unable to speak. "How? We haven't—"

"That first time took, I guess."

"Holy..." He trails off, shaking his head, staring so intently at me I wonder what's going on in his brain. If he's panicking or considering his options. Then, finally, he breaks into a wide grin that steals the breath from my lungs. "Fuck, yeah. You're stuck with me now, baby."

Lowering his face to mine, he captures my battered lips in a deep kiss, angling my head so he can slip his tongue inside and sweep around. Hoisting my left leg into his hand, he bends my knee, using his other hand to tease my pussy. And without warning, he pushes in, sinking like a capsized ship with no other choice.

Sometime later, the smoke detectors quiet. But I hardly notice, too wrapped up in the love surging through me.

29

ELIA

CAROLINE'S BODY sags against the wall as I wrench my cock from her, yanking my pants up over my hips. She struggles to regulate her breathing, and a loud knock on the bathroom door draws me from the fog I'm dragged into each time I bury myself inside her.

"Sorry, I can't seem to help myself anymore." I drop my lips to her sweaty forehead; she tastes salty and spent, and it's almost enough to make me hard all over again, but I hold back for a few reasons.

One, because I need my stamina for tonight. At least for the events to come.

And two, because we're hiding out in the bathroom of the art center where her father's holding his fundraiser. And while I don't particularly care about appearing presentable for the miserable fuck, I know Caroline needs to look composed for her part of the night.

"I'm not complaining." She sucks in a ragged breath, a wobbly smile lighting her face. Straightening to her full height, she adjusts the neckline of the gold mermaid-cut gown she has on, ensuring her tits aren't spilling out of it. They are, but I don't say a word. How the fuck can I, knowing what I do now? Knowing she's got my kid inside her, changing her body in the most glorious ways.

The knocking continues, a muffled voice of agitation joining the fray, but she doesn't seem at all embarrassed or rushed. Walking to the sink, she peers at herself in the mirror, fluffing her hair and wiping some smudged lipstick from the corner of her mouth.

I sidle up behind her, fitting my pelvis into her delectable, round ass, and place my palms over her stomach. A flutter takes hold in my abdomen, a *sort sol* within me that does nothing but inspire hope. Love. Happiness.

"Elia." Her voice holds a warning; eyelids half closed in her reflection. "We don't have time."

My head falls to her bare shoulder, knowing she's right. We've slightly altered the plan of actually killing her father —since I refuse to put her or my child in any danger—and are focusing on ruining his credibility. Making sure he never holds another office, title, or job in this entire country.

Still, something about the way her body seems to vibrate with excitement at the very prospect of ruining Dominic Harrison fills me with unease. It's a part of the reason I pulled her inside the first available bathroom, ravaging her senseless, in case she's getting other ideas.

"You know how tonight's gonna go, right?"

She nods. "In half an hour, my dad'll step up to the podium to formally introduce us as a married couple. Looking for validation in *your* community and among voters who are afraid of you. Midway through his speech, his microphone will cut out, and audio from a meeting with

Todd Davis will play, detailing his complicity in pedophilia and grooming a minor."

I inhale, squeezing her. I've been unable to tell her how I got the audio clip—she hasn't even heard the full conversation—so she still sits partially in the dark. A wave of nausea wracks through me at the pain this will cause her.

But she asked me to do whatever it took, and after finding out that Dominic had been the one to go to the police about his friends' deaths, even falsifying the reports of finding their bodies—bodies Kal had disposed of—I knew I needed to take measures into my own hands.

If I could reveal my method without spoiling the latter half of my plan, I would.

I'd do anything for this woman—for us.

For our baby.

Unfortunately, I swore myself to secrecy, so she has no idea what's to come. "And when the center erupts into justified outrage?"

"I take Juliet, find Luca, and leave. Benito will be waiting curbside in your Town Car."

"That's right. And I'll stay behind to make sure everything's worked out, that your father's adequately ruined, and meet you at the airport." I disconnect our bodies, running a hand through my hair as she turns to face me. "And you won't do anything crazy that puts you in jeopardy."

"Right."

Cocking my head, I study her: the soft makeup around her eyes makes her look delicate, though I know she's so much more than that. Fierce, bold. A protector. A damn warrior. "Are you going to be okay with this? I know you had pretty distinct plans for the men on that list of yours."

"Plans change, right?" She shrugs, smoothing one of her

hands over the left lapel of my suit jacket. Pausing over my breast pocket, on top of my heart, she smiles. "I mean, I no longer want to kill *you*."

"*Cristo*, I should hope not."

She taps me three times, a gesture I'm coming to recognize as her way of telling me those three little words she's yet to utter. Hovering over my heart the way I imagine she'd hold it in her hand, she taps out her version of a Morse code that speaks to my pulse. It makes my chest swell, even if I wish for vocalization. I'll settle for this for now.

I know the truth, anyway.

If there were any doubt in her mind about any of this, I wouldn't know a baby was growing in her. Wouldn't get the chance to feel that joy, to convince her to stay with me.

She steps closer, leaning up on her tiptoes to press a quick kiss to my lips, and then moves to the exit, flipping the lock. My father and Marco stand just outside the door, annoyance lacing their brows.

"Sorry, boys, Mr. Montalto needed some help with his bow tie." She winks, dashing past them and disappearing into the crowd.

Marco gives me a once-over. "You're not wearing a fucking bow tie."

Ignoring them, I sweep out of the bathroom and make my way to our assigned table right in front of the stage. Dominic's ugly mug is plastered around the ballroom over photocopies of the American flag, which feels blasphemous for a myriad of reasons.

Mrs. Harrison sits at the opposite side of the table from me; her nose turned up in conversation with another middle-aged socialite. They cut a glance in my direction and then quickly avert their gazes. It's just as well. I don't have a single fucking thing to say to that woman.

My father settles into the seat beside me, taking a sip of his water. "Politicians," he spits, returning the glass to the table and glaring around the room. Even the napkins have Dominic's face on them. "Fucking dogs, the whole lot of 'em. Give me hardened criminals over a sell-out bureaucrat any fucking day. At least they've got a sense of modesty."

"That's an insult to dogs," I note.

"Dogs will lick their dicks in front of anyone. Politicians debase themselves in front of anyone. It might be an insult, but the vein is the same." He glances at me, leaning back in his seat with an odd look on his face. "You seem different, son. Less ghastly."

"Oh, gee, thanks Pops." I chuckle, unbuttoning the top button on my jacket. The room is abuzz, reporters snapping pictures everywhere, and I want to make sure I appear as relaxed and aloof as possible since I know I'll be implicated later.

"It's a compliment, Elia, *Gesù Cristo*. I know these past few months have been difficult for you, on account of our shit and then adding Caroline's problems on top of it... I was worried about you, all right?"

"You have a weird way of showing it."

He nods, grasping his napkin in his fist. Unfolding it, he drops it into his lap, sighing. "It's hard without your mom. She was better at this kind of thing."

"It's been twenty-three years, Pop." I cock an eyebrow. "Don't blame it on just being bad at reaching out. You didn't make an effort, didn't want to, and that's the whole of it. The *family* was your life, and you've worked hard to make sure you left it in good hands. But at some point, I think you forgot that you had a son, not a simple protégé."

"You're right. I've been an ass. I'm sorry."

I shrug, picking at the tablecloth. Silk, lavish like everything else for this campaign. *Where the fuck did Dominic even get the money to throw this gala?* My guess is he cashed out the money I sent him and didn't spend a single dime repaying anyone.

"Don't apologize to me. Try to get to know my wife, the woman I love, so you get to be a part of your grandchild's life."

His gray eyebrows shoot up into his hairline, forehead wrinkling under the movement. "My grandchild?"

Nodding, I stay silent, eyes trained on Mrs. Harrison to see whether she heard me or not. I don't particularly care one way or the other, but it'll be a nice little send-off when I exile her ass from town to know she won't ever get to meet the baby.

A tic forms under her left eye, and I smile to myself. *Bingo.*

My father clears his throat, nodding. "Well, okay, then. She's family. I'll see to it."

"As if there was ever any question, old man. I'm the *capo*, remember?"

Caroline and Juliet finally re-enter the ballroom, Luca and Marco hot on their trail. Their only job tonight is to keep an eye on the sisters and ensure their absolute safety.

My cell phone buzzes in my pocket. I pull it from my jacket to scan the screen and see an unsaved number pop up. A virtual stranger, someone my father will be delighted to know I've formed a truce with.

Ready when u r.

Rolling my eyes at his insistence on shorthand—it's not that fucking hard to type out a full word—I let my eyes drift around the room as my wife drops to her seat at my side, gulping down a drink of her ginger ale. At the back entrance, I catch sight of Gia and a tall, hooded figure I've yet to meet formally.

I wouldn't have reached out at all had Kal not given me the nudge, saying he'd taught him everything he knows. Not to mention, there are some things Kal just won't do, and this stranger has no known limitations.

He's as vile and unyielding as Satan himself, which is exactly the kind of thing I'm looking for tonight.

So, I put my hesitation aside and gave the hermit a call. Convinced him to leave the Gothic mansion at the far end of town in favor of making Dominic pay.

Not with money, but something far more valuable.

Gia gives me a short nod, and I turn my head just as Dominic ascends the stage stairs, waving his hands dramatically to little applause.

He adjusts his blue tie, gripping the edges of the podium as he stares out at the crowd, tactfully avoiding eye contact with our entire table. Mrs. Harrison stands, going to join him, but Juliet and Caroline remain seated with blank expressions on their faces.

Leaning over, I place my palm on Caroline's thigh through her sequined dress, giving a gentle squeeze. Her hand comes down over mine, linking our fingers, and every bit of unease that weaseled its way inside me seems to melt away.

She's a balm to the chapped, burned spots on my soul.

Not the solution. Not the fix. But the provision of just enough relief that I feel like I can get through life.

"King's Trace," Dominic begins, lips grazing the microphone as he shifts his weight from side to side, appearing uncomfortable under the harsh spotlights pointed at him. I wonder if he has a sixth sense, one warning him of what's to come. "A town I've loved for what feels like my entire life. I've been so proud to serve you for the last few years. It's a privilege to be elected and even more to earn the unanimous support of your constituents."

Unanimous, my ass. Like organized crime isn't the reason he got elected.

Like he doesn't owe everything he is and could ever hope to be to us.

"I know things look bleak with the recent deaths of a couple of my closest colleagues, but rest assured, I'd have Sheldon's and Todd's full support in this campaign relaunch. In fact, in the interest of full transparency with you folks, the public I've chosen to serve and represent, I want to officially announce my anti-crime initiative. If elected, I'll be working closely with police to enact measures that ensure, specifically, our little town's safety, but eventually, the safety of all of Maine. So we can once again enjoy life without fear of harm. So we can sleep at night and not be afraid of the horrors lurking outside."

His gaze falls to mine, and a smile curves over my lips; they curl over my teeth, stretching painfully, and Dominic clears his throat, pulling against the knot in his tie.

Of course, he's reneging on his desire to align with me and instead aiming for the fear that rules the people of this town. When they're not sure if they can win the masses over with their ideas or personality, every politician turn to fear-mongering.

I'd be more surprised if he'd invited us on stage at all.

A reporter sticks a hand up, and he points at them, granting questions. "How will you combat the presence of organized crime in King's Trace? And what will you do to end the drug trade? The Montaltos won't go down easily."

"Certainly not." Dominic chuckles, and a low murmur spreads through the crowd. My father rolls his eyes, and when I glance back to see where Gia and the hooded figure are, I note they've disappeared.

Perfect. Everything's happening as scheduled.

"I'm sure many of you have noticed that it's just my wife and me on stage tonight, representing the family values I've always endorsed. You've probably also noticed that my eldest daughter, Caroline, married a Montalto a few months ago."

Gasps sound around the room, but for the most part, people seem unimpressed. My brows shoot up, surprise coursing through me at the acknowledgment. Heads turn and whispers float in the air, and Caroline's thumb strokes the back of my hand.

"That being said, I think with Elia as my son-in-law, we'll have a much simpler time convincing the Montaltos to join the effort to ensure safety to King's Trace residents. In fact, I've got a plan—"

His words become inaudible as the microphone cuts off, a crackling sound crawling through the speakers. He glances around, confused, still trying to speak into the mic. Static fills the room before an audio clip begins, and after a few beats, when he realizes he isn't regaining control of the situation, Dominic begins to panic. Pointing at an aide and talking animatedly, he rushes to one side of the stage, slightly obscuring his body. He's probably telling his staff to investigate, but it won't do any good.

Mrs. Harrison stands and smiles at the crowd, trying to appease them. Act like nothing is wrong, the same way she does with her family.

Dominic returns to the podium, eyes scanning the crowd for the IT guys, but to no avail. They've been relieved for the evening, and the media room is completely sealed off, controlled from a remote location. This campaign just became a ticking time bomb.

30

CAROLINE

MY FATHER'S face reddens the longer static fills the ballroom, giving his audience a sneak-peek into his true personality. He talks about King's Trace being full of mindless sheep, and how he can just puppeteer them into making poor executive and legislative decisions so he can continue making money off them.

He mentions his gambling and his ties to organized crime around the state. In truth, he lets it all out, and I would be stunned if it were the first I was hearing of it.

But I don't need the reminder. I've lived it.

And it's high past time for his reign of terror to end.

Todd Davis's voice filters through the speaker after a few more strained moments of crackling, immediately diving into the depravity that is the senator and his cohorts.

"You're lucky Sheldon got to fuck that daughter of yours years ago. No way would he take her now, especially after she's been sold to the goddamn mob. Imagine how many of Montalto's men are using her over there."

Elia winces at my side, and I know he doesn't like being

276

referred to as a bidder in a flesh auction. That, to him, the amount of money he paid for my hand and Juliet's safety was more of a dowry than anything else.

I'm not stupid. I knew there was something more to my father letting me marry Elia over someone else he had picked out. It was better than any alternative.

My father's raspy laughter fills my ears; it feels like someone driving a spike through my brain. "She's young enough that if I can get my hands on her again, it won't matter. Not as young as when he had her, but still. Theory of elasticity, or whatever that is. We could probably make her useful again... I think there are procedures they can do to make her..." His voice trails off, and nausea curdles in my stomach at the thought of the end of that sentence. "The problem is, the terms Montalto set up in our contract mean I can't touch her sister, either. So I don't know how the fuck I'm going to pay anyone back."

"Keep doing what you're doing. You're bound to come into a position of power high enough to just lock the fuckers you owe money to up or make those debts disappear entirely."

"They aren't exactly on the books. I doubt these gangs keep electronic records."

I watch my father pale on the stage, eyes darting between Elia and me, and he laughs, fidgeting with the collar of his shirt. He walks over to a speaker and bends, ripping the cords from the back. It doesn't stop the audio, though, and he turns to a guard and another aide, waving his arms. I can hear him—high-pitched and slowly coming undone—from my seat at the table.

My mother looks shell-shocked, as though she had no idea any of this was happening, but I know that's not true.

You can't be married to a man and be completely oblivious to what draws his attention.

I don't feel bad about exposing him. Only relieved.

"You could keep using that kid to skim from the Montalto warehouse," Todd says, and Elia's hand flexes beneath mine as if itching to go up there and beat my father himself.

A part of me wants him to. The sick, depraved part that finds his brand of violence attractive. Like he's my personal vigilante.

Still, I know why we're doing this instead. It's clean, appropriate, and more fun than letting my father rot in a grave somewhere.

Juliet turns in her seat with tears in her eyes, reaching across the table to clasp my free hand. I wish I could've involved her in the plan, but it needed to go off without any hiccups. It was tonight or never.

I take a sip of my ginger ale as the audience erupts into hysterics, the audio droning on and on, detailing the entirety of my father's illegal activities like Bond villains and their last monologue.

How Gia was able to bug my father's home office for this material is beyond me, but it's clear neither man had a clue they were being monitored.

Luca appears out of nowhere, gripping my shoulder just as my father finds an extra mic, attempting to quiet the crowd and reassure them that these recordings are entirely falsified.

Gazette reporters swarm the stage, and Elia grasps the sides of my face, dragging my gaze to his. "Go now. Before they look for your bones to feed on." I nod, and he brings me to him, kissing me quickly. My mouth opens, a confession on my tongue, but he shakes his head, pressing his hand over it. "Not here. Later."

And even though it pains me to leave him there to clean up my mess, to give control to this man who's so quickly become an integral part of my very being, I do. Because a part of ruining my father includes following through with this.

Not giving him the chance to drag me down with him.

Juliet gets up with me, hooking her arm through mine, and we shoulder our way through the elegantly dressed crowd, pushing past even when they notice us and try to swallow us whole. Luca trails close with a hand on each of us to propel us forward.

We get to a dark alcove at the back of the center, which is an old colonial-style building with a wraparound driveway. Headlights flash through the tall windows as cars pull up and away from the building, and Luca does a quick once-over of the area we're in, ducking behind curtains and potted plants to ensure we're alone.

Once he's satisfied with our solitude, he pulls the two of us into a big hug. He's not happy about the turn of events, especially considering the feelings he still seems to harbor for me, but in the interest of loyalty to his boss and to me as family, he agreed to continue helping with my plan.

It helps that I'm still aiming for ruination. That I didn't give up my plight.

"Okay, you two stay here. I'm gonna go out and make sure Benito's waiting, and I'll be *right back*." Pinning me with a pointed look, he cocks an eyebrow. "Seriously. Don't wander off."

I roll my eyes. "I have no interest in going back there."

Nodding, he turns, disarming the alarm on the emergency exit, and slips outside. Silence envelops us as we stand and wait, the clinking of glasses and indignant shouts coming from other areas of the art center.

Juliet brushes her hands over the material of her short satiny red dress, tucking a strand of hair back into her updo. "Caroline, I—"

Holding my hands up, I cut her off. "Don't. Don't apologize for things you weren't aware of."

Tears well up in her eyes, and my nose burns at the effort it takes not to join her. *Stupid hormones.* "But I *should* have known. All this time, you've been... God, what he did to you. And I've been an idiot, thinking you were being dramatic and milking the white knight complex. I called you a liar! I feel like an asshole."

"You saw exactly what I wanted you to. If I could keep you aloof and unknowing, I could keep you safe."

"I could've helped you." A tear spills over, slipping down her cheek. "You shouldn't have gone through that alone."

"I wasn't alone." Reaching out, I grip her biceps and give her a gentle shake. One hand moves to her face, wiping away the salty evidence of a lifetime of sadness and regret. "I didn't need you to know what I was going through; I needed you to get through it. To grow up without the stain of having your innocence taken away. You got to experience real life, and I don't want you to feel guilty over that."

"But I *do*, Care. Jesus. How can you even look at me and not feel disgusted? Every time I sided with Daddy over you, every time I whined about you being overprotective and overbearing. I had no idea."

Exhaling, I shrug. "I could've gone about it differently. Could've tried harder to get Dad in trouble, but I wanted to do things on my own terms. Get vengeance by myself. In retrospect, it probably did more harm than good."

"Todd and Sheldon. Did you...?"

I shake my head, unwilling to divulge that. She doesn't need to know everything. "Happy coincidence."

She lets out a shaky breath and steps back, moving to look at herself in a wall mirror. "I'm still sorry, and I still feel like a piece of shit."

"Well, I can't change how you feel, Jules. I just hope one day you can come to terms with all of this, the way I'm trying to. And I hope you know that I don't hold anything against you." I watch as she dabs beneath her eyelids, eliminating smudges of mascara.

A throat clears, and we turn around, stumbling backward. I'm expecting Luca, though I haven't heard the door open.

My father's form, standing a few feet away, shouldn't surprise me. Although, it makes me wonder where the hell Elia is since he was supposed to subdue him until the cops came to arrest him.

There's a sinister look frozen on Dominic's face. Hatred seeps through the core of his being, making my heart ache for the time before he ruined us—when he was still my father and not a power-hungry pervert.

It's fucked up, but a part of me still knows if he just apologized and worked at changing his behavior, I'd forgive him.

Maybe not right away, and not for everything, but... he's still my father, still the man I looked up to and loved at one time. The first man I ever gave my heart to—and the first to rip it into a million little pieces.

I still want him to look at me and see his perfect little girl —to want to keep me safe and happy.

But I know there's no chance of reconciliation between us. We're beyond the point of return, of forgiveness.

So why am I still searching for it?

"You always were a master manipulator." Crossing his arms over his chest, he shakes his head, watching us. The ultimate predator, finally having cornered his prey. "Got everyone convinced I'm the bad guy. Ever tell anyone how you begged me to let you sleep with Sheldon? How you refused to let anyone else go to events with me because you didn't want them to have the attention?"

I reach behind me, finding Juliet's hand and wrapping my fingers around hers. My free hand brushes against the gun Luca gave me earlier after I left the bathroom, strapped into the back of my bra beneath my dress. "*Die Hard*-style," he said as he secured it there. "*Just in case.*"

Taking a step back so I'm flush against my sister and the wall, I toss my father a short laugh. It gets stuck halfway up, fear clogging my throat despite the desire coursing through my veins.

I want this—want him dead.

But I also want to keep my baby safe.

My arm strains against my back, fingers grasping toward the weapon.

"The only manipulator here is you," Juliet spits, nails biting into my skin. "What kind of a father does that to his own kid?"

He smirks. "There isn't a shred of truth to those allegations, Juliet."

"We all heard the recording."

"And we all know recordings can be fabricated. Just like we know that your sister likes to be the center of attention." He glares at me, taking a step closer, reaching into his coat pocket and revealing the tail-end of a hunting knife. He slips it out, wielding it like a sword. "I'm not surprised you believe her, though. You never were very bright."

Her body jerks against mine, and I press back, keeping her from making a sudden move.

"Don't talk to her like that." My voice is low and deadly as rage pulses through me. A warning.

"Or what?" His grin stretches as he stalks closer, eating up the distance between us with long, deliberate steps. *Where the hell is Luca?* "What do you think you can do to me?"

I feel Juliet's hand leave mine and slide up my back, working against my bra. My spine tenses, but she gives an almost imperceptible shake of her head. Swallowing, I focus on our father, who looms closer and closer with each step he takes.

"There's no one else back here. No one to hear you two scream. If I want to correct my biggest mistake, right here, right now, I fucking will."

The gun pops from my bra and is shoved into my hand just as he jumps forward, grabbing for my arm; I twist away, spinning against the wall. He catches Juliet instead, pulling her back against his chest and positioning his knife at her side.

My breath hitches as I right my footing, wheeling on them, and lift the gun I stole from him all those weeks ago. I aim at his face, and he laughs, his free hand gripping Juliet's throat.

"Jesus, Caroline, maybe you're not as smart as I thought. Go ahead and shoot me, see if you or your sister make it out of here unscathed."

"*Shoot him*, Care." Juliet widens her eyes at me.

A tremor makes its way through me; this is it. The plan I had all along, right here in my hands. Within reach, though not without a slight blunder messing everything up. I'm not sure how long it'd take him to stab her before my bullet reaches his brain, but something tells me this won't end well, regardless.

Still, I'm frozen, hands stuck in place, the cold metal of the weapon bleeding into my skin. My index finger swipes across the trigger, and a bead of sweat pops out across my forehead as my pulse picks up.

I could do it; put an end to my nightmares. To the pull that I maintain with him, the one seeking his approval. Something I shouldn't have had to work for in the first place.

Gritting my teeth, my finger flexes, itching for relief.

For freedom.

Dominic shrugs. "If you think you're a good marksman, have at it. But you should know, I—"

He doesn't complete the sentence because Elia's standing behind him in a flash, pressing a pistol to the back of his neck. "Go ahead and finish that sentence, fucker. Give me something to think about after I paint the walls with your blood."

Luca and Gia appear from the shadows, smacking the knife from my father's hand and yanking Juliet from his grasp. I half expect Elia to rescind on our deal and shoot him right there, but he doesn't.

And I can't deny the disappointment that washes over me.

There's a tremble in my body as Gia wrenches my father's hands behind his back. Elia stands, glaring down at him, and I can't seem to make my hands retreat. I'm stuck, solidified in this space, my heart set on ending my suffering once and for all.

Gia takes a baton from his waist, cracks it against the air so it elongates, and whips the back of my father's kneecaps. He cries out, crumpling, and I close one eye, aiming at his chest.

"*Amore mio*?" Elia's voice is low in my ear, concern lacing his words. I feel his hand at my hip, trying to draw me from the spell I've fallen into, but I shake him off.

"I need to do this," I whisper, aware of several sets of eyes on me except the ones I want. Dominic stares at the ground, refusing to give me the satisfaction of even this.

"Caroline..." Elia starts, but I clench my jaw, steeling myself against him. "You don't know what it's like, what this does to you. Your soul might not recover."

"My soul is already tattered."

"Tattered, yes, but not destroyed. Not irreparable."

I swallow against the fire in my throat. "I *want* this. I deserve it." Tears prick my eyes, blurring my vision, but I don't falter. Can't. *Won't*. "He *hurt* me. He let others hurt me."

"I know."

"No, you don't. I never told you."

"You didn't have to. I found out anyway." My husband sweeps the hair from my shoulder but doesn't touch me otherwise. Doesn't try to distract me with his touch, which would have me melting like chocolate on a summer day and abandoning all reason. "But he didn't break you, remember? Everything you've done, every ounce of love and life you've poured into your existence, despite the evil he wrought on you, that's your proof. You're still here, thriving, in spite of it all. Don't ruin everything you've worked to reclaim."

My chest burns, my vision blurring.

"He *didn't win*, baby. That's all you and me." His body heat ebbs into me, setting the cold, dark parts of me alight with warmth. "Don't do this. Let me help you."

A sob escapes Juliet, and my gaze flickers to hers. She stands beside Luca, watching me with wide eyes. Eyes just like mine.

Eyes that my baby might inherit.

Or maybe he'll look like his dad, dark and handsome. Perhaps he'll be a fierce protector, loyal to the bone.

Either way, I want him to be loved—to enter this world an innocent, unaware of his parents' tainted souls.

Something shifts in me, a ripple along the blood pulsing through my body that brings me back to reality. I suck in a deep breath, relenting, and let Elia pry the gun from my hands. He sweeps me into his arms, folding me into his chest, and breathes into my hair.

"When does it stop hurting?" I murmur into his suit, letting a few tears fall. *Why do I feel so deflated?*

He runs a hand over my hair, cradling my head. "It doesn't. We just learn to cover the bad stuff with better memories." Pushing hair from my face, he gazes into my eyes, his creasing at the corners. "And you and I are gonna make the best goddamn memories."

Curling an arm over my shoulders, he ushers our group out the emergency exit. I pull against his hold when we pass my father, stopping in my tracks. He tilts his head up slightly, a menacing grin on his face. Even though there's still an ache flaring deep in my chest at his vile spirit, at the chasm between us, there's a certain pride in not stooping to his level —in proving my worth to myself.

Proving that I'm better.

Still, when he winks at me, I can't stop my reaction; my

tongue writhes in my mouth, saliva pooling on the tip, and I purse my lips, projecting it right at him.

The wad of spit lands on his mouth, and a look of pure rage washes over him. He struggles against his binds, unable to wipe his face, and I grin as Elia drags me outside to where Benito waits.

Tucking me into the back seat, my husband cups my cheek in his hand and lets out a soft smile. "You amaze me, *amore mio.*"

I tap his chest, hoping I'm conveying how I adore him, wishing the words would push past my lips. Hoping he knows how much I appreciate his unknowing participation in my plan from the very beginning.

Falling in love with him was just the icing on top.

Juliet settles in beside me, and we buckle up, watching the others turn and go back inside. Luca climbs into the front passenger seat and taps the dashboard.

"God, Caroline. You're a fucking badass." My sister shakes her head, leaning against the window, and an odd calmness washes over me as we head toward the interstate, knowing that everything is actually, *officially*, over.

31

ELIA

GIA DRAGS Dominic's stupid ass up the stairs, not stopping even as the older man's feet catch on each step, terror keeping his limbs from working properly.

Normally, we'd leave this part up to Kal, but he skipped town last week, saying something about unfinished business and claiming our hooded figure is more than up to the task.

I didn't ask questions, and he didn't offer any answers.

Shoving Dominic into the incomplete gallery, we flank him and fit him into a leather chair, binding his wrists and ankles to the arms and legs. Marco gagged him downstairs with a bandanna he found outside, and the crusty senator tries to work it from his mouth, thrashing and screaming.

The spit from Caroline still coats his top lip, and it makes my heart skip a beat.

My girl.

A back door opens and closes with a soft click, and my father approaches us, dodging the plethora of headless mannequins that fill the room. "Jesus, you guys couldn't have picked a creepier room."

I roll my eyes as Gia unloads his duffel bag, unzipping and removing tools. "*We* didn't pick it."

"Who the hell did?"

"Me."

The hooded figure from before slithers out of the shadows, hands tucked behind his back. His slightly pale face looks ghoulish in the fluorescent lighting while wild pieces of his dark brown hair peek out from his hood.

A heavy feeling settles low in my gut as he floats toward us. Unlike Kal, Kieran Ivers resembles a demon straight out of hell; not Death itself, but rather a creature created specifically for torment.

A shiver skates down my spine as I'm still unsure if I should've involved him in this.

But there's only one man colder and more disconnected than our usual fixer, and he had the technical know-how to pull off our stunt earlier, since his family owns a security empire and he spends his free time hacking into shit for fun.

Once we confirmed that it was Dominic and his men stealing from us, before we exiled Gia's brother, I realized Kieran was perhaps the perfect addition to our plan. Who better to assist in eliminating Dominic Harrison altogether than yet another person he's screwed over?

It helps, of course, that he claims to have never really been interested in Caroline at all. Just wanted his money back, and to get under Dominic's skin. Mine too, I suspect.

So despite allegedly being holed up in his house the last several weeks, Kieran was quick to agree.

I can't help but wonder if the ghost of his brother in that rotting mansion started to get to him, the way all ghosts return to the scene of the crime at some point.

Marco works at Dominic's clothing, cutting them from

his body with the knife he tried to use on my wife and her sister. What beautiful irony.

The senator squirms under my soldier's ministrations, shrinking back into the chair as Kieran stalks around him. Watching, observing. His green eyes are like lasers, zeroing in as he tries to find Dominic's weak spots.

Looking for which vein to slit first.

I cross the room to where Gia's hunched over, sifting through weapons with a strange look on his face. "You good?"

He shrugs. "I don't like involving outsiders, is all."

Nodding, I reach for a medieval-looking instrument, turning it in my hands. "Where the hell does Kal get this shit?"

"I'm not sure I even want to know."

Marco's got Dominic stripped completely naked; his chest heaves as I walk over, tears staining his rotund cheeks, making him look almost boyish. I rip the gag from his mouth, giving him a chance to speak. To repent. "If you're hoping the sad, innocent look will convince us to let you go, you've got another thing coming."

"Now, look, asshole. If you think the federal government won't come down on you because of this, you have another thing coming."

Annoyed with his lack of remorse, I shove the bandanna back in his mouth, making sure my fingers scrape the inside flesh as much as possible. "I'm not scared of the fucking government."

Gripping his left hand, I fit his thumb between the metal bars of the instrument. His eyes widen as I start to twist the screw in the middle, pulling his digit closer to the bar at the bottom of the apparatus. It's a slow process, dragged out by how he jerks and whimpers, but as soon as his skin makes contact with the metal, I twist faster, harder, putting all of my weight into it.

His wails are muffled by the gag, sweat pouring off his face as I continue twisting. I hear the soft crack where bone begins to break beneath the pressure, and I can't stop a grin from spreading across my face.

Fuck, if that doesn't give me a semi.

He pushes the bandanna out. "Jesus, *wait*." Dom pants, his face bloodred. "Can't we come up with some kind of deal?"

"You mean, like the deal you offered your friends? Sorry, but I don't fuck minors, and you're all out of daughters."

I repeat the process on the other hand, the scent of Dominic's piss permeating the air as he continues to struggle through the pain. Smiling down, I release his limp thumb, kicking him in the shin with my steel-toe. A dark purple welt forms on his leg, and a deep groan rumbles in his chest, his breaths harsh and labored.

"Should we try to get any extra information from him?" Marco asks, glancing at my father for direction.

It irks me, but I ignore the blatant insubordination, too focused on the adrenaline surging through me.

I meant what I said to Caroline. That killing someone changes you; it mars your soul in a way you can't ever erase.

But I'm already beyond saving, so this won't matter.

"I'm not interested in anything else this sack of shit has to say."

Kieran steps away, studying me. Grabbing the knife from Marco, I glide the dull side over Dominic's flushed skin, reveling in the horror reflected in his dark eyes. "What's the matter, Senator? You don't like knife play? Odd, because your daughter sure as fuck does. I could've shoved this blade up her pussy, and she would've taken it, *loved it*, because that pain would *still* be less than what you caused her."

Not that I would've ever done that. Hurting her isn't even in my fucking vocabulary.

But he doesn't know that.

I turn the tip so it slices against the end of his short, flaccid dick, and his protests resume. He kicks his head back, trying to get away, but there's no escape. "I want you to imagine her as you bleed out in this room. As the life fades from your eyes, I want the last image you have to be of me fucking your daughter. Loving her, giving her everything she needs, and never got from you. Because she might not be the one here, holding a knife to you right now, but this is *all for her*. You'll be the last fucker ever to hurt her."

Gripping his cock in my free hand, I smirk. "Uncircumcised. *Perfect*."

The sounds that gurgle from the back of his throat as I saw his shaft in half set my skin ablaze, a jolt of electricity spreading through my body the way tequila warms your insides.

He's somehow still conscious, though bleeding heavily. His eyes droop lower with each passing second. I wave Kieran over, who wields an obsidian blade with a strange look of peace on his face. *Jesus, this kid's weird.*

Stalking around Dom, Kieran bends at his back, reaching forward and cutting the ties holding his ankles to the chair. Gripping one foot in his gloved hand, he uses the opposite to drag the blade across the back of his ankle; a sharp, ear-piercing squeal comes from Dom as Kieran repeats the action on the other foot.

"Please, please don't—" the senator moans, his voice raspy and barely audible.

Marco winces. "Is this fucking necessary?"

Kieran shrugs, moving around to the front of the chair as bright red blood pools beneath Dominic's feet. He's pale and barely awake. "Maybe not, but it's pretty fucking fun."

My father cocks an eyebrow at me, and I just shake my head. We're in this now. Can't turn back.

We watch as Dominic *finally* loses consciousness, but Kieran doesn't appear to be finished. He crouches, pinching the skin on Dom's left thigh, and then glides the blade gently down the middle. A vertical line immediately begins leaking, blood pumping from the wound at an impossible rate.

"Oh fuck." Marco dry heaves, darting across the room to puke in an empty trash can. *Maybe he needs to get out of the warehouse more often.* My father sighs, and Gia looks away from the mess in front of us.

I swallow as Kieran stands, eyes trained on Dom's thigh until the last drop spurts out. Feeling a bit woozy myself just from being here with him, I nod to my men and turn on my heel, trying to focus on the success of the evening, even if it did get more intense than I'd anticipated.

As I make my way to my car parked outside, sliding behind the wheel and heading toward the airport, happiness roots itself deep in my soul, like a tree sprouting from the dirt and flourishing.

We're free, baby.

I SLIP out of my clothes silently after washing my hands in the little attached bathroom, watching my wife's chest rise and fall with soft, sleepy breaths. When I boarded the private jet, a loan from Rafe Ricci as a late wedding gift, Juliet sat in the cabin flipping through a magazine. She pointed her thumb in the direction of the bedroom toward the back, not even bothering to glance up, apparently not interested in striking a conversation with me.

Which is probably best given my clothes are covered in her father's blood.

Kicking off my slacks, I scrub my hands over my face and slide under the comforter beside Caroline, pulling her body back into mine. I tuck my chin over her shoulder as she stirs, kissing the side of her mouth when her eyes flutter open.

The takeoff signal appears on the wall, and I sigh in relief, glad we're about to get some reprieve from this awful little town.

"You made it," she rasps, rolling to face me. Having changed out of her dress from earlier, she's clad in one of my old T-shirts; it dwarfs her, skimming mid-thigh, and making me hard as a fucking rock.

"Was there ever any doubt?" I nuzzle under her ear, smoothing a hand over her stomach. "How're you two doing?"

"We're okay. Glad it's all over." She wraps her arms around my neck, drawing me closer. Moving in to press her lips to my chin, she pauses, tilting her head. "What's that?"

Her hand touches my jaw, her thumb spreading over the skin there. "What's what?"

"It looks like..." She blinks, eyes darkening into stormy seas I want to lose myself in. A shudder works over her, and I slide my hand to her ass, pulling her leg over my hip. "...blood."

I lick my lips, entirely distracted by her beauty. "It probably is."

Swallowing, she stares at the spot, hands retreating slightly. They land on my chest, a whisper of a touch, and I moan because I want them elsewhere. Want my body inside her, want to climb her hills and die there.

"What did you do?"

"What I had to." Her bottom lip quivers, and I lean down, catching it between my teeth. "Shh, *amore mio*. Don't say anything that might ruin this moment."

Her nails flex into my skin, little pinpricks that have my dick swelling, and she taps me once. Twice. Three times. Tears pool in her eyes, and she shakes her head, blinking them away. "I love you, Elia."

My heart soars, a flock of millions of starlings taking flight and filling the sky with their black bodies. I tug her on top of me, pushing up the T-shirt and pulling myself from my boxers. Slipping my fingers between her thighs, I find her without panties and soaking already. "Fuck, baby. I need you."

No time for foreplay as wanton feelings throb through me, making me feel dizzy. Nodding, she helps me strip her bare, positioning her hips over mine. I fist my dick, lining it up with her pussy, and on an exhale, she sinks down, engulfing me.

Flames of desire lick at my skin and press at the recesses of my brain. She swivels her hips, and I reach around and grip her ass in my palms, guiding her movements. Fast and hard, then slow and smooth, torturous grinding that has me gritting my teeth against my release.

My thumb finds her clit, rubbing tight circles around the pulsating bud, and she undulates on top of me, coming on a silent scream. As her pussy flutters around my cock, milking my orgasm from me, I stuff two fingers in her mouth. "Suck me. Show me what else you love, my dirty, gorgeous wife."

She obeys, eyes flaring, picking up the pace of her hips. Leaning on her knees, she bounces up and down, the sound of her ass slapping against my thighs deafening in the little room. I palm one of her tits, rolling my fingers over her hardened nipple, and she fucks me harder, showing me *everything* she's never been able to say.

I come like a teenage boy, unable to hold off as her second orgasm wreaks havoc on her body, pussy clamping down around me like a goddamn vise. My seed paints her insides, my cock weeping from the explosion, and she collapses on top of me, breathing like a track star.

Sliding my hands down her back, smoothing them over the curve of her ass, a sense of surreal contentedness takes over me, settling deep in my bones. I didn't think I'd ever get this. Didn't think I deserved it. But as she tilts her face up to mine, smiling at me like a woman destroyed by a fabulous orgasm, I realize I was wrong.

Men like me might not often know peace, but that doesn't mean we don't deserve it.

It just means we have to work harder to earn it.

I've just started to drift off to sleep when Caroline's soft voice draws me back. "Elia?"

"Yeah, baby?"

"Where are we going?"

I smile, letting my eyes fall closed again as I tuck the comforter around us, sheltering her with my warmth. "Paradise."

EPILOGUE
ELIA

"I THOUGHT we agreed we weren't gonna go overboard for Poppy's first birthday." Caroline puts her hands on her hips, appearing in the doorway to my office. She has on a rose-pink sundress with a yellow cardigan pulled over the front, looking a lot like she did the first time I saw her. Except more motherly now and a thousand times hotter. "You know, on account of her not really knowing what's going on?"

Smirking, I wrestle my daughter's left arm into the sleeve of the princess dress I picked out for her. She squeals and squirms, babbling *Dada* and making my heart swell. Like the Grinch in that stupid fucking movie.

"And *I* thought you were going to try anal before we got pregnant again. So I guess we're both liars."

Rolling her eyes, she drops her left hand to cradle her stomach; my son's the size of a deflated basketball, and *Gesù Cristo*, my wife looks fucking delicious. I don't know what primal urges her being pregnant awakens in me, but I can't seem to keep my hands off her.

Which is how we wound up pregnant again before Poppy's first birthday.

Caroline walks over to us, pressing a quick kiss to our daughter's soft blonde hair. It's just long enough to put in a single ponytail, but the ends curl and make it difficult to capture each tendril. So we went for a bright pink bow instead.

"You're lucky she doesn't repeat words yet," my wife warns, shaking her head at me. But she can't cover the smile that lights her face, and I grab her wrist, tugging her onto my lap.

Poppy giggles, clapping her hands and reaching for her mother; I lift her off the desk and into my free arm, my heart so full it might fucking burst.

News broke of Dominic Harrison's apparent suicide while we honeymooned with Juliet in Copenhagen. Exploring the countryside, we managed to experience a small *sort sol* all on our own.

I like to think it was my mother expressing her happiness for me from wherever she exists now.

There was never an investigation because Kieran barely left enough evidence to even put in a casket. Kal wasn't kidding when he said that man was a good backup. And after that gala, no one really gave a shit what happened to Dominic, too horrified by how he'd deceived them all.

Caroline and Juliet decided to have his remains cremated anyway and buried him in the family plot.

A plot neither would use in the future.

Their mom went into hiding somewhere in the Deep South, as allegations about her husband coupled the headlines of his death. The federal government is still looking for her, wanting to question her involvement.

My girl is still healing, working toward a future she'd never bothered planning out. She doesn't like to talk about her father, instead focusing on her career and being a mom.

She and Phoebe became good friends at some point during Caroline's pregnancy, and Phoebe ended up helping me pick out the storefront I gifted my wife for Christmas. Now that she's in the beta stages of starting her bakery, she's trying to poach my best bartender from Crimson and hire her for the store.

I'm putting up a fight because I don't want to lose Phoebe, but in all honesty, I'd give Caroline the fucking moon if she asked for it.

I kiss her neck, inhaling that fruity, floral scent that lives in her skin. "*You're* lucky, Mrs. *Oh, Elia, harder! Choke me! Shove your cock deeper in me—*" She clamps her hand down over my mouth, giggling as Poppy peers up at us with wide, blue-gray eyes. The perfect combination of us.

"God, shut up! Just because she doesn't repeat doesn't mean she's not picking it up."

"Then you should stop being so loud when we fu—"

"Okay!" Caroline claps her hands together, hopping up from my lap, and turns to scoop our baby into her arms. She pinches Poppy's chubby cheek, her voice lilting as her audience changes. "Let's go check on that two-tiered cake your daddy insisted on for your big day."

"You didn't have to bake it yourself," I point out.

She shoots me a look that hits me right in the dick. I grin and lean back in my chair as my girls sweep from the room. Fucking Christ, my life couldn't be any better.

Caroline planted a garden in my soul, replacing the tar and darkness from before, flourishing with each passing day I spend with her and my daughter. My family.

Heading downstairs, I enter the kitchen and find my father holding Poppy and talking to Juliet, who's living with us for the time being. Being essentially orphaned left her with no options, and I know Caroline likes having her close.

"Oh good, my daughter's entourage finally arrived."

Juliet rolls her eyes, poking Poppy's belly, eliciting bubbly giggles. "You're the only entourage around here, old man." She points at my T-shirt, and I glance down, shrugging.

So I had screen prints of Poppy's newborn photo shoot done. It's not like anyone else is wearing the shirt, even if I did get one for every guest. "If she remembers anything from today, it's not gonna be your boring attire. It'll be this bomb-ass shirt, declaring my unconditional love."

"Sure, son. *That's* what she'll remember." My father winks at Juliet, jiggling my daughter in his arms, and I exhale, clearly outnumbered.

Gia and Marco sit on the sofas in my living room, blowing up balloons, and I spot Phoebe and Caroline out by the pool, arranging pink cupcakes in a circle around the center of the patio table. It's an unusually warm day for this time of the year in Maine, so we decided to do an outdoor celebration in case the chance doesn't come back up.

Juliet's warnings about global warming went unheard.

I slip out the back door, nodding to my men in passing, and pull my wife's hips into my pelvis, unable to resist her even for a moment.

Phoebe's nose scrunches up. "Y'all are gross."

Kissing Caroline's shoulder, I grin at my bartender. "Get used to it, Pheebs. You go to work with my wife, and I'm gonna make sure I stop by all the time and pull her into the storage closet for raunchy quickies."

"Jesus." Phoebe picks up a cupcake, licking at the icing, eyes darting momentarily inside and then landing on us again. I turn my head and see Marco standing at the window, a beer in hand, chatting with Luca. "How many kids do you guys want, anyway?"

"As many as she'll let me pump into her."

"Oh my God, Elia." Caroline shoves me away, adjusting her dress and studying the cupcake display. "Can I get through this pregnancy before you start planning the next, please?"

"And can you *plan* silently?" Phoebe quips, face twisting in disgust.

"Jeez, I'm sorry my excitement annoys you."

Caroline grins. "Well, as long as you apologize for it."

Later, after the candles are blown out, the presents opened (by us, since Poppy decided she was more interested in trying to dive into the pool), and the guests have left, we sit together on a chaise lounge, watching the pool water ripple back and forth.

Caroline toys with the necklace Poppy's Auntie Liv sent from her vacation in Mexico; finally taking time off work, she decided to jet off with some woman she met on business in Los Angeles. The heart-shaped pendant glimmers in the sunlight, and my wife drops the jewelry back into its gift bag.

Poppy's light snores draw a smile from me, and I stroke her head on my chest. Caroline sits up, reaching into her cardigan pocket, and hands me a folded sheet of paper. "I have something for you."

"It's not my birthday."

"I know." She shrugs, brushing her hand across Poppy's forehead. "But this is long overdue."

I unfold it, curiosity getting the best of me, and scan the title. "Certificate of Name Change?"

She nods, a blush staining her perfect cheeks. "Keep reading."

My eyes scan the page, reading quickly. "You're... Caroline *Montalto*."

"I am." Her face beams with pride, and a surge of lust and love, equal in my feelings for this woman, renews itself in me, making my blood sing for the millionth time since she came into my life.

Like an endless ocean, I feel my heart stretch, absorbing every bit of happiness it can wrench from my soul.

I slip my hand behind her neck and crash her lips to mine, murmuring into her skin, "About fucking time." Knowing now that if I can't consume her, devour her, make her one with me, this is as good as it can get.

My soul feels cleansed, rebirthed, and atoned, despite the blackness that still lurks in its depths.

But for now, I choose to focus on the light.

THE END

EPILOGUE
KIERAN

THE SHOVEL BITES into my palm, and I already feel blisters splitting my skin, but they don't deter me.

This ritual can't be postponed.

Tossing dirt over my shoulder, I hunker down in the hole as the sound of female giggles pierces the night air, unwelcome in these hallowed grounds.

Well, kind of hallowed. By most.

Not me, if the grave I'm desecrating is any indication.

But another month's passed, and I can't let Murphy's ghost go unattended. I'm the only one who ever visits anyway. My father never really cared enough to, and it's like he didn't exist to Mom and Fiona. Like they weren't complicit in his death.

I guess their guilt doesn't run red through their veins the way mine does.

Granted, Mom has a harder time remembering, and Fiona doesn't really know better. But still.

Peering out over the grass above the grave, I scan the cemetery for signs of other people. There's no reason anyone

SAV R. MILLER

should be traipsing around the King's Trace Memorial Gardens at midnight.

There's no *real* reason for *me* to be here, either, but that knowledge doesn't stop me from coming. I can't rationalize against the eeriness that grips my bones at the thought of missing this anniversary.

All I know is, when I visit my dead brother and commemorate him, it feels like I've single-handedly diverted the apocalypse.

The girl giggles again, and this time, it sounds closer. I squint into the darkness, my eyes finally landing on an entwined couple, their silhouettes barely visible in the moonlight.

"Are you sure you want to do this here?" The other voice, a male's, bounces off the headstones, uncertainty lacing his words. "It's kinda creepy."

"This is the only place I can have sex on my dad's grave, Jace. Stop being a pussy and help me dishonor him."

Several beats pass of complete silence, and I watch their bodies twist and writhe together, blissfully unaware of a voyeur in their midst. The girl drops to her hands and knees, hiking her skirt up over her pale ass, and the guy positions himself behind her.

A low moan is the only indication of their union, and I find myself hardening beneath my jeans. I pull my hood tighter around my head and rub my palm down over my cock, trying to relieve the ache.

"Oh *fuck*, Jace. Yes! Fuck me harder. I want them to hear me in their graves." She mewls like a cat caught in a sphere of pleasure, and fuck if it isn't the sweetest sound I've ever heard.

I undo the fly of my jeans with shaking hands, keeping

my gaze trained on the pair, and yank myself out enough to wrap my palm around my shaft. Pumping it in tune to the sounds spewing from the girl's mouth and ignoring the guy's grunts of satisfaction, I can almost imagine it's me over there, unloading my seed into her until she's delirious.

Fuck, I need to get laid. It's been way too long.

But for now, my hand will have to do. I piston my hips harder, sparks shooting up my spine and to my balls at the same time a high-pitched scream pierces the night sky, filling my body with pleasure I've never known. Coming on a hiss, I pump myself dry, sticky semen dripping onto my brother's casket.

Well, shit.

Trying to regulate my breathing, I wipe my hand on the dirt to my side and swipe my free, not-gross hand across my forehead. Sweat pours down either side of my face from the exertion, and I shiver at the realization that they're still going at it.

Or at least, the guy's got his face buried between her legs, finishing her off a second time. I roll my eyes and refocus on my ritual. Reaching into my bag above the grave, I grab the salt and sage. After I light the bundle and toss it on the gold casket, I watch as the flames rage for a moment and then dissipate, kind of the way Murphy lived and died.

How fitting.

I dump the salt around the sage, repeating our family mantra as I complete the circle.

"Dia thar gach rud."

God over everything.

Not something the Ivers clan actually lives by, but we still insist on the branding.

God hasn't existed for us in years.

When I'm satisfied, I peek out over the grave again and see the couple has disappeared. Climbing out, I dust myself off and shoulder my bag, leaving the mess for the groundskeepers. They'll clean it and claim vandals have once again attacked Murph's grave, but I'll know the truth.

His murderer returned, making sure his soul stays dead.

I walk over to the grave the couple fucked in front of, studying the name in the moonlight. Something glimmers, catching my eye, and I bend down, fingering a gold, heart-shaped locket.

That guy must've fucked it right off her.

Pocketing the jewelry, I scrub a hand over my chin and wonder if she'll come back.

Excitement hums through my veins, lighting my chest up.

I hope she does return.

I'll be waiting.

SWEET SOLITUDE IS AVAILABLE NOW!

BONUS EPILOGUE
ELIA

"AND WITH THAT, the prince and the princess lived happily ever after."

Snapping the story book closed with one hand, I reach down and adjust my daughter's blanket, pulling it up to her chin. She purses her lips, watching me with her wide blue-gray eyes, and I exhale slowly, knowing what's coming.

"Go ahead, Poppy."

Her blonde eyebrows shoot to her hairline. "What? I didn't say anything."

"No, but I can tell you want to ask. Come now, don't be shy."

Pulling her arms out from beneath the pink blankets, she folds her hands in her lap, twiddling her thumbs. "It's just... all the bedtime stories you and Mommy read are the same. The good guy saves the princess, or the good guy gets the girl. The villains always lose, and it makes me sad."

"Well," I say, brushing some hair back from her forehead. "That's how life is supposed to work. Bad guys aren't *supposed* to win."

"But all the kids at school say *you're* a bad guy."

Discomfort settles over my skin, and I grit my teeth, my mind already jumping ahead and figuring out how to extract Poppy and her siblings from King's Trace Prep before their classmates soil their view of me entirely or make them ashamed of their namesake.

In the last decade, the scope of the mafia certainly hasn't lessened, though it had slowed down there for a little while. Part of the resurgence is due to the dismantling of Ricci Inc. in Boston, and the subsequent delegation of operations to King's Trace and a few other small branches spread out through New England.

The other part is because local governments found themselves in need of allies. Criminals willing to foot campaign bills in exchange for their own seeds of power, and now we're more corrupt than ever. Though most often, I confine myself to Crimson and leave the heavy work for my men. Gia and Marco have their hands full with official Montalto business, and I have mine full of five little Montaltos when I'm not at the club.

Seems like a fair trade to me.

"Something you'll learn in life," I tell Poppy, returning the book of fairytales to its place on her nightstand. "Is that good and bad can, and often do, coexist. There is no black and white when it comes to people. Sometimes, good people do or say bad things, and sometimes bad people do very good things. It's not the actions that make up a person, it's what's inside of them that counts."

She puckers her lips, contemplating this. "Are you good inside, Dad?"

Dad, not Daddy. Already, my little girl is shedding the evidence of her youth, desperate to feel older than she actually is. Her mother assures me it's not personal, that junior high looms big and bold in her near future and that's why she's changing, but it still *feels* personal.

Poppy might be changing, but she's still as small and fragile to me as the day we brought her home from the hospital. And even though her siblings still look at me as if I've cast the stars in the sky, Poppy's always been more perceptive, and I can't help feeling like her sudden burst of inquisition is her attempt at figuring out the real me.

Her question causes an ache to flare inside my chest, chipping away at a weak spot I've never been quite able to heal. I'm not sure how to explain a lifetime of bad deeds in the name of *la famiglia* to a ten-year-old, and I'm not sure how her mother would feel if I tried.

So, instead, I aim for deflection.

"*You* are, *topolina*," I say, reaching out to tap her delicate chin. "Your soul is as pure as they get, and that's really all that matters. If you do good, good things will become you."

She pulls a face, giggling as she jerks away. "That's not what *Nonno* says."

"Your grandfather says a lot of things he shouldn't," I grumble, making a mental note to ask him tomorrow to stop feeding my child's brain with nonsense. She's far too young at this point to need to know that bad things happen to good people—more often than not.

As far as Poppy Montalto is concerned, good things do, too. And it's the good that wins out, which is why I keep reading the fairytales.

Because sometimes, you get lucky.

"*Nonno* also says I'm a princess." Poppy pouts, sliding down in her bed so her head rests on her fluffy pink pillows. "Is that something he shouldn't tell me? Is it a secret?"

309

"In his eyes, you are one."

"Does that make Noah and Roman princes? Are Dani and Sophie princesses too?"

Bending down, I press a kiss to her forehead. "The Montaltos are practically their very own monarchy. Why else do you think there are so many of us?"

Her blue eyes widen, then shift around the room. "Well this new kid at school says you and Mommy have so many babies because you can't control your *urges*."

My breath catches in my throat, the vessel constricting. *Gesú Cristo, I do not want to have this conversation.*

She blinks up at me.

I blink back.

"What in the world are you two talking about?"

Even a decade after the first time I heard her speak, my wife's voice still manages to worm its way inside my soul and burrow deep, making my heart swell tenfold.

Glancing over my shoulder, I watch as she saunters into the room wearing a floor-length red satin robe, her golden hair piled on top of her head, skin glistening from the bath I know she's just gotten out of.

There's a glass of red wine in her hand, and she gives me a *look*, coming to stand beside where I'm seated on the edge of Poppy's bed.

I wrap my arm around her waist, pulling her into me, still unable to keep my hands off her all these years later—her body's somehow more beautiful than ever after having brought our five children into this world, and it's a constant battle of willpower to keep from bending her over every available surface in our house each chance I get.

She resists my grip, stubborn as ever, her bright eyes volleying between me and our eldest child.

Poppy's fingers curl around the hem of her blanket. "That depends."

Caroline raises an eyebrow. "On?"

"How much you heard," I mutter, winking at Poppy as her mother draws out a prolonged sigh.

"Okay, bedtime, you two. Little girls who stay up too late don't get birthday cake in the morning." Ushering me to my feet, Caroline bends and kisses both of Poppy's cheeks the way my father does, then tucks the blankets beneath her armpits and whispers that she loves her.

"Daddy," Poppy calls as we sweep through the doorway. I pause with my hand over the light switch, waiting. "You're not a bad guy."

"No?"

She shakes her head, rolling onto her side. "Nope. I know all about how you saved Mommy. *Bad* guys don't save other people; they only save themselves."

My chest throbs at her words, a scabbed over wound being picked at, and Caroline tugs me from the doorway, flipping on the hall night light as she drags me to our master suite. I peek in at the twins, who share a room, and Noah and Roman in their adjoining rooms, ensuring everyone is out before locking the door behind me.

At one point in time, I'd resigned myself to the notion that this house would be forever empty.

I've never been happier to be wrong.

Setting her wine glass down on her nightstand, Caroline discards her robe, revealing a white silk nightgown that clings to her every curve. She turns to me and slides her hands up my chest, pulling on the button at the base of my throat.

"Please tell me you weren't discussing sex with our nine-year-old daughter without me," she says, unlatching the button from its hole and working her way down my sternum, unwrapping me like a gift.

"*I* wasn't." A shiver skates down my spine as her fingers pull my shirt from my slacks and push it open, grazing my flesh. "Some *cazzo* at her school is trying to destroy her innocence by telling her how babies are made."

"Did you just call a kid a dick?"

Rolling my eyes, I shake out of her touch and shrug off the shirt, backing her into the bed. The backs of her knees hit the mattress, and I reach out and push her onto it, unbuckling my pants as she splays out in front of me.

Hiking her gown to her waist, she nibbles on her bottom lip, letting her thighs part slightly in invitation.

As if I've ever had to wait for one.

"If the shoe fits," I reply, shoving my pants and boxers down and kicking them off my ankles. My cock leaks a bead of precum at the sight of Caroline's breasts spilling from the neckline of her gown, and I fist my shaft with one hand while gripping her calf in the other and wrenching it around me.

She gasps, raising her hips as I sink into her, this song and dance one we've completed more times than I can count over the last decade, but still not something I've ever been able to get used to.

Her pussy grips me like a glove, wanton and desperate, and I slowly move my hips back and forth, creating a rhythm that drives her crazy. I'm coming before my brain is fully ready, spilling myself inside her and reaching frantically between us, rubbing against her until she convulses around me, catapulting over the edge of euphoria.

"That was fast," she laughs as I collapse on the bed

beside her, adjusting our positions so we're against the head-board. "Forty's really affecting your stamina, huh?"

I grunt, pulling her into my side. "I'm not forty for another three hours. Your pussy is just too fucking good."

Humming, she traces the pad of one finger down my happy trail. My stomach flexes beneath her touch, my body responding the way it always has to this nymph.

When I proposed to Caroline at her cousin's birthday party a decade ago, my intentions were only slightly altruis-tic; I'd be lying if I said I wasn't immediately drawn to her beauty and the shroud of innocence encasing her, begging to be tainted.

Even months into our marriage, our connection was born primarily of lust.

But it was her quiet strength, the way she suffered to protect her family, that did me in.

Changed me.

And I haven't looked back since.

"You seem tense," she says softly, raising her blue gaze to mine.

"Let's see how you feel when *you* turn forty."

"I popped out five kids for you. I *feel* forty now."

Chuckling, I reach over to the tabletop lamp on my side of the bed and shuffle us under the covers, rolling onto my side and hooking her thigh over my waist. My cock perks up at the sensation of her wet core, but I ignore it, burying my face in her neck.

She smells like the cupcakes she baked for my party tomorrow—a party I'm not particularly looking forward to, but that my family would likely combust over if I didn't go through with.

SAV R. MILLER

"I think it's bad luck to have an odd number of children," I mutter after a few silent seconds pass.

Caroline presses her fingernails into my stomach. "*No*, Elia. Absolutely not. You said Roman was the last. You promised."

"Don't you miss having babies in the house, though?"

"God, you're such a dad." She reaches out, gripping my chin and twisting it toward her; the silhouette of her nose is all I can make out in the dark, the moonlight drifting in from the windows not quite enough to provide more. "Once we get the five of them out, then we have *all* the time in the world for ourselves. We're less than fifteen years away from that freedom. I refuse to ruin it just because you're afraid of Poppy growing up."

"I'm not—"

"Save it, Mr. Montalto. I want no part of your mid-life crisis. Kids grow up, they stop needing their parents as much. That's the way it's supposed to work." Leaning forward, she presses a hard kiss to my mouth, and then rolls over onto her other side, settling in for the night.

Sighing, I scrub my hand down my face, the stubble on my jaw rough against my palm. She's right, of course—as usual. I'm just afraid that, like so much else, the way it's *supposed* to work won't be the way it actually pans out.

Poppy wasn't *supposed* to be so damn intuitive. Eager to see beyond the surface and expectations society puts out for her, desperate for the evil hidden beneath.

Noah, our second-oldest, wasn't supposed to be interested in my line of work, but deception may as well be his middle name.

The twins and Roman are still too young for us to be able to tell if they'll end up the way we hope, but if our track record is any indication, I'm inclined to believe we're in for a long, tumultuous ride.

Though, I suppose, that's the beauty of parenthood. Getting to watch the lives you created flourish and mold their own paths, regardless of your influence. All you can do is hope they're happy and healthy.

Nothing else matters but that.

Adjusting my position in bed, I slide my arms around Caroline's waist and yank her back into me; she wiggles her ass into my groin, waking the beast, and I push her night-gown out of the way so I can slip back into her tight heat.

Letting out a stuttered breath, she turns her head for a kiss as I rock into her. My own personal paradise.

Breaking the kiss, I drop my lips to her neck and fuck her in slow, languid strokes, my grip on her hip keeping her from being jostled too much with each thrust. She moans, and I flick my tongue over her pulse point, allowing her body to erase some of the unease corroding my insides.

After we've finished the second round, we sink into the sheets, and I focus on the even sounds of her breathing. Resisting the urge to pad down the hall and double check on all of my kids' sleeping forms.

My fingers curl against the comforter, battered knuckles shifting under my skin.

"You're *not* a bad guy, you know." My wife's voice is soft, almost reverent. Grounding, the way she's always been able to reach me. "Our kids, even if they turn out exactly like you, still won't be bad. I certainly wouldn't be mad about it. You were never a villain to me, Elia."

"That's what all the girls with daddy issues say to the bad guys."

She snorts, kicking at me. "You're ridiculous."

I reach out and curl my arms around her.

My heart raps at my ribcage, so completely full that it feels like it could burst. I press my forehead into her shoulder and exhale, my mind flickering back on the decade of our lives. The loss, the redemption, every accomplishment and trial in between.

The love.

Truth is, I didn't save Caroline from her father. She hadn't *needed* my help, was well on her way to ensuring her own freedom.

But I needed her.

And even though she's not the kind of person to dwell on others' shortcomings, we both know the truth: any ounce of goodness within me only exists because of her.

I surrendered a lot more than bachelorhood when I offered her a whirlwind proposal, and I've gotten more in return than I ever could have imagined.

BECOME A SUCKER!

Want to be the first to get important announcements, exclusive access to bonus material, and find a place where like-minded readers can share the love of all things Sav? Visit savrmiller.com for more information!

ALSO BY SAV R. MILLER

ACKNOWLEDGMENTS

They say it takes a village.

Here's mine:

To Emily McIntire: my soul sister. The reason this book exists. Thank you for being the best friend and my biggest supporter. Love you and literally could not do this without you.

To Bee: thank you for the incredible covers for this series. They're stunning, and I'm still so impressed with how perfectly you came up with them. Can't wait to create more magic with you!

To Justine and Jenny: thank you for making this book beautiful on the inside.

To Jackie and Mackenzie: thank you for your support, and for helping keep the rest of my life in order. You guys do your best to keep me sane, and I so appreciate you.

To Laura with SBR Media: thank you for your immediate enthusiasm and willingness to take me on as your client. I appreciate everything you do.

To my betas: you guys made this story what it was. Thank you for reading the original mess.

To Sarah and Literally Yours PR: thank you for handling all my publicity related things and keeping me on track for new releases. I would've forgotten to do all of this if not for you.

To my family: thank you for your support (even if you won't read the books).

To Brittany: I know you'd have loved these books.

To LB, Poe, and Arrow: thank you for quite literally being my sole sources of serotonin some days.

To the bloggers and bookstagrammers that agreed to review and promote this release, you guys are the best. Seriously, thank you for taking a chance on me.

And finally, to the readers: thank YOU. Without you, authors wouldn't exist. Well, we would, but it'd basically be us screaming into the void about the things that trouble us. So, ya know. Thank you for giving us an outlet to pour our imaginary friends into.

And to anyone I forgot, this is all for you.

ABOUT THE AUTHOR

Sav R. Miller is a USA Today bestselling author of adult romance with varying levels of darkness and steam.

In 2018, Sav put her lifelong love of reading and writing to use and graduated with a B.A. in Creative Writing and a minor in Cultural Anthropology. Nowadays, she spends her time giving morally gray characters their happily-ever-afters.

Currently, Sav lives in Kentucky with her dogs Lord Byron, Poe, and Arrow. She loves sitcoms, silence, and sardonic humor.

For more information on announcements, bonus material, and Sav's other books, visit savrmiller.com

Made in the USA
Thornton, CO
12/12/23 12:21:55